Overwatch: 1944

By Benji Karmis

Dedicated to all those otherwise good people
trapped in a horrible time, place, organization, or country.

This book contains terminology that may be new for those not knowledgeable on the setting. For your convenience, a brief index can be located at the end of the book.

Prologue: It was Them or Us
Unterfeldwebel Rupert Schmidt

Crack! The bullet sliced through the air as it left the tip of my rifle. After a split second, my poor Soviet target flinched as the rude interjection of my round disrupted him. His weapon then slowly lowered from his hands, falling to the ground as he slumped over on his stoop in the distance. I instinctively flipped back the bolt handle of my rifle up and tugged it back as a hot, empty shell casing spewed out of her right side.

It was often the only piece of consolation I could find after committing such a brutish action. The spent shell brushed against the metal receiver of my Karabiner – Ilsa, by the way – to make that familiar "*kink.*" It temporarily paused any worrying about what often could be several hundreds of meters away, so that I could tend to my rifle for a fraction of a moment. Pulling that bolt handle back has always been a wordless avenue for Ilsa and me to console each other after hacking away somebody's soul from their body. It was as if we both needed a brief slice of reassurance from each other over what we had just done. "We had no choice," we'd remind each other. This was war, after all. Ilsa and I - we held together. From preventing my men from perishing by the endless onslaught of the Allied forces. From the fanatical Nazi regime that's too focused on spreading hatred than keeping its own people alive. From not cracking under the pressure of what we've been witnessing out here. It all boiled down to one thing – we held together against losing our humanity in this brutal, modern, total war.

Our introspective moment subsided as I slammed the bolt forward into the breach, and another round took the place of the previous. I always had to be ready for another shot.

Immediately after, another Soviet soldier shy of 200 meters away caught my sight as I panned the area through Ilsa's scope. He was taking cover behind a sizeable shelled-out building. One of my German comrades was inconveniently taking shelter on the other side of a building in front of it. I couldn't tell if he knew if the Russian was so close, but I didn't think so.

I couldn't risk letting a fellow German soldier get jumped because I was too busy lollygagging around back here, so I withheld my burning instinct to relocate as Ilsa reactively snapped herself towards our next unsuspecting target. We needed to pull it off quickly because it was against my experience to stay in a spot for more than a couple of shots. I had been here long enough. Besides luck, abiding by the strict set of rules I've learnt is the only reason I've managed to survive this long.

The Soviet kept poking his head out for just a split second as if he sensed I was targeting him. Just long enough to at least get a picture of what was going on beyond his little niche. As tempting as it is to take the bait, I opted to hold my fire. He wasn't exposed long enough for me to get a clean shot, and I didn't want to alert any other enemies of my position with a resounding crack of rifle fire from my already-past-due niche.

Oh, how I longed fire anyway. If I hit the Soviet, then I did my job. I didn't, he would hopefully just run away. He would know he was zeroed in from afar. Then, I wouldn't be forced to claim another victim, and my comrade won't get killed. But that was precisely the problem with this war – retreating only held off the inevitable. Somewhere between the fanatical zeal on both sides after our ill-fated invasion, our allegiance to fight for our comrades next to us, and the primal instinct inside of us soldiers that secretly craves the rush, there was no retreat. I was probably not too different from this particular Russian. But I would be damned if he thought I was going to let him get one of my guys before I got him.

My comrade fired his rifle into the distance on the other side of his building. He indeed did not notice anybody on the other side. The cunning Soviet soldier, on the other hand, did. He readied his weapon by poking the tip out from behind his cover, prepared to dash. As it always seemed to be, it was them or us.

The weight of responsibility my part in this gave me was immeasurable, even as someone whose life was hopefully not as immediately at stake. In that sliver of a second, I was the hand of God, deciding who lives or who dies. My old priest back at home would be upset at me for having such a mentality. But I didn't ask for this responsibility, I didn't ask to take anybody's life, and I sure as hell didn't ask for us to attack the Soviet Union. It was this blasted war that had us on the brink of everything from life to insanity that really made me ask myself what the dickens we were doing out here in this God-forsaken land that we tried to conquer solely for our greed. But now that the first domino had fallen, we couldn't have just stopped fighting and said to Russia, "Hey, we've had enough war, we're sorry, we were wrong to attack you guys, we'll give you your land back, let's just all live in peace."

There were always so many of them, and the quality of our replacements was dwindling. We had already lost this war. They had defeated us long ago. But for some reason, we were still fighting. Like my comrade's arm in a futile last stand, knowing he needs nothing short of a miracle to survive.

Finally, the Ivan sprung from the refuge of his building's rubble wall like a lion after his prey, making a dead sprint to the other side of the structure with his submachine gun at the ready. Matching his pace for such a short dash this far away with the tip of my rifle for an accurate shot would be next to impossible.

Ilsa tried anyway, and I fired a round right after he left his cover, hitting the wall of his building. He didn't so much as balk.

By the time we were ready to fire another, the Ivan had made it to my comrade's building. He fought the momentum from his sprint as he approached while snapping his head towards where he assumed my unprepared comrade was on the backside of the wall. My poor comrade must have heard the Russian's footsteps and took notice, but from facing the other direction, his chance of survival was slim. He didn't even try to whip his rifle around. He just winced, falling to the ground, and raised an empty hand between himself and where the Russian would appear.

I knew my only chance to hit the Soviet was once he had stopped running, so time began lagging to a crawl as the intensity sunk in. Through my grip on Ilsa, I felt my heart pound at what seemed to be a million pumps a minute. Though by the sheer terror on my comrade's face, I could only imagine what his heart must have been like with Death, himself, exhaling a cold, dead breath down his neck.

The Russian's teeth were exposed. It was another expression I had become familiar with while on the front. This Ivan was no longer human at that moment - he was a predator, ready to eradicate the evil Nazi menace. He brandished a PPSh – those absurd contraptions could spew out more than 900 bullets in a single minute. That means, in a mere half a second, my comrade could absorb seven or eight rounds! It would be a particularly brutal reckoning from so close.

The biggest consolation I took away from that high-strung moment was that whilst Germany seems to no longer have God's assistance in the war, at least this poor German might if Ilsa and I could have our say. This Ivan may think of himself to be a God with his authority to judge if my feeble comrade trapped in his palm lives or dies, but he didn't realise that he was cornered in my palm as well. Then again, for all I knew, there could be another God with his own Ilsa about to judge my own life right now. But what only mattered right then was who could squeeze the life out of the man in their hand first.

It was bewildering to me how all those thoughts could flow through me in scantily more than a second of real-time. Perhaps that meagre glimmer of intense moral contemplation had awakened what curiously lurks in the far reaches of my sanity. Regardless, it was my turn to be the judge now, with Ilsa as my hammer, and her bullet as the jury. With my heart about to burst out of my chest, I had finally made my verdict.

When the Soviet's submachine gun commenced its hail of fire as he made it to the side of the building with my comrade, I promptly squeezed Ilsa's trigger and absorbed her kickback. The jury was out.

With the bullet soaring through the air and no longer within my control, I suddenly realised that all the God-like control I thought

I possessed had instantly disappeared. All of my previous thoughts on who had the power had become void, as who really decided where my bullet would land after it left my rifle, who really determined if I was lucky enough to save my comrade's life, who really chose life or death for *any* us lowly mortals, was none other than God, Himself.

Chapter 1

Grenadier Bruno Lindemann

It was my first day on the front lines, and I had found it hard to contain my excitement. I waited for years to be old enough to help the Fatherland! Training could not have gone by fast enough. I was too eager to get out on the field and show those communist peasants how a real countryman fights.

I was particularly excited because today was the first real taste of really being a man! No longer would I be behind the mighty arm of Germany, helping those on the front lines from the home front. I would now be part of the outer layers of skin on the knuckle of the Third Reich! Together with my comrades, we were going to push the Soviet scum back into the barren lands they were born in.

When our train came to a stop at the camp, we dismounted the boxcars in mass. I decided I wanted to get a memento to savor the moment, so I promptly snatched a pebble from the ground as I stepped off. We were swiftly placed in lines and sectioned off as if we were being drafted for a sports team.

We all huddled together, and they started calling our names. After a few minutes of waiting, I heard my name and reported to an Oberfeldwebel. He was an older man of average height with unrelenting eyes, balding beneath the edges of his felt cover. His uniform was spotless. He must know how to fight a war.

"Grenadier Bruno Lindemann?" His voice was hearty, and he delivered his words at a good pace. It was a good sign.

"Yes, sir. Are you Oberfeldwebel Martin?" I approached him and begun raising my arm for a salute.

"Show me your rifle," he ordered, turning his attention up from a document he was holding.

I hastily threw down my saluting hand and snapped my feet together, unslinging the rifle across my back and presented it to the Oberfeldwebel as if in a drill.

The Oberfeldwebel gave it a nod. "Yes, I am Oberfeldwebel Martin. Go stand by the other recruits," he ordered as he marked something on the paper he held.

"Yes, Oberfeldwebel, sir." I saluted before stepping around him to join the others.

Some of the soldiers I met on the train, the farm boy

Grenadier Weiss and shoemaker apprentice Grenadier Graf, were already waiting behind the Oberfeldwebel. Behind them were a couple of others I didn't recognize. I excitedly greeted them both as I joined them in waiting for the Oberfeldwebel to search for however many other recruits he was assigned from the train.

He called the names of a few others I haven't met before, but I greeted them all as they joined us standing by. After another minute or so, I was thrilled to overhear Gernot Huber's voice called, and then see the jolly big-boned Grenadier I talked to the most on the train make his way towards us. He said something to the Oberfeldwebel and then proceeded to fall in line like the rest of us.

"It's my friend, the crack shot hunter!" Huber exclaimed after he caught sight of me.

I ran my thumb underneath the sling of the rifle on my shoulder and gave it a brief tug upwards. "I'm beginning to think that's why you befriended me, Huber," I joked as I gave him an excited hand-shake.

"Come on, this way," the Oberfeldwebel interjected as he abruptly directed us to a spot away from the train staging area. Huber jumped in surprise as he marched through our freshly subsided handshake. I grinned at the wide-eyed Huber and fell in behind the other following the Oberfeldwebel.

The first thing I noticed about the camp as we marched away from the train was the energetic bustling of activity. The staging area where we got off was a bit crowded, but that was to be expected with as many soldiers stepping off the railcars as there were. However, the camp was only marginally less huddled, if at all. Soldiers in all different uniforms shuffled to wherever they were heading in a hurry. At one point, one of them bumped into me and didn't even acknowledge he did so!

The camp was rather extensive, too. Well, they call it a camp, but it was more of a makeshift headquarters out of the strip of stores in the middle of a small town, littered with a bunch of tents in the surrounding area. It had a larger building in the middle, which must have been a post office or something in the past, but now looked like where the higher-ups must make the battle plans. A couple of old stores around it were occupied as well, as either the medical facilities or as troops' quarters.

As we marched from the heart of the camp and into the areas less dense with soldiers, I realized that Oberfeldwebel Martin had been speaking to us this entire time. I hastily dialed in, catching something about the importance he placed on getting the recruits acclimated to combat as quickly as possible.

"The best way to do this is by placing you under the direct supervision of somebody who understands the ropes. Because of such, I am going to make you the responsibility of a soldier who knows the battlefield. Think of yourself as an apprentice under a master of war."

A *master* of war? I tried to get a bit closer to the Oberfeldwebel so I could devour every last scrap of his lecture.

"I am going to hold you to a high level of accountability, as I expect everybody within my command to be the pinnacle fighting force of the Wehrmacht," he explained.

Oh man, the Oberfeldwebel really knew his stuff. How fortunate I was to be placed underneath somebody like him. But it makes sense. I was the best shot in my training group. He will, without a doubt, know the best person to put me directly underneath.

The Oberfeldwebel kept droning on, but I couldn't help but daydream about what my "master of war." I envisioned all the recruitment posters back at home – was he blond? Brown hair?

Probably a giant guy – those always seem to do well in battle, right? Undoubtedly my mentor had to keep the sharpest of uniforms – like the Oberfeldwebel. Maybe he was one of those shave-twice-a-day kinds of people. Because they were extra disciplined. Real German soldiers were the most disciplined men in the world.

It would probably take some time for me to get on his good side because that's how the best master tradesmen are when teaching their new apprentices. Perhaps he'd act like he was too cool to talk to me as well. I thought he would be a real ice cube. Maybe I would even be so fortunate as to land one of those heroes we see in the newsreels as my mentor, like those that single-handedly hold off entire battalions of angry Russians with nothing more than a couple of grenades and a sidearm. Of course, he will most definitely embroider the qualities that make Germany great! Yes, I had decided my mentor would be a perfect German, a genuine supporter of the Reich, my mentor had to be-

"Grenadier Bruno Lindemann, this is Unterfeldwebel Rupert Schmidt," the Oberfeldwebel stated, stopping immediately in front of me. I had almost bumped into him. Grenadier Huber quietly chuckled. Thankfully the Oberfeldwebel didn't seem to notice, as his eyes were on the piece of paper, with an open palm gesturing ahead. Excitedly, I shot up.

My overwhelming thrill of the moment was put to an abrupt halt as I finally laid eyes on the man supposed to be my guiding light through the strange dimness of war. To my front was a scrub in his mid to late twenties, leaning on a wooden pole in a mudded uniform as he wrote in a book. He had long hair for a soldier – probably a couple of centimeters too long to fit underneath his cover – a smoke in his mouth, and stubble that had gone at least two days without being shaved. But despite this, his eager facial gesture when he heard his name called suggested that he hadn't seen combat since the start of the war, if at all. My heart simply sank.

He must not have had the same feeling because his cheerful light brown eyes lit up as he caught sight of me. "Grenadier Lindemann! Pleased to finally meet you," he exclaimed as he snapped his book shut and threw his cigarette on the ground, all with a mischievous smirk on his face. "I have been eagerly awaiting your arrival so I can show you what it takes to become the best chef east of Germany! We are going to cook some exceptional dishes together, no stomach within a thousand miles will go unsatisfied."

"Cook?" I gasped. Thank goodness, there must have been a mistake. I glanced over at the Oberfeldwebel. "I'm not trained to be a chef…?"

"Gotdamnit, Schmidt," the Oberfeldwebel sighed as his hand crept up to his forehead, all while rolling his eyes. "Not the chef thing again! Take your job seriously for once, could you?"

Some of the other soldiers sitting around us began to chuckle. One laugh, in particular, was more noticeable to me. It was made by a soldier who was rubbing his already red eyes underneath silver glasses. With a desperate grimace, his chuckle sounded more like that of an injured wolf, as if some looming sadness prevented him from laughing normally.

My situation sunk in at once. It must have shown because Oberfeldwebel Martin took notice. He placed a hand on my shoulder. His scowl let slowly let up, but just a little, as he shared, "This man is a pain in the ass, Lindemann, and I'm sure you'll find out soon enough."

The Oberfeldwebel sighed, and then sort of winced before taking his hand off me. "But *something* has allowed him to survive this long in this war, and whether that is if he's doing something right, or if he's just plain lucky, under him, you'll have a decent chance of figuring out how to survive out here."

"Keep stroking the shaft, chief," Schmidt threw in as he put his book into a pocket. His wisecrack made the men around laugh a little bit heartier, as if the sadness that burdened the soldier with glasses down earlier was uplifted ever so marginally compared to before. Even so, it still wasn't very motivating.

Oberfeldwebel Martin violently stepped between the toes of Schmidt's feet, pushing him back a half step while jabbing an open hand right underneath his subordinate's chin. The sides of Schmidt's mouth lowered from a carefree smirk to an off-guard frown.

"You *will* respect me in front of the troops, Schmidt! Especially after all I have done for you!" the Oberfeldwebel growled. Our area of the camp went silent. He soaked in the awkwardness he had created for a few more seconds before huffing, "And shave. Your gotdamn. Face."

The Oberfeldwebel held his hand up at Schmidt for another second. Underfeldwebel Schmidt's eyes narrowed. His face has considerably more resolve as he raised his chin before dropping it down, giving a single nod to his superior. "You are right,

Oberfeldwebel. I apologize for stepping out of line. Thank you for both looking out for me and for bringing me Grenadier Lindemann."

The Oberfeldwebel's hand lowered, but he kept his eyes locked. Schmidt took a step back and played with his hands before pointing at the other recruits. "Oberfeldwebel Martin is one of the only Obefeldwebels left still leading a platoon. He cares too much about us to do anything different. Saved me – well, rather, us all – countless of times. You're in the best hands."

The Oberfeldwebel grunted. He raised his chin high, further squinting at Schmidt, before marching off towards some of the other men sitting around. He beckoned at the other recruits to follow with an aggressive wave. The other recruits followed in a confused gaggle.

I caught Huber's eyes right before he followed the rest of them and shot him a crooked "uh-oh" face. Huber picked up what I meant as the distance between us grew, and he blinked with a shrug. Optimistic of him, but I was still worried.

With his attention now entirely switched to me, Schmidt grabbed my shoulder as he excitedly gave out introductions to the gloomy crew that laughed at his mockery of the Oberfeldwebel.

“This is Gefreiter Burkhard Kuhn, that is Gefreiter Udo Sommer, next to him is Obergefreiter Karl Moller…”

Almost every introduction was matched with either a nod or grunt, except the first guy, who reached out for a handshake with an oddly pleasant smile. He seemed like a friendly one.

Another man with a narrow mouth approached me before being introduced and grabbed the rifle strung around my shoulder. “You know how you can always tell if someone is a fresh recruit?” he smoothly quizzed.

I lowered my arm so he could examine my rifle. “I, uh, less ribbons?”

The man pulled the bolt back and looked at me with piercingly green eyes. “They’ve got the shittiest weapons,” he jabbed with a smirk.

“Not even as much as a hello to the new guy first, Herrmann?” Unterfeldwebel Schmidt kept the smirk of his own as he raised his chin.

The man pushed the bolt forward on my rifle and cackled lightly. “Thought you were against leadership positions.”

Schmidt shrugged. “They still think I need more volume of

fire."

The man gave back my rifle and punched Schmidt lightly in the chest. "Can't hurt. Hopefully, he does better than the last guy." I didn't see him do it, but I just felt as if his shrewd, green eyes had already looked me over from head to toe. I just knew that he had already sized me up.

As he strolled away, Schmidt brushed his forehead and muttered, "He sure has a way with words," before abruptly starting to prod me with questions.

"So how was your ride here? Where are you from? What did your father do before the war? What do you like to do in your free time? Do you like it when you get asked a bunch of questions by strangers? Does it make you nervous?" Okay, so maybe he didn't go that far, but he might as well have.

One by one, I'd answer them. "Uhm, great, West of Munich, he is a professional hunter, I like sports..." He must have liked my responses because he kept up the probing. Schmidt was oddly energetic for somebody who had supposedly seen so much of the war. It was difficult for me to comprehend.

Schmidt's warm gaze soon turned into a slight frown as the

tone changed. “Alright, I have to see you shoot. Drop everything but your rifle next to my gear, and come follow me.” I wasn’t expecting his order, but I did what he asked. He said a blanket goodbye to the squad as we got up and started trekking through the camp towards the outskirts.

“What do you think so far?” Unterfeldwebel Schmidt’s eyes glistened with excitement as if he was the host of a marvelous party.

I decided then was the time to show him how excited I was to be here. “I’ve been waiting for this day since before I can remember. I enlisted on the day of my last birthday,” I boasted. “I can’t wait to do Germany’s bidding against those filthy Soviet pigs!”

Schmidt’s eyes narrowed, and he turned his head away. “Ah, right,” he muttered.

For somebody as lively as him, I couldn’t understand why he wouldn’t at least pretend to be glad I was going to fight right under his wing. I had the ideal mindset for a German warrior. He should be excited for someone like me to come about to help his war efforts! At the very least, he should be pleased that somebody could act as energetic as him, if even for just a flash.

Silence overtook us as we walked through the camp. It could

have been a bit weird if it weren't for the constant movement of others around. Their noise provided a barrier to prevent any awkwardness from setting in.

As we hiked past some other vehicles, a gigantic tank stood out from the mix, and I couldn't help but admire how statuesque it appeared in the setting sun. I remembered seeing such a tank while watching the newsreels. I believed it was a Panzerkampfwagen VI. An actual Tiger tank! They had an exclusive news clip when it arrived on the battlefield. I brushed it with a hand as we made our way past it. It indeed was a marvel of German engineering: its boxy shape, its huge cannon, her crew having a smoke on its other side – the whole scene was exactly how I pictured the true might of mighty German army to appear. It reassured me as we wandered by.

The camp got less and less busy until we eventually made it to an area open enough to fire my rifle. Schmidt had me shoot a couple of tire-sized logs in the distance, all in the realm of a hundred meters away. His reactions were a little generic: "Great shot!" "Good!" "Nice hit!" Of course, they were nice hits. A hunter raised me and I knew my way around a rifle.

After a couple of more shots, we embarked back towards our

spot in the camp. Not too long after, we again passed the Tiger tank. Even though her crew was no longer in sight, it still retained its projection of prowess among the environment.

It made me a bit upset. How come my mentor here couldn't be as stoic and powerful as this tank? He was just some scrub who had somehow managed to survive so long. But you can avoid combat and survive. Maybe that was his secret – he could just avoid the battle. That would explain his softened face. He would never see a fight if he hid like a coward the whole time. Something about him, about all of this, just agitated me.

We eventually made it back to the squad, where we both sat down on the grass by our gear. I started to dissect Schmidt's uniform. A random button on his shirt was not closed. He had a pistol of sorts on his belt. A big one, too. One I didn't recognize. It couldn't have been one of ours, so how did he get it? It must have been scavenged. Maybe he was a scavenger, too busy looting corpses to fight like a man?

Schmidt must have read my expression and decided to tackle it head-on. "Lindemann, something is obviously wrong. What does that face suggest?"

I scratched the back of my neck. I was unsure at first about if I should go for it, but Schmidt's magnetic charisma made it peculiarly easy to decide to mount an attack. I propped myself up from behind with the hand that was on my neck and let it out.

"Are you sure you know what you're doing out here? I mean, I've seen a lot of newsreels with interviews of successful war heroes, and you're nothing like them."

Schmidt's expression changed from one of concern to one of surprise. He didn't respond immediately, so I continued. "Look, Oberfeldwebel Martin said that he wanted recruits like me to be placed under experienced men on the front, and from what I've seen so far, I am unsure if you are suited for command of anybody else." I used my hand to reference his unkempt face and uniform. "You can hardly take care of yourself, from the looks of it."

Schmidt's head bobbled back. He silently produced a cigarette, lighting it up as he processed my words. The air grew thick with discontent as the seconds passed where Schmidt didn't say a thing.

Just as he put his lighter away, one of the men we were sitting by from the squad walked into our sub-circle of conversation and interrupted us.

"Excuse me, Schmidt, I'm sorry to be bothering you if you're in the middle of something." It was the man who forced the laugh when Schmidt teased Oberfeldwebel Martin earlier. The gloomy one. He was older than me, but not as old as Schmidt, with circular glasses seated in front of hollow, reddened eyes. He had probably shaved yesterday.

The man took a knee before noticing me and introduced himself again, which I was grateful for because I was so swamped with new faces earlier that I had already forgotten most of their names. "Sorry, I'm Gefreiter Udo Sommer, in case you forgot." He raised a hand, and I shook it.

Gefreiter Sommer then turned towards Schmidt again before immediately fixing his eyes towards the ground. "About earlier. I, uh…" He coughed as if to cover his uncomfortableness and continued. "I… I accepted death out there."

There was a brief pause, and I became aware of how serious of a turn this conversation was about to take. "By now, I'm sure we all have at some point," Gefreiter Sommer explained, "but today, I really, genuinely thought my time had come." His troubled eyes glanced up to identify how Schmidt was reacting thus far.

Schmidt carefully nodded. His lightly squinted eyes gave away a complete fascination in Sommer's words. Sommer picked this up but snapped his back to the ground.

"I saw every bit of my most treasured memories scroll in front of my very eyes, as if in some newsreel," he revealed, rubbing an arm with one of his hands. "It was at that very moment I saw my family. I felt their warmth. And I saw our restaurant back at home…"

There was a moment of silence. Gefreiter Sommer wanted to break down further. But for some reason, he couldn't. Maybe because he had a reputation to uphold, but at this moment, I doubted he was concerned about his status in the slightest.

Gefreiter Sommer's eyes drifted up towards the sky. "I never felt a stronger feeling when your bullet hit that Russian soldier, especially over watching somebody go from living to dead so quickly within a couple of meters from me." Your bullet, as in *Schmidt's*?

Gefreiter Sommer gulped and faced his head away from us. His eyes focused on nothing specific far, far away. Birds chirped as he thought about what to say.

He soon spoke up. "You asked me a long time ago what I wanted to do after the war, and I couldn't answer you because I couldn't imagine anything beyond being a soldier. Fighting has become our life. It's become all we know." His words came across as stressed as he again took comfort in looking towards the ground. "I've wanted to die for such a long time now. I can hardly remember when I wanted to live."

That's when it clicked – the forced laugh earlier, the evident pain of his words. Gefreiter Sommer had no energy left to fight the hopelessness draped around him. He couldn't even make tears anymore. He's had too many hardships to fend off the sorrow that seemed to also come from within. On one knee before us was a broken man.

But then he started fidgeting. Something inside of him sparked and began pushing out of him as if he was the class dweeby kid who has been picked on enough and finally decided to fight back against the schoolyard bully. That dreary shell around him earlier – it was fracturing like brittle pottery.

With the cloak that dragged him down with the horrors of the world driven off his shoulders just enough for him to breathe, Gefreiter Sommer snapped towards Schmidt, armed with much more confident eyes behind his wire glasses.

"But at that moment, right before I almost died, I saw my loved ones at home. I saw my family's restaurant." His eyes teared up ever so slightly, but their lock on Schmidt was unbreakable.

"I'm sorry it's taken so long, but if there was no war, I would have wanted to work at my family's restaurant my whole life. I don't care if I would never leave my hometown. I would have been happy there." He ended his speech with the slightest expression of optimism he could muster. It was as if the girl he had a crush on but never talked to many years ago had moved back for his last years of schooling. Sure, he still may never speak to her, but at least that possibility could now exist.

Schmidt had a most sincere demeanor. "I'm glad to have finally heard that, Udo," he reflected as he gave Gefreiter Sommer a respectful pat on the shoulder. "And someday, you'll be able to return to it."

"Yeah, yeah, but on my own terms," he quietly shared, imaginatively fixed off on the horizon. As he was pretending to wipe the soot from his eye, Gefreiter Sommer's concern to appear tough had started to come back as he claimed, "I would have told that Soviet soldier because I guess this all was technically his doing, but I can't now, so you're the next best thing."

The two men let out a faint chuckle. Gefreiter Sommer's laugh had become more human. He didn't have to force it out this time around. It was the first genuine laugh I had seen him do. He still carried deep pain, but I felt that he'd have a good chance of being able to deal with its weirdness. In fact, I felt considerably more optimistic about the future of this new Sommer in front of me as opposed to the one I had met mere minutes before.

"Anyways, uh, I'll leave you two to it. Sorry to interrupt. Thanks again, Overwatch," remarked Gefreiter Sommer as he got up, and went back to his spot in the circle. *Overwatch*?

"I appreciate that, Udo," Schmidt followed. Sommer had almost made it back to his spot at the camp when Schmidt called on him again. "Hey, hold on a second!"

Gefreiter Sommer turned around and mirrored his quizzical face by responding, "Yes?" Schmidt jabbed his chin upwards as he declared, "Call me Rupert."

Gefreiter Sommer's new guise was subtly childish as he smirked, "Whatever you say, *Underfeldwebel Rupert*," before he turned away.

There was something about Gefreiter Sommer's new face. It was the same one that initially turned me off of Schmidt when I had first met him. It was never a face that demonstrated a lack of experience – it was one that shrugged it off, tempered enough to dampen any hardships that affect a person's wellbeing effectively. I just may have begun to understand how such a seasoned individual like Schmidt could maintain such a pleasant demeanor despite the war ravaging on around him. Maybe, after all of my doubts, there was hope with this man after all.

Schmidt peeked at me, and I realized that I was staring deep into the unknown. He let out the dirtiest shitbag of a smirk and commented, "If you want to submit a request to change squads, by *all* means, feel free to take that up with Oberfeldwebel Martin."

He took a long, deliberate puff of his cigarette before casually leaning back into his gear and cracking open his book. That bastard probably wasn't even really reading.

Chapter 2

Unterfeldwebel Rupert Schmidt

These blasted bugs were relentless in their attempt to further drive me into insanity. It wasn’t easy to keep a keen eye on the horizon when you had them flying by your face. Ordinarily, you could light up a smoke which puts them at bay, but not out in the field. Every second you look at the flies around you to properly swat them away is a second you are not paying attention to your surroundings, just to wave to the enemy. But it didn’t matter if we were moving from place to place, because no matter where we went, there seemed to be more than a ration’s worth of our little insect friends, trying to get a slice of the action. Believe me, little buggers, you wouldn't want it.

Equally as frustrating as these bugs in my personal space were my new protégé of sorts, Grenadier Lindemann. After a little tiff when he first got here, he had quite quickly become casual. I usually am quite fond of having someone out here close enough to be on casual terms with. Udo Sommer comes to mind. I’ve grown quite an admiration for him as of late. But with Lindemann, it's a bit different. It's tougher to take orders seriously from a friend over a superior, so he has interpreted that voicing his displeasure over my instructions is acceptable.

Our closeness should not be mistaken as friendship, however. When he speaks to me as he would to a friend, it's in a casualness that doesn't acknowledge that he is supposed to respect my commands because, at the end of the day, I am his superior. I always hated having to pull rank, but if he didn't follow through with my instructions, he could get my comrades killed. I usually don't mind being a teacher – in fact, I generally quite enjoy it – but he's been quite a pain during this whole ordeal.

I noticed the bulk of our men in front of us move from behind giant bales of hay to behind a small stone wall, so I notified Lindemann that it was time for us to move forward from the brush we were covered in.

He stopped fumbling around with the rocks by his feet to unenthusiastically respond, "Yep," sounding like a child given a chore by his parents when he'd rather play outside with their friends. Admittedly, he could be grumpy because I forbid him from firing his rifle unless either I explicitly told him he could use it. Or, unless otherwise absolutely necessary. It was his first contact with the enemy, so I'd be lying if I claimed I wasn't worried that he could become a liability.

We caught up with the others on a stone wall, which was a good 30 meters from the gaggle of buildings we were supposed to assault. I carefully peeked up from behind the stone barrier and snagged a glimpse of the extensive building that supposedly was occupied by the Soviets. The wall we were hiding behind bent slightly around the barn to our front and continued to the front right. It stopped not too far to our left, where the only somewhat viable cover would be a very shallow drain ridge beside the barn.

Feldwebel Pfeiffer, our squad leader, also noticed the building. He stopped peeking above the stone wall and begun quietly barking out orders.

"I want you three fucks with me, and I want some gotdamn cover as we get close to that building!" he aggressively whispered.

One recruit underneath him scrambled to acknowledge his order as quickly as the others, which did not please Pfeiffer. "Did you hear me, you pigly looking fuck?"

The boy's eyes widened as responded swiftly and immediately, "Yes, Feldwebel Pfeiffer, sir!"

The recruit's name was Huber. If I remember correctly, his first name began with a 'G.' Maybe Gernot? Anyway, Grenadier Huber had quickly become close to his fellow rookie, Lindemann. A relatively stocky man for the front lines, he had a face as green as green could be. Meeting him gave me a sense of joy – people as innocent as Huber could still exist in this war-torn world. Even so, it's still a bit sad. His face will be cold as the stone wall we hid behind after this battle. If he made it even a few months out here, his mother will hardly recognise him. That is, of course, if he even survives. Pfeiffer was particularly hard on him, which was a bad sign. He also sensed he'd need more work.

I noticed Lindemann was taken back by the way Pfeiffer talked to his men, specifically to Huber. I shaped my face to say, "You really want to find another person to show you the ropes?"

Lindemann must have noticed this telepathic thought because he flashed back at me with a facial gesture that irrefutably implied, "fuck off." If that's how my mentee treats me, then maybe I am the bottom shelf rum of mentors. But hey, even bottom shelf alcohol can do the job. And believe me, I would know.

Pfeiffer forcefully beckoned that he wanted us all to gather around him to share his plans for the attack. I nodded to Lindemann, and we both shimmied along the stone barrier to where the rest assembled.

Feldwebel Uwe Pfeiffer was a short man and always had a frown on his face. One of the quickest men to pull his rank in any argument, he suffered from short man syndrome, where he felt as if he had to compensate his smaller stature with his other accomplishments. I'm on the slightly taller side myself, so I am not necessarily a conductor on such a train of thought. I don't quite understand why some short people feel as if they need to act all strong and mighty. It clouds judgement. I'll be your friend no matter how tall you are, even if you can't reach the top shelf. Maybe that's why Pfeiffer is so mean. Perhaps his comradery with the relatively taller Oberfeldwebel Martin was so somebody else could reach the top shelf when he couldn't.

Once we were in a tidy circle with the others, we saw Pfeiffer attempting to forge a map on the ground. The diagram was probably not Pfeiffer's idea – he is way too dense for maps and the like.

Though it definitely wasn't Moller's, either. Perhaps Kuhn politely suggested it to help with the new guys.

I used to think all soldiers fight for something they love, whether that is for their love of country, their comrades, or their families and friends back at home. I don't quite think that is true anymore because of the conscription and such, but I credit Pfeiffer with showing me that some fight because they simply love fighting. I'm unsure if he actually hates the Russians, or if he just loves to hate them because it's a way he can justify fighting them. Either way, it's a completely different mindset from that of my own and probably why we're not the closest. You have to respect the guy who loves the job when he's in charge, though.

While Pfeiffer was preparing the rudimentary diagram, I used Ilsa's scope to scan the house the Russians were supposedly in. Sure enough, I saw some bobbling heads.

There was indeed a machine gun on the second floor of a building past an open courtyard between the barn and us, dominated by a well in its centre. The ground around it was checkered with one or two artillery holes. Not too deep though; either from lighter artillery, or general neglect of the land. To the right of that building was a one-story shop of sorts, which allowed us to peer into its empty storefront from our angle. Pfeiffer would likely want to take that. The only other building in our section of the town before it crossed over to where the other squads were attacking was far back and to the left of the one with the machine gun. I panned it through my scope but still couldn't tell if it was occupied or not.

Keeping our future battlefield in mind, I made Lindemann peek above the stone ridge before I decided to test his knowledge. "Where do you think we should go?" I inquired after a couple of seconds.

Lindemann glanced at me, and then back above the ridge before I justified my task. "I want you to think. Don't just follow me into battle – you need to know why I chose where we're heading."

Lindemann hummed in acknowledgement, so I added, "And eventually if I ever become a good enough instructor, I'd like you to find an even better spot than me. That's when I will have fulfilled my teacher's duties." Sure, I loved goofing off, but I learned to take teaching very seriously.

It took him a couple of seconds, but he finally came up with an answer. "The long ridge on our left is our best bet. It will lead us closer to the machine gun." He must not have assumed the building further to the left would be a threat. Or, the little bastard must want us to catch as much fire as possible so I will be forced to let him use his gun.

Either way, I wasn't going to push it. "The building far back and to our left could be a threat if we go there. Our safest bet is behind the stone wall to the right. That way, we'll also have an open view of our environment."

"We didn't see anybody in it!" Lindemann was getting too loud, so I shot him a glare and put a finger to my lips, urging to keep quiet.

"You'd rather possibly get shot at by a second machine gun? And, you'd be forced to go prone. If they know exactly where you are, you don't want to go prone, because once you are on your stomach, you can't get closer to the ground to take more cover," I replied.

Lindemann was still unconvinced, so my hand was forced to torch his proposal. "Also, your sides are more exposed, you can't change directions as easily, and you can't evade if you need to without standing up and exposing almost all of your body. Plus, over there is too close for my scope to be as effective."

With a sassy huff, Lindemann finally agreed. I would need to address his attitude at some point soon. What a shit he could be.

As expected, Pfeiffer's plan turned out to take the empty house to our right by splitting our forces into a smaller distracting force down the middle by the barn, well, and crater holes, and send the majority to the right by the empty store. Moller and his machine gun would take up a position on the stone ridge by the store, giving the bulk of our men some suppressing fire. After he consulted the rest of the squad, I debriefed him on what my plan was to support the men, and naturally, he got irritated.

"Why can't you help us take that house? I want all of our manpower focused on it," Pfeiffer argued. Maybe he would have been a better mentor to Lindemann. They both really love to complain.

"If we split up, I can draw some of the fire from you guys while you take the house," I reasoned. While that was true, I primarily wanted to go back behind the wall because my abilities were best suited in the more open terrains. I could pinpoint places of interest that needed my assistance, instead of confined areas where any soldier will do. But Pfeiffer had a narrow mind, so I needed to come forth with a reason that suited his plans.

It worked. With a nod of approval, Pfeiffer grunted, “but if you’re going to be back there, make sure you fuck them up. You got that, *Overwatch*?”

He loved to mock me. I just put on my war face and grunted with a nod. I knew he’d like that.

Pfeiffer then waved me off, so I tapped Lindemann on his shoulder and gestured for us to halt as the rest of the men shimmered along the stone wall to get into proper positions.

Udo Sommer followed Pfeiffer and a few others had soon made it to their spots along the right. Once he made it, he glanced back at the other chunk of men to our left going straight. Then he saw me and shot unsure but hopeful eyes, so I gave him a nod. He had been working on regaining the spark that he once had. I was proud that he sought to improve himself.

Pfeiffer, too, scanned the area one final time. I advised Lindemann to stay low until he was ready. We were already in a position where we could effectively engage the machine gun once Pfeiffer began the attack. I signalled to Pfeifer that we were ready, and he gave us a gesture of acknowledgement before he diverted his attention to Moller, who was preparing his machine gun.

Although we have not been getting along so well, and despite his aptitude to become the single-handed biggest boulder of shit known to man, my biggest concern right now was Lindemann. Though he was hot and bothered over doing "Germany's bidding against those filthy Soviet Pigs," as he recently put it, there was no way he would be ready for whatever the war has devolved to on this forlorn eastern front.

I swatted away another group of flies by my face. Those damned buggers might become the death of me.

Chapter 3

Grenadier Bruno Lindemann

It was a beautiful day. The sun was shining, there was hardly a cloud in the sky, and it was just warm enough for a picnic. I couldn't miss out on taking advantage of such perfect weather, so I made plans to meet up with Annette.

We had been seeing each other for a couple of months, but it hadn't gone anywhere, even though we'd hang out with just each and other for hours. So long, that I was frequently getting home late and my father would berate me for it. All very worth it, of course.

But I was distraught. I had already enlisted, and my date for training to begin was quickly approaching. I would never forgive myself if I didn't tell Annette how she makes me feel when she is near. Maybe this time, I would tell her. We will only have a few more picturesque days like this to spend time with each other before I ship off.

I trekked up the slight hill in the vast meadow of grass. She had beaten me to the lone tree at the top we always met up at. Her

French braid holding down her otherwise wavy blonde hair, her dainty white shirt, her oversized hat – she was stunning, and always knew how to dress when she wanted to. Her eyes caught mine as I made my way up the slope, and as always, my heart skipped a beat. After all of the times we've met up, she still had that ability over me.

I could hardly think of putting together a proper greeting, but I somehow pulled it together enough to spit out, "Good afternoon, Annette! You sure look lovely today."

Annette grimaced as she gandered at the vastness of the meadows. Her freckle-covered cheeks seemed to get ever so slightly rosier as if I had embarrassed her.

"Oh, stop," she jested as she fixed her gaze back at me, and gleefully went in for a hug.

When we touched to embrace, time seemed to slow down until it damn near stopped by the time we were in a full lock. The world may as well have stopped functioning around us for all I cared. My concern about how the day was going to pan out, how Germany was doing in the war, what it might be like on the frontlines – all of it completely vanished. Besides an overwhelming feeling of euphoria, I couldn't think of anything, really.

I read somewhere that we dream several times a night, and one of those dreams was usually just a feeling, repeated for several minutes. Since we forget most of our dreams, I, for one, can't say I remember them every night. But I've remembered bits and pieces of those dreams. No light, no sound, just a feeling. That's exactly what this moment was like – a dream of pure bliss. No thoughts bustling around, just a few seconds of simple happiness to enjoy within such a tumultuous world. Honestly, I imagine heaven as being a similar feeling, because I could enjoy that moment with Annette for the rest of eternity.

Time regained just some of its momentum as the warmness of our hug came to a close. We began pulling away from our heartfelt embrace, but she held on to my sleeves to keep our hands locked around each other as if she had wanted to say something.

My stomach picked up on what was going on first and immediately started doing backflips. Oh shit, here? *Now*? I built the entire day around this moment, but I didn't know if I was ready for this to happen already. I mean, the plan was to build up the courage throughout the day and hopefully tell her at the end. Ideally, even be a glass or two of liquid confidence deep.

But on the flip side, we could go about our day as a couple, which could add a whole different dynamic. But no matter how I reacted, I hoped I didn't stutter! Please be smooth when you finally talk, Bruno, please be smooth.

Our faces were pointed slightly down with our foreheads within a centimeter to each other. There were a couple of seconds of silence, which could not have possibly seemed to last longer. Maybe she was waiting for me to speak. Already? I hadn't fully prepared what to say. I mean, I had fantasized about this moment for the better part of forever and played out what I should mention countless times, but I didn't fully put together which phrase I was going to use.

Forget this, I decided. I was just going to say what comes to mind. I opened my mouth and took a deep breath. My palms were starting to get sweaty. Hopefully, she didn't pick up on it. My knees were becoming weak and my arms grew heavy. My hands were sweating profusely now, and my forehead started to perspire. I had to be drenched in sweat right. Oh, and at the worst of times, too! At the peak of my breath, I hesitated and started closing my lips and completely fumbled at the goal line. I felt as brainless as a caveman asked to cook Italian food.

Okay, round one was a failure. But I was just testing the waters. Let me give it another go! Round two, I had this. Just let her know what's on your mind. It really shouldn't be this difficult.

I had just started opening my mouth again when she managed to take the leap before me. "Bruno, there's something I need to tell you," she hardly louder than whispered as she goggled up at my eyes. I was hopelessly lost inside the captivating color of irises. They were the clearest of blues. I could see the entire vastness and beauty of the ocean when I was caught daydreaming inside them.

I was so lost it took a second for me to react, but I managed to let out, "Me too," in the same whisper she used on me.
Annette smiled as she shook her head, and I managed to steal a glance at her hair as it flailed behind her. There was something about that French braid. Still, she started poking at me.

"Oh, you do now?" She could be so sassy, and I was obsessed with it. "And what would you have to tell me?" She leaned back and cocked her head slightly as she let out a dainty laugh.

I resonated off her style, so I smirked and shot back, "Well, you said you have something you needed to tell me, first." We both giggled.

Her head stopped jostling around as our gaze into each other's eyes intensified. Glancing down, for a split second, she looked up to about where my mouth was. Her mouth opened a sliver as she inhaled, but remained silent, as if she was trying to spit something out, but had also discovered the same difficulty as I had just experienced. That was exactly why she is the best - she did the same things I do. I had been anticipating this moment for years, and despite my flop earlier, it was going even better than I had imagined.

"You're going to be off so soon," she eventually breathed. I noticed Annette and I's faces had been slowly drifting closer together. Our grips around each other had tightened. The only feeling I had was pure bliss, like our hug before but with dialogue, too.

I entered the striking distance of her lips, but I couldn't go in for the kill until I finished letting her speak. Annette pulled a centimeter or two away, just enough to comfortably make eye contact.

"Go on, Annette," I crisply whispered. Staring at my right eye, then switching to my left, then back to my right again, her eyes began to glisten as if she was completely mesmerized with this moment. My eyes expanded in eager anticipation.

With an indescribable amount of passion, she boldly declared, “I need you to start using your rifle.”

What the fuck did she just say? I pulled my head away in shock as she repeated with the same sincere face, “I need you to use your rifle.”

Suddenly, the colorful bits of the world around us started cracking like shattered glass and falling away in little pieces to reveal a black background. Annette still had the same innocent look on her face as she softly whispered, “Lindemann, do you hear me? Your rifle...” Blackness began to overthrow the elegant environment around us.

Then, Annette started fading through my fingers, and I fell to the ground in a desperate attempt to keep holding on to her. Terrified I was losing her for good, I shouted, “No, Annette, no! Don’t leave me!”

She continued to drift through my fingers into nothingness as she verbalized, “Lindemann… Your rifle… Lindemann…” After a few painful seconds, there was nothing left but blackness around me.

No, no, no! Anything but this! I jolted my hands towards my

face to wipe my eyes but immediately felt a shooting pain by my brow as I felt a bump. I winced, and when I opened my eyes, the harsh world had returned to me.

"Stop hitting yourself with your rifle and start hitting *them* with it!" Schmidt roared. He was violently firing his rifle off beyond the rock barrier we were behind.

Still bewitched over what in the name of fuck almighty had just happened, all I could do was watch Schmidt's rifle as he fired it. It was the somewhat dated Karabiner 98k, but a particularly interesting one with more character compared to the rest of our weapons. "Ilsa" was carved in the upper part of the wood by Schmidt's front hand. It had a scope, I'm pretty sure an older one with four times magnification, rigged up on the top. Paired with the little bit of tape around the slightly worn wood of the stock, it was truly more at home here on the battlefield than at camp. I didn't think much of it when I first noted it, so watching it in action was much more apt than I had imagined.

Equally as enthralling as his rifle was Schmidt. He operated so precisely. His painted helmet would expose a subtle underlying tan base as it rotated with his head a split second after every shot was fired, so he could get an idea of what was happening surrounding him. He'd even check behind him every once and a while. After a couple of shots in one position, he would duck behind the stone wall, top off his rifle with a few more bullets, and scoot to another position a few meters away before rising again to engage the enemy. When his eyes would change targets, Ilsa was always so quick to follow. He was tackling several different positions at once, judging by the areas he was aiming his rifle at. Their fittingness on the battlefield was a remarkable sight, and the duo's synced harmony reminded me of what I hoped Annette-

"Lindemann!" Schmidt again interrupted my thoughts with a shout as he slammed his back behind the stone wall to shove more bullets into his rifle. His voice was coarser. A far cry from the warm tone he had when I first met him. "Your friend, Huber, *will die* if you don't pick up your fucking rifle, and start using it!"

Huber was in danger? I raised my head above the stone wall we were behind on the other. The battle had begun and had not been going well. Pinned behind the well in the center of the courtyard was Grenadier Huber, audibly terrified as bullets peppered the ground around him. To the right and left of the narrow safe zone his well provided were two unfortunate comrades, limp and sprawled over the dirt. The one on the left was covered in blood. Feldwebel Pfeiffer was barking out orders with the rest of his men surrounding him on the outside wall of the store to our right. Behind Pfeiffer were our machine gunner and his assistant, who occasionally fired a burst at the enemy before being forced down by the incoming fire. Both groups were of little use to Huber.

A burst of machinegun fire ripped through the wood holding a bucket over the well, exploding the surrounding area with splinters. Huber let out a resounding shriek that even I could hear from so far away.

The spurt of fire found its way up to the rocks in front of us, which instinctively made me take cover. The sound of enemies shooting at us, Pfeiffer shouting commands, and Schmidt firing back – it was all so much to handle all at once. Just like my daydream, my hands were sweating. I couldn't move. I felt paralyzed. I did not imagine my first glimpse of combat right. It was horrendously more frightening.

Schmidt was right though. Huber was out there. He must have been far more frightened than I was. Just like Schmidt said, I needed to do something. I breathed in. Mouth open, I hesitated. Okay, next time. I breathed in again, gripped my rifle with all my strength, and let out a roar as I swung it over the rocks and took a shot toward the enemy building.

I was hardly aiming. I'm pretty sure my bullet missed the house entirely. But that didn't matter. I had reached the milestone of taking my first shot at the enemy. There was no going back now. I was officially a soldier. This was my new life.

I still mirrored Schmidt by scanning around us. The battlefield was bleak – another one of our comrades had caught a bullet by the house and was being tended by one of his friends. Pfeiffer was now leaning at the edge of the wall of the house, periodically engaging the closest machine gun, all while still barking out orders. Russians were shooting out of most of the windows of the building with the machine gun. The limp man on the dirt to Huber's side was in a much bigger pool of blood than I remember when I first caught sight of him. To top it off, Huger was uncontrollably sobbing right now. He was a complete mess. The situation was truly dire.

Schmidt's rifle cracked next to me to seek vengeance for our wounded as the head of the man on the machine gun sprung backward with an oddly satisfying red spew behind him. What a shot! Their machine guns had a metal shield covering their front, so hitting somebody on one of them would be a tricky one to pull off, especially with as much adrenaline pumping through our veins.

"Men! Suppressing fire!" Pfeiffer commanded. He had noticed that one of the machine guns had been temporarily silenced and decided to take advantage of the opportunity. "Huber! Get your ass over here! Now!" They made it inside the closest building on the right. Their rifles poked out of the front windows after Pfeifer's order and started firing at the enemy's position.

Huber, hearing Pfeiffer, trembled before bracing to run. Come on, Huber, you could do this. But the terror-stricken Huber remained frozen, long enough where Pfeiffer yelled at him again. "Huber! *Now*!"

The petrified Huber stuttered another second before he jumped from his cover in such a hurry, he left his rifle behind. Hands almost above his head as he dashed, Huber screamed in terror as tears overtook his face.

The German rifles that stuck out of the window began to

withdraw as the Soviets adapted to the barrage of fire. Oh no, did Huber hesitate too long? Terrified at the sudden possibility that I could lose my closest friend, I start shooting ferociously.

My assistance could not prevent Huber from stumbling over the carcass of our fallen comrade, which delayed him just long enough for a Soviet to hail of bullets from one of the windows at the unarmed recruit. He picked up a bullet in his leg, which forced him to the ground, right beyond our fallen comrade. He twitched as another bullet hits his shoulder, and Huger screamed even louder.

Gotdamnit! Weeping on his back, he needed help, quick. I had to get to him! Forgetting what I was doing moments before, I rocketed over the stone wall and made a mad dash towards my wounded comrade.

"Lindemann! *No*!" Schmidt's booming voice pleaded as he fired another shot. He was shocked at my act of bravery, but if anyone would understand, it was him. Like how he saved Gefreiter Udo Sommer, I wanted to save Huber. I needed to prove that I was worth my weight, too.

Another Ivan jumped on the previously silent machine gun and began raining its bullets in my direction. The Bolshevik's death-seeking metal sprayed the ground around me as I charged, which forced me to take cover in one of the shallow artillery holes. I quickly learned that my valiant sprint might have been too bold. Bullets tore up the dirt to my front and sides, and I was a terrible position. I couldn't hug the ground anymore, as I was taking as much cover as possible in the small crater.

Ping! ping! Two bullets hit the ground centimeters away from my ears. I could hear Huber's stressed sobbing just a few meters away from me. Just like that, things had turned for the worst.

I knew I really did it for myself. The only thing I could do was to start daydreaming again. I thought about my family, my schoolmates, and of course of Annette. I wondered if I'll ever get to-

A bone-chilling scream suddenly arose from behind me that captivated the entire battlefield as the machine gun shifted targets to behind me. I could hardly turn my head, but I managed to twist it just enough to catch sight of Schmidt in my peripherals charging over the stone wall to the barn. The enemy machine gun switched from me to trail him. This time, I was glad he interrupted my drifting mind.

Disturbing grunts seeped out from the close side of the barn

were paired with gunfire that randomly rung out of some of the small windows on the side facing us. One of Schmidt's rounds produced an agonizing scream from the enemy's house in front of us. I craned my neck vigorously enough to see him just as he raised his head from his rifle and looked towards the rest of the men.

"Pfeiffer! Push when I draw them to the other side!" Schmidt boomed. Schmidt snapped an eye back into his scope and took a hasty shot before ducking away.

"Preparc to advance!" Pfeiffer shouted from outside my view.

I only got a brief glimpse of Schmidt before observing him through the corners of my eyes, but for the first time today, I notice Schmidt's face had completely hardened. He was baring his teeth. His brows touched from such a determined frown. But the biggest change was his eyes. I could have sworn his normally light brown eyes turned engagement ring gold. They were more than just the eyes of a soldier – they were eyes of a killer, just as willing to force an unfortunate enemy to part with their life as he was accepting to lose his own in the process. This was the face of an entirely different person. Supplemented with the terrifying cry he had let out, I could hardly believe this was the same man who had earlier joked about being a chef instead of a soldier.

Schmidt carried the attention he had drawn from the enemy back with him to the very ridge on the other side of the barn he was ragging on me for suggesting earlier. With the communists' fire now drawn to him, our men in the house on the other side finally had an opportunity to push forward.

"Close the gap!" Pfeiffer ordered. Some of the other men echoed the order. Others, in a similar fashion to Schmidt, let out their battle cries as they threw grenades and pressed on the attack.

I pulled my rifle out of the hole and aimed. Explosions rocked the building as our men peppered it with fire. The defense of the enemy's position to our front was now breaking. There are two dead by the machine gun, with its current Bolshevik operator visibly wounded on his left arm. Two bodies had fallen out of the building on the left side, and there was a man slumped over on a wall within view through the main door. Besides the dead and wounded, bullet holes plastered the building's exterior.

As a final desperate act, the wounded Bolshevik at the machine gun of the breaking house made a roar and desperately strafed the area one final time. Noticing my terrible position, he swept his weapon towards my position. I ducked right before it reached me. The communist's horrifying yell carried on as he shot up the area surrounding me. I nimbly poked my head out after the salvo ended just in time to hear the crack of a rifle pair with the Bolshevik's head popping back with a spray of gore behind him. What a terrible final act for him to go out with. The enemy position was now completely compromised. Hardly any other resistance was put up as Pfeiffer led his men inside from the front.

Oh shit, Huber was on the ground right by me! Now safe from the enemy, I vaulted out from the crater towards where Huber was. My heart sank as I witnessed what was the grisliest sight I had ever laid my eyes upon. I knew it was him, but if I didn't see him trip in the same spot earlier, I wouldn't have been able to recognize him.

It was horrible. Just… Horrible.

Unable to hold myself up anymore, I fell to my knees, and my eyes started to water. He was unarmed and already hit, why would they shoot him like that? What kind of sick monsters would do such a thing?

Those fucking pigs. Those fucking communist pigs. Those people who shot him weren't men, they weren't even human. They were dirty, *disgusting* animals. They will pay for what they did, and I will deliver them justice for their crimes. They didn't deserve the right to live. They needed to die. It made me want to kill every last one of them.

They could still be around! I sprung up, rifle in hand, and darted to the side of the building the now-silenced machine gun was in. Schmidt was taken by surprise. "Lindemann? Lindemann!" he shouted from afar. Maybe I could get one of them. Make them atone for their sins. I'd avenge you, Huber. I'd make them pay for what they did to you.

I reached the side of the building to see three of the filthy Bolsheviks cowering away, probably 150 meters out. The first man had a rifle, but the other two pigs must have left in too much of a hurry to grab theirs. Fools. I thought more might remain inside, though, so I charged in through the back entrance and into the cellar of the defeated Soviet stronghold.

A wounded Bolshevik animal stumbling around inside caught my sight as I stormed inside the building. He had been shot through the thigh and could hardly hobble on one foot. His pathetic eyes widened as he raised his hands.

I lowered the butt of my rifle from my shoulder to my waist and let him soak in his defeat. He tried to plead his way out, but it was too late. I fired a round into his stomach. A satisfying, red puff splattered on the cellar walls behind him. My round went through him so quickly that it didn't even make him shake, even with only one leg to stand on. After a second of standing with his hands still partially raised, he fell to his knees, and then the ground.

"Clear!" I heard our men from above shout as I stood with my rifle in hand. Clear maybe, but I wanted more. For Huber. So, I decided to take another shot at the filthy animal on the floor of the dimly lit basement. I racked the bolt handle back and raised the butt my rifle from my shoulder to my hip to aim.

Out of nowhere, a hand swooped in, yanking my right shoulder back and forcing me to discharge my rifle off into the wall. As the bullet pinged in the confined basement, the same hand swiftly came upwards into my gut. I dropped my rifle and put my hands on my knees.

"You *callous* brute!" Schmidt stood in front of my hunched-over body. Being on the receiving end of his golden eyes was much more chilling. "You shot a wounded, unarmed man trying to surrender? Do you think that shit is *ever* okay?"

Confused over what just happened, but still fuming with rage strong enough for my eyes to water, I shouted back, "They shot Huger, and he didn't even have a gun either!" The punch, paired with everything else I had just gone through, kept me bent over. I wanted to throw up.

"Those defenseless men share nothing with that asshole who executed Huger but the country they were forced to fight for! How does committing the same atrocity as him make you exempt from the same sin?" Schmidt's face was overshadowed by a demanding scowl.

"Answer me!" he commanded, shoving me on the floor. I bounced off the basement wall and collapsed to all fours. I was speechless. I could only just stare at the ground.

Thick silence contaminated the air for a couple of painful seconds before Schmidt slowly spoke, "I'm sorry about Huber, but I don't care this war puts you through. We've all lost people out there. But as long I have any say in it, I will *not* allow you to sink to that level."

Schmidt grabbed me by the front of my shirt and yanked me off the ground, very close to his face. His eyes shined an even brighter gold for a wink as he stared into my soul. "And if I *ever* see you shoot a defenseless soldier again..." He threw me to the floor. I looked up at him, and he growled, "…I'll kill you myself." He scowled in comptempt for a second before turned around and took a few steps away from me to look around the rest of the basement.

The battle was over. There were no more fighting Russians left in our part of this town. For the first time in what seemed like forever, there was no sound of rifle fire. Except for the clamor of footsteps from our men above, it was silent. However, the otherwise welcomed silence was unwholesome with Schmidt lurking in my vicinity.

"When we receive word that the other squads have taken the rest of this town, I want you to go dig a hole outside and bury your first kill," he muttered before marching off outside.

I gazed past where he previously stood to see the Russian I had shot still lying on the ground, with a puddle of blood oozing around him.

Schmidt wasn't around anymore, but the silence remained about as thick. The weight of my actions wrapped around me like a tattered cloak as a circle of deep rose blood grew from underneath the soldier that I was responsible for felling. I ripped that man's soul away from this earth, separating him from the terrible cause he believed in enough to fight for.

Frankly, I was befuddled. He was a communist. They did terrible things to our soldiers. To Huber. He could have grabbed a gun and shot me. I thought shooting him would pay them back for our fallen.

But I didn't want to mess with Schmidt. He scared the shit out of me. I'd have to watch my actions, or maybe even he would kill me. Combined with just losing my best friend out here, it was just so much to worry about.

My gut still ached, so I rubbed it. Then I realized that I understood the burdensome weight that Sommer had draped around his spirit when I had first met him. I was wrong before when I thought I had become a man during the battle. Worrying about what had happened, what I was going to do next – that what it meant to be a man, and it was decidedly less fulfilling.

Chapter 4

Feldkuchenunteroffizier Johannes Buhr

It's quite popular to despise mornings. But honestly, I found them to be quite relaxing. In my youth, I noticed that the elderly tended to wake up before their younger counterparts did, but I could not quite comprehend why. Now, in my old age, I have realized that it is simply a natural progression to grow fonder of dawn.

Perhaps it is the silence in the wee hours of the morning draws us in. There is less ruckus from the youngsters while they are still asleep, after all. Regardless, it was convenient for me, as I had to get up before the others to prepare a proper breakfast for our hungry men.

Supplies always seem to be scarce, but I was always confident I could make do with what was at hand. I cooked long before my days with the military, even during the depression after the first Great War, so I picked up a couple of tricks to ration our resources. Plus, nothing on the Eastern Front could be as bad as North Africa. More optimistic times perhaps, but hardly anything to cook with. There was hardly any water, either, which I learned can be the most crucial ingredient for stretching your limited food supplies to feed all these soldiers. It was a desert, though, so a lack of water was expected.

For today, I planned to use the remnants of beef from yesterday's dinner. We were taught to use the meats right before a big fight, but I do what I can to prepare the best meal possible right after intense combat with recruits as well - even if that means beef for breakfast. I like to think it gives them a reason to make it back. So, I use some sway I have with the command to secure some extra meats for before a battle to use for after it.

I don't often see combat anymore, but I've seen enough faces to know how the fighting went. Even if it goes well, the troops are generally dreary. But everybody likes a good meal, and even though they often forget to acknowledge my especially distinguished dishes after a hard fight, I know they appreciate it at heart. Some of their otherwise empty faces soften just a bit when they smell the food.

Just as I was about finished cooking my beef broth, Rupert approached my station. He isn't usually up this early, so he probably wanted to talk. His eyes fixed on the ground could have given that away even if he woke up when he normally does.

As Rupert closed the distance, he gazed up, and his face sparked upon catching sight of me. “Ah, my favourite person in the camp!” he exclaimed with an invigorated laugh. “Spotting that moustache always means a delicious watered-down meal is in the works.”

“Unterfeldwebel Schmidt! So, they still haven’t locked you up for that stubble,” I reacted. We cackled at our exchange. Rupert knew my cooking better than almost anyone, and specifically, as of late, he became less attentive when it came to regulations. He had a heart of gold, though, so I was glad to see him.

“The less Rommel there is, the less I’m inclined to deal with our military’s beauty standards,” he joked.

Our grins soon subsided, so I decided to dive into the meat of the conversation my inferring aloud, “You are up early. Something must be on your mind.”

Rupert’s lighthearted mug reverted into contemplation and he again scoured the ground. “It’s my new guy, Lindemann” he divulged, shifting his weight to one leg. “He’s incredibly brief with me and consistently finds displeasure to voice over my requests. And then yesterday, he had his first fight, and…" His head lifted to display lost eyes. He didn't have those often. "He lost a mate and then shot a wounded, unarmed Russian, just trying to surrender."

"Good, kill them before they can crowd the world with more of their sodomite children." Schmidt ripped around, and his embarrassment that first arose when caught with his guard down transformed into irritation when he noticed Oberleutnant Ross had decided to be one of the first to get breakfast this morning.

Rupert was quick on his toes this time. "Sodomite? Wow, that's a pretty big word for you, Denis," Rupert retaliated.

"Ah, but getting soft this early in the morning is nothing new for you," Denis shot back. He was always quick with the comebacks. The two stared at each other with familiar frowns of determined competitiveness.

Rupert and Denis had a confusing history spanning several years, but their relationship has grown more aggressive after Denis' latest stint. First, it was from Denis becoming an officer, and now it's with his even closer ties to the Nazi party. Though still technically in the Heer like the rest of us, Denis has also been working on being a Nazi party political, called the

Nationalsozialistischen Führungsoffiziere, or NSFO. In addition to constantly throwing salt at Rupert, now his role requires that he spews Nazi ideology at him as well. But somebody as self-concerned as Denis couldn't have actually cared about Nazi idealism – he joined the solely to boost his career.

"It's a shame such a promising recruit is wasted on a softie like you," Denis prodded, removing his cover to brush his well-kept, blond hair. "Such a dedicated soldier would be exactly what the Reich needs."

"Oh, how unsurprising, you're trying to steal him away to take credit for his dirty work," Rupert reflected. "Even in Africa, you were only ever concerned with advancing your career."

"You could learn from me," Denis smirked as he put his cover back on. His piercing blue eyes found their way to my warm meal, and he promptly changed gears. "Mmm, beef for breakfast. What a surprise, after the recruits' first fight," Denis observed. He, too, was familiar with my cooking. "Is it ready to eat?"

I grabbed the ladle and stirred the pot. Bringing some of the broth up from the depths of the heated water, I declared, "You are in luck, Oberleutnant. It is ready."

Denis procured his mess tin and cut in front of Rupert, who rolled his eyes. I filled the Oberleutnant's dish and he nodded his thanks before he patted Rupert's shoulder and headed off.

After Denis was out of earshot, I chuckled and pointed out, "After all of these years of butting heads, you still can't bring yourself to despise him, can you?"

Rupert's frown changed into a sly grin. "Nothing ever gets past you, does it, Johannes?" We chuckled it off as some of the other troops approached my table, now smelling breakfast.

To nobody's surprise, Obergrenadier Gunther Herrmann led the pack. He had gained a reputation for being a scavenger, anticipating he could acquire a warm meal early. Rupert sensed a growing presence behind him and procured his mess kit.

I pulled the ladle out of the pot to issue him a serving. "After knowing you for this long? Of course, nothing can. Stop by the kitchen later, if you can," I told him.

Rupert politely smiled and gave his thanks before leaving to dine. Obergrenadier Herrmann was next in line, and I couldn't resist giving him a hard time. "Did not expect you to be one of the first for breakfast, Herrmann."

The soldier's green eyes lit up as he displayed his signature crooked smile. "I couldn't resist, knowing you whipped up something special."

He undoubtedly had scrounged some new trinket, so I curiously asked him what he reclaimed as he pushed forward his tin. "So, what did you find during yesterday's skirmish?"

Without saying a word, he rose and shook his wrist. His sleeved pulled back to display a second watch. I could not prevent myself from grinning while nodding side to side at the lengths he goes for the spoils of war.

But he needed to be ragged on for disrespecting a corpse by looting it, so I tore into him as I poured him a serving of breakfast. "Oh, I didn't know you required more than one watch to tell the time." He cackled as he turned away to find a seat.

I continued serving the soldiers in line. Oddly enough, most of the men were a bit more upbeat than usual. The battle must not have been as difficult for everyone as it seemed to be for Rupert.

There were numerous new faces within the past few days. New men frequently fill in the open spots on the front, but despite the constant arrival of fresh recruits, I always try to at least greet them. If nobody else was going to be nice to them out here, they can at least count on me. My food doesn't discriminate between experience. I'll feed you the same no matter how long you've been out here.

I try to invite as many of the new soldiers as I can to eat with me one-on-one in the kitchen. Even though many of them won't be around for long, I want to be an open resource for anybody who needs it. I guess that's what years of working at a bar had done – it made me a people person. It was also fascinating to hear them describe the veteran soldiers with their sets of fresh eyes. It made it easy for me to figure out what they were like outside of my mess station.

Rupert's concerns were weighing heavily on my mind, so I decided I would get to know that recruit of his. Hopefully, I would be able to offer better insight about him to Rupert. I remembered his name was Lindemann, so I kept my eyes open for him.

I continued serving the troops when the oversized Obergefreiter Karl Moller lumbered in front of my cauldron with two tins in his gargantuan hands.

"Moller, I've told you a thousand times, I don't care how

heavy your machine gun is, you can only have one serving until everybody else gets theirs," I explained. He could eat more than most, but I couldn't let him get two servings right away.

Moller's eyebrows rose. "But I'm bigger than everybody else! I need the extra food," he complained.

He was right, but he knows the procedure. "So, what if you get two servings and somebody else doesn't even get one?"

My question didn't stump him for long. "Then they should have arrived earlier," he suggested with a grin. I filled one of his bowls to the brim. It was the least I could do. A compromise, if you will.

Gefreiter Burkhard Kuhn decided to chime in from behind Moller. "Nonsense, Karl! Even if you are larger than most, you should at the very least be honourable enough to ensure everybody else had their first serving before you take a second." I was always impressed at how strong of a character Kuhn maintained. He was an incredibly noble man.

Moller rolled his eyes as he reluctantly realised that Kuhn was right. "Alright, fine, I'll wait." His eyes shifted to me, again armed with his cheeky grin. "But I'll be first in line if there is any left."

I found his adamant hunger to be humorous. "Maybe I'll put some laxatives in the leftovers. Then you won't want to eat as much."

Moller was stumped at my rebuttal, but he managed to maintain the slightest of smiles as he growled and began walking away. Just as I poured the breakfast into Kuhn's dish, Moller must have figured out my quip and thought of a comeback, so he turned around to let it rip. "Maybe then I'll be small enough to be the chef!"

I grinned disapprovingly as Feldwebel Uwe Pfeiffer decided to chime in to scold Moller from a few spots back in the line. "Stop harassing gotdamn the chef, Moller! I'm hungry!" Moller hastily turned around and promptly sped away from his temperamental superior.

Sure enough, a slightly taller boy with freshly-cut brown hair and moderately brown eyes shuffled in front of me and nonchalantly handed me his tin. I recognized him from yesterday's dinner. "Lindemann?" I inquired.

My words disrupted the boy's deep thoughts, and he glanced up. "Yes?"

I poured his meal before I continued. "I like to meet all of the lucky chaps I forge these meals for, so I'd appreciate it if you would be so kind as to join me for breakfast."

Somewhat surprised, one of the boy's brow lifted. "Yes, Feldkuchenunteroffizier. Shall I wait for a table until you're finished?"

"Nonsense!" I exclaimed as I beckoned towards the seats behind my serving station. "Sit in one of the chairs behind me and start eating right away. I can catch up." The boy nodded and hurried around my station with his steaming tin.

Everyone else was served after a few more minutes, so I poured myself a bowl before I announced seconds were ready. Otherwise, I would never eat. There'd be nothing left. I proclaimed everyone could have another portion while supplies last, and without missing a beat, Moller immediately pushed another soldier out of his way and charged towards my station. I served him and a few others again until there was no more food left in my pot before I finally could turn around to find that the boy Lindemann had been sitting with a cooling-off bowl of food.

"I thought I told you not to wait," I recalled as I sat down in the chair across from him. "It is rude to start eating before the host is ready," he politely replied.

"Ah, of course. Manners seem to be a lost art, especially during a war," I hinted. Though my first bite was a tad hotter than I had anticipated, I still decided that I outdid myself with another well-cooked meal.

The boy nodded and took a bite, so I continued when I finished my first spoonful of breakfast. "You must have a proper upbringing. Tell me about yourself, Grenadier, uh…"

Lindemann caught on and finished my thought. "Bruno, sir, Grenadier Bruno Lindemann."

I put him at ease by being as warm and friendly as possible. "Bruno, my boy! Just call me Johannes. Now go on – help me learn who you are."

Taken back by the kindness of an elder, Bruno leaned back in his seat and took a moment to process his thoughts before speaking. "I'm, uh, 18, from the western suburbs of Munich." I casually nodded, and he carried on. "I did track in school. Long-distance running. I wasn't the best, but I really enjoyed it."

"Ah, track! A thousand years ago, I used to be a runner," I interjected. A good start, but I wanted to dig a bit deeper. "So, were sports your passion? Is that what you miss?"

Bruno shifted around in his seat before facing the ground. After a pause, he quietly lied, "I don't miss anything."

I cocked my head and disagreed. "That's malarkey, of course you do! Everybody has something they miss."

Eyes searching the ground for nothing specific, Bruno repeated his story. "Maybe everybody else does, but not me anymore."

I knew where his head was at, but I decided to ask to push my question anyway. "And why don't you anymore, Bruno?"

The poor child looked up at me and weakly let out, "I don't know." He was still processing his first taste of combat. These kinds of things are hard to witness on an innocent child such as him, especially as a father. I couldn't help but think of observing my stepson after a few months away – he, too, had changed. I grew worried about who he had become. Poor Bruno was likely on a similar route.

I kept our eye contact. One of my greatest tools to get more details out of someone is silence. It tells the other person that you are still waiting for them to finish their thought. Less can indeed be more, especially in this circumstance.

After maybe ten seconds, I still had no response. But I had one last subtle trick of my sleeve, so I cocked my head to the side. It would show both my interest in hearing the rest of his thoughts and would politely imply, "Well?"

It worked. "I don't know if I can go back to what I love." The poor boy wiped his eyes. He wasn't crying, but it was a precaution some tended to make.

I held my bowl between my knees and leaned in to show he was the only thing I was focused on. With a lowered voice, I inquired, "Did you see something out there?" I knew the answer, but I wanted to hear from him.

His head pivoted away, but he whimpered, "Yeah."

Ordinarily, I pride myself on being able to read people well. It was a skill I picked up at the bar. But I'll admit, this time I cheated. I knew what to ask because Rupert mentioned it earlier in the morning. "Did it make you do something you regret?"

Eyes hollow, but still not contain any trace of tears, he muttered, "I don't know." He was a tough boy.

I decided to give him the Johannes special. I had done it a

thousand times before, so it was sure to work.

So, I leaned forward even further and reached out to ruffle his hair. With my hand on his head, I stared into his eyes and proclaimed, “This is war, son. Out there, you become a person you ordinarily are not. And you do otherwise unthinkable things because it’s an instinct to survive.”

I stopped ruffling his hair, grabbed my bowl, and leaned back. “But I’m glad you feel this way, as it means you’re still human.” I took another spoonful before adding, “And I’m sure that someday you’ll tell me what you miss.”

Words like that take require time to process them. So, in the meantime, I opted to change the subject to get his mind off it. It is not as fun to eat with somebody who is lost in thought, anyway. “So, is my cuisine royal or what?” I queried.

Bruno’s eyes lit up. He was relieved to not keep talking about the terrible world around him. He remarked, “It’s delicious. I’ve never had beef for breakfast.”

I chuckled. “Don’t get used to it. It’s only for special occasions.” I took another hearty bite, and after I finished chewing, I remembered to ask him about Rupert. I might be able to finagle something interesting about him. “So, what do you think of Unterfeldwebel Schmidt?”

Curious about my question, Bruno tilted his jaw and cautiously commented, “He’s fine, why do you ask?”

I snickered again when I pointed out, “He’s an odd one, that Rupert. He has an uncommon outlook on this war and a most unique method of coping with it.” I took another bite, and with a little bit of food in my mouth, I challenged him. “Do you get along?”

He very diplomatically stated, “We are two different people, and while we aren’t necessarily two peas in a pod, I recognize that he is a very capable soldier.”

Capable. What an interesting choice of words. I frowned slightly. Maybe it was time to shed some light on my dear friend.

“Rupert is one of the few who have survived this long,” I revealed. “With a few others who managed to survive, were once both stationed in Africa together, under Rommel’s Afrika Korps.”

Bruno’s face flickered interest. His eyes opened to twice the size they were before, and he sputtered, “Really?” Just mentioning Rommel was enough to get his young, nationalistic mind turning. Rommel was a much-respected hero in our homeland. The entirety of Germany grieved over his death earlier this year.

I tilted my head up slightly. “Oh yes. That is where he learned his devotion to keeping his men alive,” I claimed. “Command in the Afrika Corps didn’t encourage sending soldiers to their deaths for no reason. Rupert very quickly learned to recognize the importance of living to fight another day.”

The gears turned inside the young Bruno’s mind. “Is that why they call him, ‘Overwatch’?” He was also a smart one, that he was.

“Precisely,” I stated. “Rupert developed a knack for keeping his companions alive.” Taking another spoon of breakfast, I added, “And the lengths he’ll go for his comrades is even more admirable than his skill with that rifle of his. He’s borderline fanatical about it.”

As if I was telling a story by the campfire, Bruno disregarded the meal in his hands, leaning forward and grasp every shred of detail from my tale.

I opted to add to his imagination. Perhaps it will help him bond with his superior. “I remember a young Rupert Schmidt, who had to be not much older than you. So eager to fight, so fresh.” Bruno was captivated, so I went on. “We met long ago, but we grew close in Africa. Combat in Africa wasn't easy, and we were always low on supplies." I chuckled, recalling having to learn how to ration. "That's how I figured out to cook with so little."

The boy grinned, but I dialled it down. "Not having enough supplies gets people killed, though. Despite having competent leadership, we still took quite a few losses." I shuffled around in my seat before drawing my hand up to make a point. "Rupert wanted to stem the losses at almost any cost, which built him a reputation for empathy very early on."

I stood up and made my way to the empty pot that once held the morning's broth before continuing my story, back towards him. "There was something inside of Rupert that wouldn't die, even after countless battles. But when he would return from the field, he would always find a way to be the same person he always was."

I turned my head and looked at Bruno out of the corners of my eyes. "That same gotdamn goofball." We shared a light chuckle.

Chapter 5

Unterfeldwebel Rupert Schmidt

Soldiers like to win. Or, perhaps it's that we don't like to lose. There are exceptions, sure. But no matter the perspective, we soldiers are usually a competitive breed. Even if we prefer to not fight, most of us like to sharpen that competitive spirit, regardless if we are in the heat of battle or boondoggling around at camp.

Such explains the intense atmosphere when someone procures a deck of cards. We play card games for all kinds of different reasons: to pass the often-mundane free time that often takes over, to relieve the stress of war as a morale booster, or even to assert dominance and settle scores.

I drew from the deck of cards in front of me. Shoot, another worthless one. I couldn't let the others pick up, though, so I swiftly shuffled it amongst the other cards in my hands to disguise it as a different card before placing it in the discard pile. Oberleutnant Denis Ross must have picked up because he gave me a cocky sneer.

Since Denis opted to play with us, it was a particularly

competitive game. While I prefer playing games with a larger crowd so everybody is involved, I didn't mind playing this western version of Skat we picked up long ago with a medium-sized party. It's usually the equilibrium for where luck and skill coincide. Plus, our German Skat game can only be played with three players, so it would be rude to force one of us to sit out.

To my left was my apprentice of sorts, Lindemann, who was carefully deciding which card to discard. Across from him was SS-Obersturmführer Milo Otto, a blond-haired man with relentless pale blue eyes, probably not much older than I. He probably used to have a slightly less withered face, but as with everybody else exposed to enough of this war, it had hardened. The SS tended to appear angrier than us in the Heer did, probably from all that hatred they rub over each other at their gatherings. But it could be from being forced to work alongside Denis. He really could get under your skin.

Obersturmführer Otto was one of Denis' mates, but he was also a member of the Nazi party, sent here to judge Denis's progress in the position he took as Nationalsozialistischen Führungsoffiziere, or as we call them, NSFO's. They were Nazi political officers whose job it was to spread their propaganda that is somehow supposed make us actually want to fight this useless war. We didn't pay much attention to them, but Denis was keen to take the position, almost certainly just to advance his career.

Lindemann finally chose a card to contribute to the face-up discard pile and the keen Denis immediately switched Lindemann's discard with one from his hand. "You should know by now that you'll never be able to beat me," he asserted, primarily towards me. "Even if you insist on deviating from our classic German card game."

"We all know you prefer our version of this card game to our own because you can't do basic math," I quipped. He gave me a low-key glare but dropped it before Obersturmführer Otto could glance up at him with a suspicious eye. Denis smoothly nodded side-to-side to act like I was not speaking the truth, but Obersturmführer Otto kept his eyes on Denis.

Denis and I had a very odd relationship. We constantly attacked each other, but we'd avoid getting each other in trouble. Oddly enough, he had even stuck his neck out for me a couple of times. Today, we had an unspoken agreement not to disclose that this version of Skat was one we learned from the enemy in Africa.

Denis could get in trouble if they found out that he allowed his men to enjoy an "inferior" Allied card game over our highly preferable German one, even though ours allowed for more than three players.

Though nobody usually minded what card games we played while our lives could end at any given moment out here while fighting for Germany, today he wanted us to be especially careful while being reviewed by Otto for his potential new position. So, I diverted the attention by promptly cracking, "Plus, hey, at least my family loved me."

It worked. Obersturmführer Otto snapped towards me, and without missing a beat, Denis countered, "Oh, how funny, because your mother *really* loves me." Obersturmführer Otto and Lindemann chuckled. His snappy comebacks were his strong suit.

"Hey, I'm glad at least *somebody* likes you," I replied. Sorry, mum.

He smirked. Obersturmführer Otto placed a card down, and right before I drew, Denis scratched his head and pitched us all a proposal.

"Say, Rupert, how about we put some skin in this game?" His eyes narrowed as his chin rose. He was up to something, but I still decided to humour him.

"We're already wagering a couple of smokes, but I'm keen to listen. What do you suggest?"

He cracked a dirty smile as he offered, "How about the winner of this game also gets an extra man for the rest of the day? Until nightfall, you can have Obersturmführer Otto assess your alignment to the Reich, and if I win, I'll get to show Lindemann what the Nazi party has to offer."

Denis knew I had a knack for plinking at Nazis because there usually wasn't too much they could do to affect me. Maybe some paperwork at worst, but my day would still be great if I could ruin Obersturmführer Otto's. So, I shook my head with a squint and shot back, "You have to deal with my pupil, *and* I get the rest of the day to myself? I might try to lose on purpose." They all grinned. Even Lindemann, thank goodness.

"But what do I get if I win?" Obersturmführer Otto, of course, immediately needed to know what he would get in return. A true image of Denis. Lindemann must not have thought of his reward right away but was glad Obersturmführer Otto asked, as he nodded in agreement.

Denis already had an answer. “If either of you wins, we’ll each give you eight cigarettes.” Eight was a hearty bunch – he was seriously upping the ante.

Lindemann scratched his chin as he nodded in approval. “Sounds like a pretty good deal to me,” he decided, looking for my approval.

Admittedly, I was a bit concerned over what he would see while under the piece of shit without my supervision. I didn’t want any SS animosity to further compromise his integrity. But, I couldn’t help recall a conversation with Johannes around a week ago when I had voiced my concern for Lindemann.

“He’s charged full of something,” I recalled Johannes concluding.

I countered, “but what about what happened the other day? He callously executed a defenceless soldier.”

Johannes made a brief hum as he responded, “Hmm, Rupert, don’t force him,” before he leant towards me. He always did that if he had come to a verdict on what stance to take on a subject he had previously taken some time to ponder. “If he’s a lost cause, then there’s nothing you can do to change it. The more you crowd him, the more he'll want to be anything but you. Just be an open resource. He needs that. Don't force it, and he'll learn to respect you enough to model part of himself after you." After all these years, Johannes still consistently proved to be my best supply for anything I was troubled over. Johannes then added, "You should know this best after all. I recall something similar happening between you and Denis."

I snapped out of my flashback and shot down a sharp look to Lindemann that said, "fine, fuck you then," before I faced Denis. "Alright, let's do it," I agreed. I glanced at Obersturmführer Otto. He had no idea how much he'd hate today if I won. Plus, any day away from Denis would be good for him. I'd still probably teach him how to bother Denis, though. "Does that seem fair to you, Obersturmführer Otto?"

Obersturmführer Otto gave me a once-over to size me up, and with his head slightly tilted up as his eyes met mine, cockily demanded, "Ten cigarettes."

I rolled my eyes. "Ugh, fine."

"Then it's settled," Denis stated with a concerning gleam. I was confident in my abilities at Skat, however, Denis was a worthy adversary. The other two didn't realise it, but it was improbable for rookies like them to win when facing seasoned veterans like ourselves. It was really just a match between Denis and me, and the other two were just cannon fodder. Even so, Denis and I went head to head often, and he had won a fair amount of time. It would be a tough match.

I drew a card. Dammit, nothing useful again. Rough start. Lindemann took his turn. If he was not doing well, he was at least decent at hiding it.

Denis went, and without even drawing a card, slyly gleamed at me as he declared Skat, making him the winner of the round.

"You gotdamn degenerate," I exclaimed. "You specifically waited until you were doing well enough to make that bet."

Denis's laughter roared before our eyes locked, and his deviant smile cracked, "That wasn't against our rules."

I must admit, even knowing how much of a scoundrel he could be, I was impressed by how he could still pull the wool over my eyes with this sort of trickery after I've known him for as long as I have.

The next five rounds went a bit better. We were playing with three lives, which was just short enough of a series to not take up too much of the day. I won the next round, Obersturmführer Otto won one, which took out Lindemann, Denis won the next round, which knocked out Obersturmführer Otto, and I won another, which tied me up to Denis, both of us with but a single life left.

Our competitive spirits were under a full load as our final round carried on. My hands were sweating and Denis' sneer was more infrequent than usual. Even if I lost, it was comforting to know that at least I put the pressure on him.

My turn. I had two alright hearts and a pretty good diamond, and I needed three of a kind. I could use another heart, or could completely flip my strategy and set my sights on diamonds if I pulled a good enough diamond.

The suspense of pulling another card from the pile was a bit nerve-wracking. My new card revealed itself as a garbage diamond, which now made it equally possible for me to win with either diamonds or hearts. I just needed to choose a suite to stick with.

I eventually decided to stop fighting when I didn't need to by taking to "heart" the advice of the old chef, placing my diamonds in the discard pile.

Denis eagerly drew a card. "Say, Obersturmführer Otto, how do you think Lindemann will fair with the SS?" Denis beefed as he placed a diamond I could have used in the face-up discard pile. Then he knocked on the ground, signifying I only had one final turn to get the best hand possible.

"It's hard to not like," Otto excitedly responded. "I am without a doubt that he will enjoy his time under the superior leadership of the Schutzstaffel." Otto was really working the shaft. Denis has a huge head (in multiple senses of the word), so he always ate that kind of stuff up.

I was too focused on pulling another card from the deck to react to their quip. Johannes' voice still echoed in my head. "Rupert, don't force him." At least I would be able to put his advice to the test if I lost.

The peace I made with losing came at an impeccable time, because right after I flipped over a new card to reveal yet another diamond, which was not the heart I needed.

"Let's see what you have," Denis taunted. He placed his cards down to reveal a hand I could not beat. Not letting him get the first strike after viewing my losing hand, I placed my cards down in front of him and immediately went on the offensive.

"It's probably actually a good thing that you'll have Lindemann for a day. He knows how to read, and the SS must need all the help they can get if they commission illiterate retrogrades like you," I cracked with an endearing tap on Denis' shoulder so Obersturmführer Otto knew it was not meant to be taken seriously.

Lindemann was just figuring out how hard I ride Denis's simplemindedness and only mustered up a face of confusion before I found another avenue for attack.

"You know, Lindemann, Denis couldn't read a full page of the Bible if his life depended on it," I claimed. Obersturmführer Otto actually chuckled. Lindemann picked up and followed before I interrupted with, "And even if he was able to, he would just burst into flames." The entire crew howled, including Feldwebel Uwe Pfeiffer who overheard as he walked by within earshot, which I found as amusing because he, too, probably couldn't read. Denis did not laugh, however, but at the very least he smirked at my zinger.

Quick to dish it out but never too quick to take it, Denis hastily started to close up shop. "Well then, it looks like we have had our fun for the day. Grenadier Lindemann, grab your rifle." We all stood up, but I was sure to squish my left hand in the soft mud in the ground behind me before rising.

"Remember, he likes his milk at room temperature, and will you have to read him a bedtime story before he goes to bed," I informed Denis as he was about to head off.

"Ah, so he takes up after you," Denis retaliated with a squint.

I grinned, and I reached out my right hand to shake his. "You remain living proof that you don't need to have anything going for you to be successful."

Denis let out a quick, "Hah," before reaching out to grab my hand. "Whatever you say, Rupert."

As we were finishing up shaking hands, I gave the lower back of his tunic a friendly, inconspicuous pat as he turned away to smear dirt on his otherwise pristine uniform. I loved getting under his skin, especially if he didn't know I was the one that was messing with him.

Lindemann stepped in front of me with his rifle in hand, and unexpectedly stood at attention. "Unterfeldwebel Schmidt, this Grenadier requests to shadow Oberleutnant Ross for the rest of the day." How formal of him. We never did this, but so he probably wanted to show his discipline in front of a new officer.

I stood in attention and formally responded, “Granted, on the condition that you return with some of the Schutzstaffel’s rations.” Without giving him time to respond, I raised my hand for a salute, forcing him to as well. Finishing the salute, I declared, “Dismissed,” and I turned to pack up the deck of cards.

Both Obersturmführer Otto and Denis rolled their eyes. “Come on now,” Denis ordered as they began to march away. Lindemann quickly followed.

I swiped some flies out of my face as I noticed Lindemann gave me one final glimpse as he hurried to catch up to the Oberleutnant. I hoped Johannes was right.

Chapter 6

Unterfeldwebel Rupert Schmidt

It was a rather unproductive day. I cleaned Ilsa, even though I never really needed to. She was a reliable weapon and would always function, regardless of how much debris she had accumulated. Even so, I was always sure she was in tip-top condition, just-in-case. I hadn't gotten a haircut in a few weeks, and it had been three, maybe four days since I last shaved. But Ilsa was my lifeline. She was much more of a concern to me than how much hair my face grew. To boot, I relished irking command by pushing what was acceptable. They weren't as keen on dragging men slacking on regulations off the front because they needed all the help they could get – especially after so many years of war.

Besides tidying my rifle, I played some more cards, got some dinner with Udo, and even managed to find some time to write in my journal after I composed a letter addressed to my sisters. It was hard being without my family.

It was about half an hour after dinner when I grew curious

about Lindemann. I guessed he would be gone until at the very least until least dinner was over, but I was unsure when exactly he planned to return. He had not the slightest idea when I bumped into him briefly during the Sturmbannführer's falsehood-instilling speech.

Time with Denis was going to be a real test for my newest recruit. Despite my constant belittling, the Oberleutnant admittedly was a fantastic salesman and had a very quick wit. Even so, I hoped there was some form of ethics aligned deep within Lindemann that was polished enough to realise that the Nazis are not the final evolution of us Germans and were, in fact, just criminals using their blatant racism as a scapegoat to further gain power for themselves. Though I was disappointed to admit he was sort of my friend, the Oberleutnant was the epitome of a dirtbag, and I would never forgive myself if he instilled his morals (or lack thereof) into my newest protégé.

All the uncertainty eventually led me to ponder about what kind of person Lindemann is. He sure seemed to drift off when the fighting started the other day. Enough to bop himself in the face with his rifle. So, there must be something he has a deep affection for.

People react different ways when they're first indoctrinated to combat, but his was most definitely a first.

I have always tried to make sure to keep an eye out for as many of my comrades as possible. Knowing whether or not that is the right thing to do has been a struggle, especially witnessing the horrible things that some of us Germans have done to the enemy. Even more so with the Nazis. But with how large my squad was, I usually had my hands too full to worry about every single German on the same battlefield as me. I ultimately realised that it was impossible to make sure that everybody made it home. Unfortunately, I have failed before, and especially with how the war seems to be going, I am bound to fail again. I just hoped at the very least I could figure Lindemann out a slight bit more before either I failed at keeping him alive, or if my luck finally decided to run dry. I had been living on borrowed time after surviving this long anyway, so who knows how much longer until the clock strikes midnight for me.

As I soaked in the remainder of the sunshine from the setting sun, Lindemann turned a corner along the path towards our part of the camp, within shouting distance. I was oddly glad to lay eyes on him again, but I couldn't act like I cared too much, so I played it cool and made fun of him instead.

I stood up and hollered, "Hey, you made it back from the Nazi party!" Double meanings and puns were my lifelines. "Did they put fingers in your butt? I heard that was Denis's speciality." The squad around my spot made a muffled cackle as Lindemann's cheeks turned a dark rose. As usual, I got the biggest kick out of the dainty grin that crept up on Udo's face.

Even after embarrassment, he still managed to compose a comeback. "He must have stopped doing that after you left his direct command," he retaliated. Denis must have told him that I was the old squad leader.

Even so, I joined everyone's hoot in admiration of his crack back. I patted him on the shoulder when he got close enough. "Welcome back from fantasy land, Lindemann."

The rookie winced at my gesture before glancing away as he rolled his eyes. "Yeah, that was sure something," he admitted. The sarcasm of his words made relief hit me like a tidal wave.

"What makes you say that?" I inquired as casually as possible.

Before explaining himself, Lindemann reached into a bulging pocket I somehow missed the opportunity to make poke fun at earlier to pull out quite possibly the most beautiful apple I had ever seen. It was a juicy shade of scarlet and was plump enough to have been pulled straight from a book of a toddler. All of the other men in the squad snapped their heads to catch a glimpse of the miraculous fruit from their new favourite rookie and promptly gathered around to steal a bite.

Lindemann, overwhelmed at the new popularity a simple apple could provide, must have sensed his time with his treasure was limited. He should have taken the first bite right away because he was almost immediately harassed by the old factory worker Obergefreiter Karl Moller. He was the first of the squad to reach us, and apparently, the hungriest.

"How does a little boy like you get your hands on something as beautiful as that?" Moller's pupils grew to be as large as coins as he approached the red delicacy. Pfeiffer, not even second in line for the apple, shouted from behind, "The first bite is mine, Moller! Don't even try it."

Moller turned back to yell, "The hell it is, that apple is all mine!" He raised his claws to abduct the apple of his eye from Lindemann's hands.

As Moller's self-righteous tentacles got close, a hand darted in to block him from swiping the apple. "Hey now, Moller, he must be hungry, I'm sure he deserves it." Obergrenadier Gunther Herrmann, right behind Moller, made it seem like he couldn't let poor Lindemann get swamped right away, so he stepped in to defend the recruit. But Herrmann was a shrewd operator, so his 'nice guy' approach was just to earn a bite. Moller tended to be a little abrasive, especially with the new guys, so Herrmann knew he could use it to his advantage.

"What do you know about being hungry, Herrmann?" Moller's aggressive bronze eyes dug into Herrmann with a chubby finger referencing his adversary's smaller stature. Even though Herrmann was by no means a wee man, compared to how bulky Moller was from moving large boxes around in a factory for years, he might as well have been Pfeiffer's size.

But Moller left the door wide open for a sassy comment. "Oh, that's right, if we're not as fat as you, we don't get hungry. That's how our bodies work. Thanks for the biology lesson, Moller,"

I teased.

One of Moller's bushy eyebrows raised as he flashed me his eyes. Now fighting a war on two fronts, he was overwhelmed from trying to think of anything to say, so I continued to address the situation as the entire squad closed in. As much as I hated doing it, I could still use my rank if I needed to.

"Alright, everybody, we all want a taste, so let's go one at a time, and make sure you take small enough one so everybody can get a bit." I looked at Moller specifically to call out, "Especially you, mate."

Lindemann assumed I would go first, so he poked me with the apple after I finished my statement. I figured I would get one of the first nibbles, but I was still delighted nonetheless. If this was any other situation, I would have made sure everybody else had a bite before I did, but since I specifically told Lindemann to take something from the SS for me, I had to bask in the glory of the moment. It had been much too long since I had seen such an exquisite fruit.

I plucked the apple from Lindemann's hand with a thank-you and took the smallest of samples from the wondrous delicacy. I might as well have entered a state of complete solace as my mouth was rushed full of its scrumptious flavour. Despite experiencing the full might of Johannes' exceptional cooking abilities (even before supplies were not as scarce), the understated juiciness of the simple fruit was quite possibly the best experience my taste buds have gone through that month.

As soon as the apple dropped from the attack range of my teeth, the slight Gefreiter Burkhard Kuhn snatched the edible gold from my hand and promptly took a disproportionally broad bite. Moller and Herrmann's jaws dropped as they realised they had allowed anyone, especially the wee Kuhn, to get a bite before they did.

It was a surprise to everyone. Besides Kuhn being smaller and not aggressive at all when it comes to food or rather virtually anything else, he was universally known as one of the kindest men to ever grace this horrid war. It took him forever to start actually shooting at the enemy, and I swear to goodness, when he finally did, I once witnessed him yell, "Sorry!" after he fired his rifle. He probably still missed on purpose. Such a quality guy.

Kuhn's chewing stumbled to a crawl as he noticed the

perplexed stares he was getting from everybody else in the squad. After a second of silence, he justified his actions. "I just really like apples, okay?" The entire squad roared, even the unbearably hungry Moller and Herrmann.

As the others continued divulging in the fruity delicacy, I figured it was a good time to proceed to ask Lindemann about his time with the Nazis. "So, was your experience today as dandy as this apple?" I queried after a beckoning jab at him with my elbow.

Lindemann rotated his head away from the others to respond, "I wouldn't necessarily say it went '*dandy*,' but it wasn't horrible."

Udo Sommer was hardly finished chewing before he decided to weigh in on Lindemann's trip. "Did you talk to the Sturmbannführer after his speech today? I can't believe he just got back from meeting with the Führer himself."

Lindemann returned Udo's gaze. "Yeah, I spoke with him briefly afterwards, which I guess was cool, but it was also kind of weird," responded Lindemann as he scratched the back of his neck.

Burkhard asked the empathetic question, "Why do you say that?" He was indeed a benevolent one.

Lindemann shifted side to side. "Well, there was just a weird vibe surrounding the whole thing." Burkhard nodded in complete absorption, so Lindemann further divulged. "They make it sound like everything is perfect there, and I don't know. I got this really weird impression with the relationship between everyone in command, like between the Oberleutnant and the Führer, and Oberleutnant Ross and the Oberleutnant."

I couldn't help but let out a chuckle, knowing both of them from long ago. "I'm pretty sure I know what you mean, but I want your take on it."

Lindemann glanced at me, and then to the ground. "I felt like… Like they were always… I don't know…" He searched me for approval as he carefully let out, "…Trying to show off who was courting the Führer the hardest...?"

Udo and I locked gazes as we might as well have died from laughter. Well, I sure did, and Udo gave a comparably as hearty chuckle. Udo truly had lightened up as of late, and I was charmed with who he was becoming. I treasured his renewed sense of humour.

Removing his glasses to wipe the tears from his eyes, he still snickered as he remarked, "What an incredibly vivid description,

Lindemann."

Gefreiter Gunther Herrmann, a quieter soldier, decided to add his two cents. "Well hey, it worked out then." He must have been referencing the apple, of course. "Schmidt had his underwear in a bunch, worried sick about you all day," he jested.

I didn't anticipate a wisecrack and scrambled to assemble a retaliation long enough for Moller find an opportunity to avenge being chaffed at earlier. "Yeah, he was writing all day. They were probably poems about you, Lindemann."

Finding an opportunity to make fun of his macho-man appearance, Udo stepped in to take a shot at Moller. "Actually, I heard they were poems about you." To my surprise, Feldwebel Pfeiffer joined the snickering from the outskirts of our circle. That would have been a joke I could have pinned being used on him.

Our lively chortle died down as I added, "I'd let you see them, Moller, but they use pretty big words. You wouldn't understand." It's a go-to insult, but it was nonetheless effective.

"Hah," Herrmann added to the banter. "Those poems are something even I wouldn't snatch from the battlefield."

I admire somebody who makes fun of themselves, and even

though the reputation of such a looter was generally frowned upon, the confident humbleness that Herrmann radiates beneath his street-smart exterior breathe at least some humanity into his soul.

Nonetheless, Moller liked Herrmann's crack, and slapped his knee before pointing at me to say, "Gotcha." I shrugged to play off the joke when I noticed Lindemann grinning at me. It gave me a revelation that perhaps the chef was right - there just may be hope for him yet.

Chapter 7

Grenadier Bruno Lindemann

The surrounding city must have been stunning a few years ago. The use of rock as a building material was a terrific choice. The granite bridge beyond what must have been a market area to our front repeatedly caught my eyes. We also had to watch it for incoming enemies, I still thoroughly enjoyed the architecture, even if there were was rubble sporadically scattered across it.

There were two apartment-style buildings on top of empty businesses to either side of the front of the bridge. The one on the left was bombed out, leaving a trail of rubble that one could climb to a hallway on the second floor. Slightly in front of that building, and almost immediately to our left, was a cozy alley. It surely once contained fond memories from the inhabitants of this town. Now, it would just be a narrow hallway of death. Gefreiter Herrmann and Grenadier Graf locked it down to prevent any Russians from advancing through it. Gefreiter Herrmann didn't seem like the type of person I'd enjoy working closely alongside. I decided I'd have to ask Graf about it later. Us lowly Grenadiers were close.

A short, stone fence advanced alongside the walls of the bridge and to the right of it, leading to a slightly damaged but still relatively still intact building. On the bottom floor of that structure were the remnants of a store. I couldn't help but think of what kind of business was there before the war had made its mark on this land. I wondered if the store's owners were still alive, and if they were, what they would do after the fighting here had stopped. Would they return to their old workplace and decide to repair the damages? Or would they cut their losses and move to a less destroyed townt? Perhaps a store in another town would have a vacancy. That was the only piece of consolation I could find about the decimation of such a romantic town, although I did enjoy the destroyed building. It suggested that maybe it was okay to be damaged.

Our building was surprisingly intact, which was peculiar because it was smack in the middle of the market area. Schmidt and I were on the second floor, with one small, unoccupied window in the attic above. Obergefreiter Moller and his new replacement recruit, Grenadier Weiss, were on the machine gun on the floor below. Weiss was previously the pupil of another veteran, but he had fallen in battle, so they paired him under Moller, whose recruit had too perished.

Scattered around our building was the rest of the squad. There must have been a railroad somewhere nearby because there were bits of track and a few train carriages almost kissing the right corner of our house. The squad decided to use them as cover. It offered protection from the bridge to our front, and to the open street to the right of us, where the marketplace closed up to a road.

We had been positioned in the market area for the better part of the day, but the few weeks since we had first entered this town seemed like an eternity. It was a hair colder now as well – not anywhere near snowing, but not as comfortable as it was when I had arrived.

I cast my eyes to the kneeling Schmidt on my right. He tended to be silent when on watch, probably so he could concentrate on the battlefield. But I'd also bet he was lost in thought about something. As much as I give him grief, we were at the very least similar in that aspect. I, too, get lost in my mind during the lulls. Hell, even during battle.

It made me miss Annette. I thought about her at every chance

I could afford to, and many times I really shouldn't. Occasionally, I would get to write her letters. But in the days since being held up in this city, I haven't been able to find the time. I hoped she was okay. Maybe when we are done fighting this war, we can open up a shop or a business together. After all, I would bet my day's ration of cigarettes that there will be some empty businesses by the time this war ended.

But what if I didn't return a hero? Would Annette still care for me if I couldn't prove my worth on the battlefield? It worried me because I wasn't operating at peak performance. My irregular sleeping pattern didn't help. Again and again, I would have reoccurring nightmares of my first battle. Huber's cries for help echoed in the ambiance as that machine gun spat its lead towards his niche until it eventually caught its prey. Every time, my stomach goes in knots as I laid my eyes on Huber's mutilated remains. As if under a trance, I couldn't stop myself from pulling the trigger on that wounded Russian inside, despite Rupert's harrowing threat. I would repeatedly wake up with my hairs on end, topped in a frigid sweat after absorbing Schmidt's blow as he witnessed the execution. I would tremble as I remembered the certainty of his words: "And if I ever see you shoot a defenseless soldier again, I'll kill you myself." I could never tell Annette about what I had seen out here. How could I ever burden such an innocent person at home with such haunting experiences?

We had had some light skirmishes since, but that monster inside of me that came out after Huber died hadn't yet come out again. But whenever he did, I wasn't sure if I could hold him back. And if I could ever hide him again whenever the fighting stopped. The worst part of it all was that I knew I would eventually have to kill again, no matter how hard I tried not to.

But the real evil was not inside of me - it was the Soviets, and I would need to learn how to tame this monster to crush them. Taming it would be required to make Annette proud.

An enemy tank rolled through an intersection at the end of the street, far beyond the bridge. Behind it followed some Russians. Most of them kept following the tank, but a handful of them turned to head in our direction. We could see them, but they were well out of range. Nonetheless, I propped up my rifle and aimed for when they would be close enough. Schmidt stomped his foot twice to let Moller and Weiss below know that the enemy was en-route. We heard their footsteps before they signaled the others by banging the wall to alert the others outside.

"Back up. You're letting your rifle stick out of the building again," Schmidt calmly whispered. He had been doing everything in his power to micromanage me, and my fear of him promptly found a way to morph into irritation. While he meant to be useful, he more often than not just tested my nerves.

Even so, I knew he was right, so I did as he asked. If my rifle stuck out of a window, our enemies could spot me easier from the side. They could even spot me easier from the front because I would be closer to the natural light shining down from the outside.

Despite heeding his warning, Schmidt opted to repeat the rationale of his lesson. "Remember, the best armor in battle is invisibility. If they can't see you, they can't shoot you."

Keeping my rifle pointed towards the approaching Ivans, I still decided to mock him by continuing his lesson in a higher-pitched voice. "Second is *speed* because they can't shoot what they can't catch, and *armor* is third, which is useless to us because we have no armor." We could technically count the cover we hid behind as armor, but I just felt like giving him a hard time.

Schmidt grunted. “Heaven forbid I try to keep you alive out here, hey?” Even the heaviness of combat encroaching couldn’t prevent Schmidt from shooting back a sassy comment.

The Bolsheviks were almost within our effective shooting range. We were higher up than everyone else in the squad, so we got first pickings. A gaggle of men advanced towards us, but three men led the pack. The veterans would have to lead from the front, as their senses of the battlefield were the sharpest and could most easily sense when something was about to happen. They were to be our first targets.

Schmidt and I could have probably hit them already, but it was of little use if we engaged them before anyone else could. Schmidt always took the first shot, which usually signified everyone else to join in. The rest of the men would generally wait for him because his first bullet was most likely to hit an unsuspecting victim, and he had the best pick of who to go for initially with the perk of our vantage point. We would try to hit leadership and gun crews first because losing them causes the most disarray.

Schmidt interrupted the encroaching tenseness of the up-and-coming battle. “This one is all yours, Lindemann,” he smoothly denoted with a tap on my knee. The first shot was a big deal to me, so I was determined to show him how competent I was, especially with the new scope.

When I came back from spending a day with Oberleutnant Ross around a month ago, Schmidt dug into his supplies to present me with a gift rolled up in cloth. I carefully unrolled the corners and uncovered a scope smaller than Schmidt's with a front mount made to replace the front sight on my rifle. With very little information elsewhere, he briefly mentioned it was something he'd been "holding for a friend," but he'd allow me to use it in the meantime. He then joked about how the advantage it'd give me at range would hopefully help me not blindly charge into battle like my first engagement.

I aimed my newly-modified Karabiner 98k at the Russian in the front of the group of three. The new scope so small and far away from my eyes, nothing like optics of the hunting rifles I had used back at home. My field of view was much less. It was also was not as hefty as Schmidt's and offered only 1.5x magnification compared to his 4x. Even so, it was more than enough to gain a foot up from this distance, especially compared to the iron sights I had before.

The Soviets had entered our effective range. I selected my target to be the first man leading the pack. Schmidt had taught to avoid aiming for the head because it was a small target and easier to miss, so I pointed my rifle at the upper portion of his chest.

The lead Soviet had almost made it to the other side of the bridge when he began to act suspiciously. It was as if his experiences had hinted towards his grave future. My rifle started wobbling. I took a deep breath out and then inhaled as much air as I could. Huber's horrified face flashed in my brain, and I shuddered. Whether or not that memory forced me to forget how to breathe at that instant, or if I was holding my breath, I could not decide.

None of that mattered now – I knew it was time, so after finishing triple checking everything from my positioning, to my cover, to the men around my target, I rallied my strength and nervously squeezed the trigger.

The rifle kicked back into my shoulder. My bullet took less than a fraction of a second to travel through the air before it hit the lead Soviet in the upper left part of his torso, right underneath the shoulder. An arm jerked back as he let out an agonizing scream. The blood oddly satisfyingly splattered behind and around him as his body twisted from absorbing the impact of my bullet. He dropped his weapon right as the men around him dissipated among the walls of the buildings on the street. Moller's machine gun below us immediately began spewing out rounds, and the rest of the squad joined in as if they had been eagerly anticipating this moment.

It only hit by the Soviet's shoulder, though, and hardly at it. I couldn't understand why I didn't get a cleaner hit. He wasn't in cover, nor was he far away. He had even stuttered, giving me a second to aim. Even so, I should have been able to hit him again if I wanted to, but I was preoccupied with the others.

I took a few more fruitless shots at the scurrying men behind the wounded Red before I noticed that he was bleeding a lot for just a shoulder wound. Left and right around him, his comrades were being mercilessly wiped out by our men. His morale had to be inconceivably low.

The man I had shot first laid behind the stone sides of the short wall beyond the bridge, positioned relatively safe from most of the fire the squad was putting downrange. The strained Bolshevik was still screaming, and the heavy fire around him prevented anybody from effectively helping him.

I further debated firing another round at him to put an end to his suffering. Part of me still upset sought revenge for Huber as well. Maybe if I avenged him, my nightmares would subside, and I could sleep. I almost justified shooting him again, but Schmidt's death threat after I shot the last soldier a while back deterred me.

Enough was going on around my first victim to stop worrying about him for a while. Schmidt had topped off his rifle with more rounds twice before I had even once. I had some catching up to do.

There were a couple of other men I could have aimed for, but I found it best just to only focus on one. My next target was a Bolshevik behind and to the right of the first man I shot. He was taking cover in the doorway of a bombed-out building. He would occasionally pop out and fire a burst from his submachine gun before taking cover. He wasn't the closest to us, so he probably assumed he was safer than the others. Schmidt taught me the other day to not always focus on the first Russians to engage unless they were an immediate threat. The ones behind the leaders of the pack often took less care in taking cover, thinking they were not the first ones we would aim at.

He popped out again, and I fired a shot. The wall behind him exploded bits of brick. It startled him, and he retook cover inside the building. He knew someone was zeroing in on him, so hitting him was going to be a bit harder of a challenge.

Moller's machine gun below us kept spewing out bullets. Such a weapon could dominate the atmosphere, and even though Schmidt and I could perform on the battlefield just as well (if not better), the high rate of fire provided for a deterrent against any bold Russians willing to advance on our position. It was the most important weapon we had.

The weapon was an MG-42, which was the improved version of the legendary MG-34 we used earlier in the war. It could shoot out somewhere around 15 rounds a second, which was more than twice of the Russian Maxim or their pan-fed machine guns. That was as many bullets per minute as an entire squad of men using my rifle. Maybe two squads. There was no doubt in my mind that it was the best weapon of the war. Its distinct noise made while firing visibly instilled fear in any overhearing enemy. It made me jealous, in a sense. I couldn't imagine terrorizing the enemy like Moller was with a mere bolt-action rifle.

My target popped out again, but less than before. He had just finished a burst when I squeezed off another round.

That time, it hit mere inches away from his hands. Dammit, I missed again! His weapon sprung away as a reaction from my projectile hitting so close, and he buried himself behind cover yet again.

That moment reminded me of why Schmidt stressed changing cover. Schmidt's instructions indicated that if the first two shots missed and the target remained in the same spot, it was because of luck that they missed. The third would be almost guaranteed to land because by then, the shooter would be zeroed-in. So I knew that my next shot was most likely to hit.

With that in mind, the man popped out a third time, and I calmly fired again, instantly scoring a hit. My bullet bounced off his PPSh and slammed into his arm. His weapon almost comically flew through the air as the man's arm ingested my round. It wasn't the cleanest hit, but he would now have trouble firing his weapon.

Another scream originated from my first victim. Somebody else managed to hit him from behind the stone wall. He took one in the thigh as well from trying to crawl to a safer position. I stared at the deep red puddle draining from another wound on his leg. Almost immediately, his screaming had become more stressed as he grew closer to the brink of life. Again, I debated firing another round at him. He was likely to continue writhing in pain until he eventually nodded off and entered a slumber. For a second, I thought that was why that Russian machine gunner killed Huber. So that he wouldn't suffer anymore.

A rifle shot popped off in the distance as the 'ping' of a bullet contacting metal echoed from below us. The machine gun below us sprayed the rest of its burst upward and then went silent, and I realized the worst had happened as fellow rookie Grenadier Weiss screamed below us.

The round had likely gone through the steel helmet of Moller, interrupting the machine gun's reign. Weiss let out another distressed yelp as the situation sunk in, which prompted Schmidt to take control of the situation.

"Get that MG running again!" Schmidt's voice grew deep and uncharacteristically severe again. "Lindemann! Change to the window in the attic!" Schmidt fired another round off into the distance as an enemy's bullet zoomed through the window he was firing out of, obliging him to jolt within the safety below the window. We shared a mutual guise of concern as we gathered how close he had just come to death.

Almost instantly, his eyebrows dropped, and an agape mouth tapered to the sides of his face once again. He kindled his fighting spirit and shifted to the window one further away from me to continue the conflict.

I sprinted to the stairs just as the MG-42 begun continuing its reckoning below once again. Grenadier Weiss was genuinely showing his grit - the recruit almost immediately remanned the machine gun after watching yet another one of his mentors take a bullet before his very eyes, all besides being a priority target for the Russians. Just like us, the Russians had learned to aim at the enemy they deemed most dangerous, which was usually the machine gun.

I made it to the window upstairs, which was much smaller and octagon-shaped. It should offer me a bit more protection than the windows below, which I was fortunate for. I bashed through the glass with the stock of my rifle so the glass wouldn't affect my aim. I then hid for a couple of seconds to keep the suspicion away from me.

The tip of my rifle was about half a meter away from the glass of the window when I soon took aim, to keep my new position as concealed as possible. I had an even better vantage point than before.

More Soviets had begun pouring in from the intersection at the end of the street. But before worrying about them, I glanced at the Russian I had picked off first. He was no longer yelling. Now, he was just coughing up blood as the internal damage from his wounds further took their toll on him. For the third time, I debated shooting him. I knew I wasn't supposed to feel anything for these filthy Soviets and had grown a callous attitude in the few weeks since I had first arrived. But witnessing a man's gruesome struggle to stay alive amidst our ambush was still a challenging watch.

The man finally stopped screaming to stare blankly into the sky. I definitively decided against firing another round into him. He was moments away from death anyway, and by now was making a final peace with his memories before he finally perished.

Enemy soldiers endlessly poured in from afar as Grenadier Weiss had let out a ferocious battle cry from downstairs. My hairs stood on end as his machine gun continued to displace rounds downrange. I took note of his bravery, knowing I would need to channel a similar part of me to return home distinguished.

I fired another round off into the horde of enemies when another crack in the distance when a particularly long burst from the machine gun strafed towards where none of them were. Another lull in the machine gun fire confirmed my fears. Son of a bitch, they hit Grenadier Weiss, too!

But with a tremendous howl, the machine gun below began firing yet again. It wasn't the scream from before, though. It was like the one from the communist who gunned down Grenadier Huber. This terrifying roar was a shout that called upon all of the loved ones, brothers, sisters, mothers, fathers, and all comrades. It simultaneously gave them all a final goodbye while drawing from their strengths to carry out a last act of heroism. Grenadier Weiss had taken a bullet. But accepting death, he had decided to fight until his last breath, knowing he was likely to catch a fatal round like Moller moments before. His last stand was truly remarkable.

Schmidt interrupted Weiss's reckoning. "Lindemann! First floor, now!" he shouted from beneath me. I fired another round when I saw a grenade lobbed into the distance from his floor.

As I passed through the second floor, I heard the distinct sound of a smoke grenade popping off as Schmidt trailed me down to the first floor. He directed me to where Grenadier Weiss was still screaming, still shooting off the MG-42 into the growing cloud on top of the bridge.

I entered Weiss's tiny room and immediately caught an engulfing, horrid whiff of human gore. Turning towards the middle of the small room, pure fear over swept my body as I stumbled upon the distorted remains of Huber scattered across the ground in front of me. My jaw dropped as I tripped and collapsed to a knee, and I retreated backward until my back hit the wall. It couldn't be him! Isn't it enough that these memories dominate my dreams? Can't they just leave me alone when I'm awake?

After I tried frantically wiping my eyes, they lazily refocused on the room to reveal the remains of Obergefreiter Moller on the ground. Although his body remained larger than most even after death, his head was disfigured and covered in so much blood that I wouldn't have recognized him otherwise. To the wall behind him was a gruesome spray of the burgundy-blasted innards of Moller's head paired with the blood expunged from Weiss's wound. I had seen this scene before, but coming this close to such a grisly corpse still made me dry heave. Especially because that corpse belonged to a member of my squad.

Schmidt, however, was undeterred and made it downstairs, hurrying around my recuperating self. He brushed past me and crouched by Moller's body with his back towards me before spinning around with dog tags. He calmly held them in front of me.

"Take these," he demanded as the trance I found myself caught in subsided. I snatched them out of his hands, and then he added, "And make sure Grenadier Weiss gets to safety while I man his gun."

Before grabbing the dog tags, I observed Schmidt's eyes for a split second. They had further lightened from their ordinary shade of light brown. Though not the same gold I thought I saw during my first fight, they were undeniably out of the ordinary for Schmidt. How a man's eyes could change so suddenly was beyond me, but I was too overstimulated to think much about it.

"Weiss, comrade, today isn't your day," Schmidt declared as he placed his hand on Weiss's good shoulder. His other shoulder could only remain stiff after being pierced by a bullet. Weiss did not even acknowledge Schmidt. He just continued to let out a frightened yell while holding down the trigger of his machine gun.

Schmidt pulled on his shoulder again, this time strong enough to pry him away from the weapon. Grenadier Weiss wrestled him at first but soon stopped putting up a fight. With tears strolling down his cheeks, he snapped out of the valiant mode that had made peace with parting from its soul. What replaced it was a shocked state of confused innocence.

Schmidt didn't waste any time processing his face like I did, and got right to the point. "Lindemann will take you back to base. This world will need people like you alive after the war."

A cannon boomed in the distance from the end of the street. My blood froze as an explosion from the front of our building shook the ground. The remaining beauty of the marketplace was compromised.

Pfeiffer instantaneously picked it up. Realizing how futile the situation had grown, he shouted, "Enemy armor! We cannot win here! Fall back! Fall back!" The squad echoed his orders as they hastily began scurrying to safer ground.

Schmidt thrust Weiss towards me and readied the machine

gun. “Get out of here! Before the smoke clears up!” His newly glided eyes shimmered as he hastily loaded a fresh belt of ammunition and began firing into the thinning smoke covering the bridge. I wanted to say something to him, but I was too entranced by the situation. I couldn’t think of anything worthy enough.

I speedily positioned Weiss’s unwounded shoulder around my neck to help him move. I had just made it outside the back of the building with a delirious, weeping Weiss when we met up with some other members of our squad, including Sommer, who hastily asked, “Where is Schmidt?” An explosion thundered from the store to the right of the bridge I was pondering about earlier.

Before I could respond to Sommer, the MG-42 stopped firing, and Schmidt yelled my name. “Lindemann! You’re Overwatch while I’m gone!”

Sommer’s slowly widening eyes behind his wire glasses gave away his piecing together of the situation. He gathered that he may lose yet another comrade today. But his face tightened up, as if he was still upset, but had accepted what was likely to happen. Without any warning, he sprinted across the street, then stacked up on the back of a building on the other side to cover our retreat.

I quickly regained my bearings as well. With Weiss's weight over my shoulders, I swiftly darted into the street, back towards where we initially entered the. Despite the thinning cloud between us, some marketplace of the Russians had begun returning fire over the bridge. The bodies from a few of the brave savages that tried advancing through the smoke laid dead on our side of the bridge. The Soviet tank wasn't fully visible, but we knew it was pushing up. Schmidt's machine gun remained hailing bullets into the rapidly dissipating smoke by the bridge, covering our retreat.

After salvo of machine gun fire, we heard a final request echo from inside Schmidt's building. "If I don't make it, tell Oberleutnant Ross that he is a piece of shit!" he insisted. Schmidt briefly persisted hailing rounds downrange before pausing another time. "A literal *piece* of *shit*!" The sounding off of his weapon again carried on.

Sommer's eyes grew glossy from being situated between realizing that he may never see Schmidt again and at the dark humor that his potential final words were a friendly insult to make a venture at lifting the breaking spirits of his comrades. How could Schmidt find any humor in being the last man here, in the same cramped room as his butchered, lifeless comrade?

One by one, the rest of the squad crossed the bridge and begun heading back to the rally point. Sommer was the last of the squad to leave the marketplace. He might have been the last one out anyway, but I believed he had trouble leaving Schmidt alone in the face of death. He provided cover by frantically firing his bolt-action rifle into the fray. A massive explosion tore apart the top of Schmidt's building, scattering rubble across the entirety of the road between us and the marketplace. Sommer was finally obliged by the blast to fall back with the rest of us.

We could hear the armor in the distance. For once, I wasn't thinking of Annette. Surprisingly, I was thinking about Schmidt. I wondered how long he would last in such a place. The smoke must have been dissipated by now. Surely the enemy tank could see where Schmidt was holding out.

We shuffled for blocks and blocks past various buildings, some damaged and some completely untouched. I realized that Weiss had stopped crying on my shoulder. He was having trouble moving from losing so much energy from his bleeding wound. I was starting to do most of the work in transporting him. Sommer caught on, and carefully tried assisting him from the other side without touching his shoulder wound.

After an anxious ten minutes or so, we finally reached the next line of our defenses. Another squad with an anti-tank cannon had already dug in. Most of our men joined them, but along with Pfeiffer's approval, my priority was fulfilling Schmidt's final request by finding someone who could treat Weiss's wounds.

Weiss had hardly enough energy to stand at this point, let alone move. I began repositioning him to carry him entirely by myself. Sommer wouldn't allow me, and after shouldering his rifle, we both lifted Weiss by the back and legs, so Weiss no longer had to use up his remaining energy from traversing.

After about ten more minutes of carrying Weiss past various soldiers hurrying to and from the defenses, we crossed paths with a medic who was on his way to the front. He took notice of Weiss' condition and directed us into the protection of a nearby building where it was slightly safer to patch him up. We shuffled inside and carefully laid him down on the floor, where the medic had begun doing what he could. Weiss couldn't talk, but his glistening eyes blankly stayed open. He was still conscious, which was a good sign.

The medic had cut around Weiss' uniform. He was doing his best to position a bandage over the wound by his shoulder effectively but was having trouble finding a suitable spot. It made me wonder how that first Soviet I shot was doing right now. He, too, had a wound in the same place.

After a few seconds of watching, Sommer put his hand on my shoulder. The blood of our comrade's wound had stained his uniform. I knew his distressed eyes were equally as concerned about leaving Schmidt back there. Those two became good friends since the first day I met him. Sommer always seemed to admire him. I hardly got to know Schmidt.

After looking at Sommer for a well-needed second, we both turned back towards Weiss. I probed my fingers in the pocket I put Moller's dog tags in to make sure I still had them. I figured I should probably find someone to give them to.

Chapter 8

A letter by Unterfeldwebel Rupert Schmidt

My Dearest Sisters,

I apologise for not writing to you as much as I had wished. Waking up each morning to carry on this pointless war is a struggle. Unfortunately, none of us has any choice in the matter. But I do still think about you two every single day.

I suppose I should tell you how things have been as of late. You've always teased me about being skinny, let's just say I've got even more of an "athletic" build now. There isn't much to eat nowadays, but Johannes works his magic with every dish, so the taste is usually something to look forward to. His old self is doing well, which I am thankful for because he always provides me with valuable insight. Every time I think I've seen it all, he gives me another way to look at things. I don't have many people to look up to out here, but it's safe to say I am still learning from him. I wish you both got to meet him.

Speaking of friends, Udo Sommer and I have grown

especially close lately. He started making a point to be around me more often, which is great because he used to be such a loner. I still worry about him, but I think he's adjusting a bit better nowadays. Udo's usually on the quiet side, but he can be quite lively when we get his mind off the war. He'll mention his family's restaurant back at home, and how he used to love cooking for it. I can only imagine his dishes, however, because Udo will eat literally anything. I once caught him eating spilt beans off the muddy ground beside the Chef's pot! Still, he's one of my favourites out here.

Pfeiffer is the same, always being so quick to argue. He is always so intense. Just like Oberfeldwebel Martin. That's probably why they're so close. I still wonder where they would fit outside of this war. Nonetheless, at this point, They've become family to me, and I'd rather have them in charge of me than anyone else. I'm just glad they're on my side when the bullets start flying.

Gunther Herrmann is still doing what he does best – finding the goodies littered throughout the battlefield. I caught him toying with a silver pendant I didn't notice on him before the other day. He shouldn't mess with the dead, but I suppose someone else would have taken it anyway, and there's a lot worse going on. He fits in well with the rest of the squad and has retained his close companionship with Moller.

Speaking of Moller, I had a terrific conversation with him the other day! I caught him starring a little bit too intently into an abandoned flower shop the other day. So, I went up to him and casually asked him if he liked flowers. And after some friendly pushing, he admitted his family ran a flower shop! Apparently, he comes from a long line of florists. But he isn't so good with colours, so he took up the job in the factory instead. I must admit that I look at him in a completely different light now. Who would have thought that such a rugged man like Moller had an affinity for something as delicate as flowers!

Unlike a flower, however, the little shit Denis Ross is still out here as well. For some reason, I just can't seem to hate him, despite how close he is with the Nazis. Johannes pointed it out recently, explaining that everybody comes from different backgrounds and that Denis simply never was taught any better. A long time ago in Africa, he shared that he's not too close to his parents. Either one or both of them. From a young age, he learnt that he needed to look out for himself. We really lucked out with how great Mom and Dad were. They'd always teach us right from wrong. I'll never forget when Mom caught me stealing from the candy store and made me go back in and pay, or when Dad quit his banking job because they were doing something unethical. They gave us a moral compass. So, Johannes said I should cut Denis some slack because he never even knew about one. All he knew was to take care of the people around him, which I'll admit, he does a damn fine job of. He's always looked out for me, even when the Sturmbannführer is hot on my ass. And apparently, he's got a sister who he cares for as well. But don't let that fool you, as that man is without a doubt in anybody's mind still the most fitting example of a textbook piece of shit.

I witnessed the funniest moment the other day! My newest pupil, a child around the both of your ages named Bruno Lindemann, managed to procure the most alluring apple I've ever seen. The entire squad surrounded us, trying to snatch a precious bite. But, the person to steal it out of my hand right after Lindemann and I took our portions was none other than the ordinarily selfless Burkhard Kuhn! You should have seen Moller and Herrmann's faces. They were yearning for a taste harder than anybody else! Well, anybody except for Kuhn, apparently. It was quite an act from him, easily the most generous man amongst us.

That brings me to my newest recruit, Lindemann. It would be hard to describe our time together without mentioning the mixed signals he radiates. On one end, he seems to love that gibberish Nazi ideology. He mouths off at my orders. Despite continually drifting off in thought, he still hasn't told me almost anything about him unless I specifically ask, which always seems a bit forced. Worst yet, I witnessed him commit a terrible act during his first battle, one I will not compromise the innocence of your ears by describing. He's just not somebody I want to be around.

But on the other hand, he earned some points with me the other day. After the rest of the squad was done eating the apple and had dispersed, we had some one-on-one time to shoot the shit. I took the opportunity to ask him what his opinions were on the Nazis their role in the war. He started to lose me as he began mentioning how elite the Reich's soldiers were and how the Russians were beneath us "mighty Germans." But his demeanour changed when he said something along the lines of, "But the Nazis are just concerned about winning, not keeping me alive." I previously vented my concerns to Johannes, and as always, he seems to have proved himself as savvy with people. If I can give the little shit Denis a pass for being raised to not know any better, then perhaps I can provide the child Lindemann with something similar. And maybe with time, I can teach him what is right. Mom and Dad would be proud if I could.

Even so, I wish he'd tell me more about him. He still has a mark on his face from when he snapped out of some daydream amid his first battle, just to smack himself with his rifle. I really wish I knew what he was thinking about. Bending over backwards to teach a new recruit is quite the challenge when he remains somebody I hardly know. I haven't quite excelled in similar roles in the past.

Today, I chuckled quietly to myself when I remembered the last time we went ice skating. I can't understand for the life of me why I couldn't do it as well as you two – I resembled a baby giraffe taking his first steps while out on that ice. I wish we could have done that more before I left. I regret not having been there for you two as you both grew up. I'd do anything to go back in time and be there with you two. But it's too late now. I just hope I have been a good enough role model for you two. The military has awarded me many different ranks and awards since I have joined. Still, the most important title I've ever owned is that of "older brother."

By now, you must also understand that there remains no guarantee that none of us could survive this war. As time carries on, my chance of keeping my life grows progressively bleaker. So, if there's one closing thought I could leave you with, one final thing I could mention before my possible demise, I'd give you a final declaration of what I've already proclaimed a million times before, but I'll say again for emphasis: to the core of my being, I love you both more than life itself.

With love from your favourite older brother,

Rupert

Chapter 9

Grenadier Bruno Lindemann

As I brought forth my mess tin for lunch, Johannes caught sight of my disoriented face. “Bruno, my boy, you’re getting a meal from the best chef on this side of the Danube! This is when you should be excited, not distraught,” he exclaimed, dipping his ladle into the steaming cauldron.

Johannes was right, but a meal would be hard-pressed to get me out from the depths of my mind. I scratched the back of my head and explained, “Yeah, you know, still just a little lost, I guess.”

He put his weight on the other foot, shifting his stance. Johannes’ voice lowered as he sensed the displeasure in my words. “You can’t get too bent up over what happens out there. If you don’t let it go, you’ll never be able to appreciate the wonders of life,” he advised. Johannes poured my bowl to the brim before adding in a more upbeat tone, “Like my wondrous cooking!”

He let out an infectious cackle, pleased by his own humor. It admittedly made me grin. His smile faded as he leaned forward.

"You need to give me that letter back soon… So I can send it off. You've had it for long enough."

I reached in my breast pocket to feel it. I could use more time with the letter, but Johannes was right, so I nodded to let him know. "That's true. Can I give it to you at the end of the day?" I proposed.

Johannes played with his mustache, bouncing his head from side to side before deciding to compromise. "Get it to me before I serve dinner." He shrugged and again leaned forward to admit, "I really shouldn't have procured it for you in the first place. Fair?"

He was convincing, so I agreed with a soft smile. "That seems reasonable. Thanks, Johannes."

The Feldkuchenunteroffizier gave out a nonchalant, "Yeah, yeah," before he waved me off with his ladle.

I didn't buy the rouse Johannes put on. If anyone cared about how everybody was doing, it was him. But I waved nonetheless and departed his station to begin scouring the area for someone to sit with. Since Schmidt's absence, I had been spending more time with Udo and Graf, so I took an open spot on the ground by them.

"I like the old camp more," I remarked while sitting down on the trampled grass. "We had seats back there. Now, we only have the grass to sit on."

"I'm with you on that," Graf agreed, taking another spoonful of the broth. "I can't remember the last time I ate inside a building."

"At least we get the grass to sit on instead of the snow. You both haven't been here during winter. That was the worst," Udo pointed out. He had been out here for longer than us and had fought during the previous winter. He played with his spoon as he reasoned, "Or maybe the best. Nothing tasted better than a warm meal in winter."

"I'm sure we'll get a taste of the snow eventually," Graf noted with a roll of his eyes. He wasn't wrong – it was only going to get colder for the rest of the year.

"Yeah, we sure will, won't we," I replied. I didn't mind the autumn weather we were having right now, but I shuddered when I imagined how terrible fighting in the cold would be.

Udo slurped up some of his stew from his spoon before he tapped me on the front of my arm to get my attention. "Hey, did you hear anything about Schmidt?"

I couldn't look at Udo, so I just stared into my broth. But I knew I had to pull myself together, so I stuttered, "Uh, n-no, not yet… I ask around every day, and so far, nobody's heard anything."

"Oh. Sorry to ask," Udo reacted. He was equally as troubled as me about the whole ordeal, if not more. They had grown an entrenched bond that repeatedly held as time waged on.

After a moment of staring at his food, Udo's glasses almost flicked off his face as he looked up and blurted out, "Maybe he's out harassing the enemy behind their lines!"

Graf cackled as he brought Udo down from the clouds. "That's a little farfetched, Sommer," he reasoned before taking a loud slurp of broth.

He was probably right. The Soviets were swarming the city like ants as we retreated. Even Schmidt, the renowned survivalist of our group, would have trouble staying hidden in such a scenario.

Even so, I was still feeling optimistic after the Feldkuchenunteroffizier revitalized my spirit by letting me keep the letter a few hours longer, so I countered Graf, "You never know. He did a great job of annoying us, so the Russians might find him to be equally as irritating."

Udo found that to be an amusing thought, so he commented, "The Sturmbannführer has been hot on Schmidt's ass since even before I got here, and he's seemed to elude him so far." His piercingly blue eyes sparkled as he chuckled, "Well, most of the time. I remember once, right after I arrived, The Sturmbannführer caught Schmidt mooning Oberleutnant Ross."

A smile crept on Graf's face, sparking his interest. "Really?" he questioned, putting his spoon into his mess tin and resting it on his leg. "What did the Sturmbannführer do to him?"

Enjoying the newfound popularity, Udo did his best to make his old story sound as dramatic as possible. He casually finished another bite while nodding, and leisurely swallowed before carrying on. "He wanted to have a drumhead court-martial. There were talks of sending him to a penal battalion."

Udo milked the moment by taking another drawn-out spoon of broth. Graf and I couldn't help but be drawn towards the story, willingly feeding into Udo's ego to do so. We glanced at each other before fixing our eyes on him again.

Udo finally continued. "Oberfeldwebel Martin talked down the Sturmbannführer's proposed punishment with help from by pointing out Schmidt's actions in the days before. He aided a wounded crewman of a damaged panzer. Apparently, he had broken rank, ran into enemy fire towards a burning tank, pulled a crewman from its burning carcass, and dragged him to safety. All while under fire." Udo smiled out of the corner of his mouth as he finished his story. "Oberleutnant Ross gave testimony to Schmidt's character, and the Sturmbannführer eventually conceded. He reluctantly only dropped him in rank and temporarily assigned him for manual labor to dig holes for bunkers. That's why he's an Unterfeldwebel. You don't see many of them nowadays."

"Wow, he really dodged a bullet," Graf reflected. "Hardly any survive in the punishment battalions." Penal units had a reputation for being similar to the Russians for their lack of regard for human lives. We'd all heard stories of correctional units being the last ones allowed to retreat as the rest of the soldiers fled from the drowning amounts of the Soviet forces.

"Yeah. The Feldwebel knew he would need Schmidt around because he was going to have to watch over this guy in the future," Udo added as he pointed in my direction with his spoon.

"Sometimes, I wish they had just sent me to a detention unit instead of being under him," I somewhat honestly cracked. We all chuckled.

We finished our meals and headed back to where our stash of gear. Udo went to mail a something, while Graf began to clean his weapon. Now finding myself with a bit of free time, I reached into my pocket for the piece of paper tucked inside.

It had only been a few days since I last saw Schmidt in that marketplace, but I still found myself tugging the letter tight as I reread it. I knew I had to give it back to Johannes so he could send it back to his family sooner or later, but I couldn't give it up just yet.

Maybe it was because Schmidt had directly mentioned my name in the letter. Or perhaps it was because since I had met Schmidt, I had learned more about him in this letter than from him directly. I knew he didn't care for the Nazis, but I didn't think he outright hated them. That might explain why he didn't talk too much with me. Maybe he just didn't see things the way I did.

I eventually decided to go to the medical facilities and check on how Grenadier Weiss was doing. He got hit pretty bad, and would typically be sent further behind the frontlines. But between our hasty retreat from the city the other day and Russian aircraft managing to destroy a few of our convoys behind our lines, and we were behind schedule on getting the wounded to safer areas. Even so, at least it made it easier for me to visit my injured comrades, notably Weiss, who I had visited every day since our retreat. Schmidt's last order was for me to keep an eye on him. "Lindemann! You're Overwatch while I'm gone!" His words remained etched in my memories.

Schmidt sure could be irritating, and we never quite got along. But as difficult as he could be, I was still just a bit jealous of the bond that Udo had with Schmidt. He had taught me so much about fighting, but I was disappointed that I hadn't learned much of anything else about him.

Come to think of it, there was still much more he could teach me about fighting, too. I never understood why the intensity of his eyes varied depending on the pressure of the battle. Was that something I needed to learn? How would I excel in war without him? I needed to make it back to Annette, and he was my key to do it.

Still nose-deep in Schmidt's letter, I made my way to the tent that contained the wounded Weiss. I lifted open the flap to the medical station over my head and stopped dead in my tracks as it fell behind me when I noticed, of all people, Rupert gotdamn Schmidt was sitting on the edge of Weiss' bed. How the fuck did he make it here?

"Who would have thought a florist?" Schmidt mused aloud as he started to get up. "But regardless, you deserve that."

In Weiss' bed was a black leather holster, and in his hand was one of our issued pistols. On the side of his bed were two apples. They must feed the injured well.

"I appreciate this, Unterfeldwebel Schmidt," Weiss acknowledged while Schmidt stood up. Weiss looked better than he did yesterday. His face had regained some of the colors it had lost. He wasn't doing well when we first got here.

Though he had already stood up to depart, Schmidt's eyes remained focused on Weiss. Most of his uniform was stained a dark maroon. "Well, Moller didn't need it anymore. Plus, you earned it."

Weiss held the gun with the hand he could move. His other arm was immobile, locked in a cast from catching a bullet. He continued to examine the pistol before Schmidt insisted, "And please, Joachim, call me Rupert."

Weiss faced up and agreed, "Yes sir, uh, Rupert."

Schmidt smiled as he picked up Ilsa from the side of Weiss's bed. “I’ll be seeing you, Weiss,” he remarked. The two held their grin as Schmidt committed to walking away, finally catching sight of my utterly stunned self blocking the exit.

I was too shocked to say anything quick enough, so Schmidt beat me to the punch as he placed an arm around my shoulder. “Oh, hey, Lindemann.” He peeked down at the open letter in my hands, raising an eyebrow when he noticed it was one of his. His eyes back met mine before he cocked his head to the side and quizzed, “So, do you always read other people’s letters, or are you going to swear up and down this is the only time you’ve done it?” Without adjusting his gaze towards anything else, he whipped his arm back from around my shoulder and snatched the paper out of my hand. Only after he had taken a step around me did he looked towards the flap of the tent to lift it and exit, patting the side of my arm with his fist that held his rifle.

I remained paralyzed in the same position for another second or two. I was overwhelmed over not only seeing Schmidt but also at now needing to figure out a way to explain how I ended up with one of his letters. Weiss, observing my complete surprise, beckoned for me to go after him with his new pistol in-hand.

When I finally figured out how to move again, I nodded at Weiss and stormed back through the tent flap without even trying to open it with my arm, like a bull running through the cape of a Spanish bullfighter. I caught up to Schmidt, but couldn't figure out how to say anything beyond, "How?"

Schmidt, noticing I made it to his side, glanced in my direction before explaining in very little detail, "I had a very nasty first date with a Russian." He stopped to survey our new makeshift headquarters. He pointed at me and asked, "Hey, where is everybody else? You could consider me new here."

After I provided another second of silence, I gestured down the path we were walking. "We're, uh, right up there, right before the trees," I informed.

"Thanks," he responded as he leisurely continued his stroll. Suddenly, his shoulders rose, and he stopped and whirled around. "Oh, I almost forgot!" he exclaimed. He took a palm off Ilsa to dig into one of his bulging pockets that I had not noticed until that very moment. He peeked up towards the corner of his eye with a squint before an expression of excitement overtook his face. A hand removed itself from the pocket, grasping two beautiful red apples.

They were promptly thrown my way without warning.

I struggled to catch them both as he explained, “I owed you one, but you could consider the second one as interest. Thanks for investing in me, Lindemann.” He gave me a friendly nod before turning around to continue his journey. “The rest of them are for my other stakeholders,” he chirped as he patted his still-bulging pockets. “It’s a bull market for the Sturmbannführer’s favorite squad!”

I stared at the apples for a couple of seconds as the situation registered. Okay, so Schmidt *was* alive. He had snagged Moller’s sidearm and gave it to Weiss. He was covered in blood. He had stumbled upon a cache of apples. And he was walking away after days of being missing in action.

Wait, he was walking *away* from me after being gone for so long? A sudden vision of Huber’s corpse sprung in my mind. The horror of seeing a friend die invaded my system. The fear provoked quickly turned to resentment as I remembered experiencing the same bitterness from when I had accepted that Schmidt, too, had met his demise. Resentment towards him sparked in my system like the fuse to a firework. How could this asshole think it was okay to toy with me, his *loyal* subordinate, by disappearing for long enough to assume he had died, and then hardly give me an answer on where he had been? How was I going to survive this war and get back to Annette without receiving the answers I needed? That I *deserved*? He was fortunate to have a recruit as fierce as me, and this was how I was treated?

Enough was enough. Engulfed by the frenzy I had built up, I sprinted up to Schmidt and shived his arm with enough force to spin him around. "You've been gone for days!" I exclaimed. "We all thought you were dead! Even Johannes did – that's why he gave me your letter!"

A shocked Schmidt gave me a cockeyed look as he lifted a hand to cover where I had just punched. Another soldier looked inquisitively at us as he walked by. Schmidt took note and deflected, "Damn, so I left one in the mess room again," before shrugging and spinning around to carry on his trek through camp. "Turns out Soviet armour is allergic to me," he added, slinging Ilsa over his shoulder.

What a buffoon. A self-righteous buffoon. All I wanted to do was figure out what happened to him, and he could hardly give me any information. How of all people could he leave me out of the loop? And somehow, he thought a joke would be fitting.

"Schmidt, come *on*!" I pleaded as I launched one of his apples at him. It hit him with enough force to almost make him trip. I screamed, "Tell me, gotdamnit!" as I caught up to him.

Again finding an opportunity to jab at me, he winced in pain before teasing, "Oh, did my favorite recruit miss me?" He picked up the apple and cracked a sideways smile.

My determined eyes pierced right through his asshole attitude, which made him realize how serious I was. He sighed, dropped his defense, and put the arm that held the apple around my shoulder, suggesting that I walk with him. I quickly brushed it off but matched my pace with his.

Schmidt briefly raised the insides of his eyebrows as he turned his head forward. "I carried Moller's body to a field far, far away, deep in the outskirts of that city," he described. His tone was serious now, which was a stark contrast to his previously sarcastic tone. "I buried Moller near an apple tree, because of how much he wanted that apple you once procured. Put flowers on his grave. You might not think it would be a terribly fitting move for Moller, but it was the least I could do. I've known him for so long."

We came across a Grenadier getting berated by a senior

enlisted. Something about the recruit's laces not being tied correctly. The commanding loudness shadowed any words Schmidt could have created, so he waited until we passed the duo until he carried on. I considered how petty some silly laces were compared to Moller dying. Would they yell at Schmidt for his unkempt uniform after he had just buried our comrade?

"While digging Moller's grave, I discovered a Russian marksman had stalked me all the way out there. The rest of the day, I moseyed along with my business as best as I could before I slipped from her grasp." He had lightened up towards the end, not letting such a somber story appear too disheartening. He glanced at me, and he jesting again like a jokester, "I wasn't kidding, it really was a terrible first date."

Schmidt tripped over a hole he didn't see coming. He regained his balance before finishing his story. "Finding you all took longer than I wanted. I had to sleep outside, and I was low on water. But by some miracle, I stumbled upon one of our convoys, where a kind truck driver offered to give me a ride to our new post in exchange for an apple or two. Such fantastic people, those truck drivers can be. They really deserve more appreciation."

After a few seconds of silence, he finally ended his story with a shrug. "Now, I'm here." Schmidt then snapped his head towards me with a squint. "Is *that* good enough for you?"

Even though he presented the conversation in a very Schmidt-like way, it detailed all of the questions I had. Though still upset at how brief he had been earlier, it put me in a better mood. I needed it. So, I responded, "Yeah. I guess."

Without any words, we both faced ahead, continuing to lumber towards the others at the same speed but not entirely together. Maybe I was going about dealing with Schmidt the wrong way. We sure didn't see eye-to-eye on why we fought this war, and he didn't react desirably to my seriousness. But I could still find it in myself mess around with him. Maybe that was the best way to bond with Schmidt, by attempting to communicate in a way he'd appreciate. And I needed him. So, I decided to give it a go.

I turned my head towards Schmidt. Ilsa rested on his shoulder, allowing the setting sun to reflect the small dents and marks on her traveled furniture. Just like Schmidt, she, too, had her secrets.

"But one more thing," I asked, finally switching my attention to Schmidt.

Schmidt craned his head towards me, acknowledging my request as we strolled down the path. “Yeah?”

I smirked as I quipped, “Try to find some steak next time you decide to go missing.”

Schmidt let out a relieved chuckle. He seemed to resonated with my change of tone. It worked; he liked my lighthearted joke because he was more accustomed to humor. This is how I would unlock him.

Schmidt placed a foul-smelling, bloodied arm around my neck and handed back the apple I had thrown at him back as he admitted with a smile, “It’s good to be back, Lindemann.”

Chapter 10

Gefreiter Udo Sommer

I hated digging. When they urged us to join the so-called "mighty" Wehrmacht, I didn't picture digging this much. It didn't matter where we were. We always ended up manning our shovels. We dig in the snow, we dig in the dirt, we dig in the gravel, or we dig in my least favourite, the mud.

My entrenchment tool must not have the same opinion as me. It always somehow ended up finding the wettest pockets of ground – the gotdamned mud. It reeks. It has bugs. It is like jelly and will shift right into the deepest part of a pit, forcing us to dig in the same spot multiple times over. It made my already shitty vision even worse by getting all over my glasses, and I'd get yelled at if they found it on my uniform.

But the worst part of mud was the wetness. A muddy pit will keep you in a constant state of damp. Being damp makes you cold. Being cold gets us sick. Especially with how strained our medical staff has been, the attention we would get from being sick is not anywhere close to what we need. I could easily lose a foot if we spent too much time making trenches. I didn't want to die slowly with a fucking foot missing. Fuck that. But sometimes, even after digging a good half a meter down into topsoil that was reasonably assumed to be dry, the dirt could turn into mud! So, fuck digging.

As I bored into the ground, I wondered how my family was doing back at home. My mother was a phenomenal cook. I worried she wouldn't be able to run it without me, but I doubted she was having any issues running the restaurant. I could still smell her beef stroganoff if I focused hard enough on it. So what if it was a Russian dish? I bet she could go toe-to-toe with any Russian cook. If anybody could, it was her. I'd do anything for her beef stroganoff one last time.

My head began to hurt, and reality squirmed its way back in. With all the rationing that likely takes place back at home, I could imagine the restaurant having trouble. She's short of staff, too, with dad gone and me off far to the east. I'm sure she's still surviving, though. She'll learn to do it without us. I've seen what the Feldkuchenunteroffizier can whip up, and she *must* have more than he does to cook with, right? *Right?*

The memories of my mom's beef stroganoff made my stomach growl. My shovel unanticipatedly uplifted a giant, juicy worm. I toyed with the idea of cooking it with my mess tin. How would it taste? Perhaps I could salt and dry it, making a jerky-like snack. But it was juicy, so maybe it would go well in one of the Feldkuchenunteroffizier's broths. It could be best just to bite the bullet and eat raw, no preparation necessary. I could save it from this hell and make it all end, little worm. I could spare you the burden and take the choice of life out of your hand.

"Hey, Udo!" My eyes lit up, and I instantly dropped the worm. I snapped my head around to where Rupert was beckoning me from. "You've been digging for long enough. Come play a quick round of cards before the Oberfeldwebel comes back to scold us!"

I was equally as happy to leave the mud as I was to catch up with Rupert. We really thought we lost him. We were forced to pull back from the city almost immediately, which diverted him into trekking through unfamiliar ground alone. But he somehow made it, which at least put an extension on the borrowed time we all live on. I was glad I was still alive when he popped up.

I left my unsavoury mud-filled crevice towards the more

finished parts of our trench line by the bunker Rupert had called from. He was outside talking to a few new wide-eyed soldiers I had not yet met.

"Just punch the shark in the fins or eyes, and it will swim away." Rupert turned around as he heard me approaching. "Speaking of sharks, there's my favourite one! How goes it, Udo?"

I couldn't help but grin a little bit. "Just sniffing out the wettest mud like a shark smells blood," I responded. Used to his shenanigans by now, I never really let the oddness Rupert's conversations delay my response. Rupert did a fantastic job at keeping our minds off everything else, so I always welcomed the distraction.

He chuckled, "Some things never change," as he addressed the new recruits. "Alright, lads, I'll leave you two to return to your diggery." Was 'diggery' a word? I wasn't sure, but knowing Rupert, he probably made it up to further baffle the unadjusted recruits.

He had faced me before he could witness their startled reactions. "Come on, Udo, let me show you around our new luxury hotel," he encouraged as he disappeared inside the concrete doorframe of the pillbox. I wish he could have seen the recruits' faces.

I sucked my cheeks in and gave them kissy lips. It was my best fish impersonation as I followed Rupert. One just shrugged and walked away, and the others soon followed.

The small bunker we had entered was far from an actual hotel, but for us soldiers who have spent all day outside, it may have well been a Ritz-Carlton in downtown Berlin. Besides a handful of crates, the accommodations were on the lacking side. But that didn't matter. The re-enforced concrete protecting us was just as welcomed as the break from the mud outside. Even the wet, dewy scent of the concrete walls was a nice change of pace.

Already gathered in a circle around a crate with a deck of cards on top were Bruno Lindemann, Gunther Herrmann, and Burkhard Kuhn. By the fixed machine gun at the front of the bunker was a new face I had not seen before, an Obergefreiter by the ranks on his sleeves. Grenadier Graf accompanied him, whose first name I believe was Frank? Fuck, we had spent so much time together, and I still forgot his name. I was terrible at remembering names but trying to recall everyone sort of lost its purpose. So many new faces would show up, just to disappear as you started to get close to them. Good on the Chef for making such an effort to remember who everyone was.

Rupert took a spot between Herrmann and Bruno, so I approached an open place on Bruno's other side. I didn't want to get to know Bruno when he first got here. I was close to the guy who was under Rupert before him, and it gutted me when he died. Fuck, I missed Hans.

But when Rupert disappeared, Bruno and I found something to mourn over. I told him I'd call him Bruno if he called me Udo because I thought Rupert would have wanted that. So we got closer. Bruno was a lot more idealistic than Rupert and I, but we all were when we began life out here. We were all just trying to figure out where we belonged, if anywhere. I thought Rupert was too hard on him for not knowing any betters, so I was open to spending more time with him while Rupert was gone.

"About time you showed up," Herrmann exclaimed with a smoke in his mouth. Herrmann stopped fiddling with a German-made submachine gun, a Machinenpistole 40, propping it up on the wall beside him next to the submachine gun his submachine gun, a scavenged Russian PPSh -41. It was ironic how he had gotten his hands on such a weapon after how much of a fuss he made when they tried issuing one to him.

Not long after I arrived on the front, the Sturmbannführer decreed that all of us must now use German firearms unless absolutely necessary. Naturally, the Sturmbannführer only cared about our gear being German-made because he just *couldn't* imagine the Russian equipment being up to our *superior* quality. Oberfeldwebel Martin tried bribing Herrmann to stop using his Soviet submachine gun by offering him our alternative, ironically also a Machinenpistole 40. But Herrmann wouldn't swap. He preferred to use his PPSh because it was a better weapon, and we didn't blame him. The PPSh had a faster rate of fire, made use of a colossal drum magazine, and could still use scavenged Russian ammunition as well as our 7.62x25mm ammunition. We had heard that our Machinenpistoles could explode when using the Russian ammunition, despite a bullet that appeared to be about the same size. The Sturmbannführer didn't know this when he issued the order, so he kept after Oberfeldwebel Martin to keep his men up to his standards. Oberfeldwebel Martin soon put his foot down, citing the flexibility the Soviet weapon had over using both ammunition types lessened the demand on our struggling logistics. Eventually, Herrmann was allowed to keep his PPSh.

"We were about to play without you," Hermann claimed without even looking at us. He started acting like he was the coolest guy around after he got his way with the Sturmbannführer.

Kuhn clicked his mouth as an understated way to disagree with Herrmann. Kuhn had our back. He was much too considerate of a soul to start without everybody being ready.

Rupert noted only two men in the bunker that were not sitting in our circle. "Hey, Keller and Graf, why don't you join us? You could use a break." Ah, Keller was the new Obergefreiter's name.

Graf had already come and sat down before searching for approval from Keller, his senior. Noticing Graf had left him, the Obergefreiter nodded side-to-side, possibly over his dissatisfaction with Graf's abandonment. "No thank you, Unterfeldwebel. Somebody has to keep watch in case Ivan attacks," he grumbled.

Not content with his answer, Rupert responded, "Nonsense!" as he stood up and poked his head out the side window of the bunker. "Hey, you!" he shouted while pointing at a digging recruit outside.

A baby-faced recruit sprung up like a dog that had just heard its name called. He pointed at himself and blankly stared back at Rupert, who clarified, "Yeah, you, high roller! Want to stop shovelling for a bit?"

The recruit's nod was slow to start but progressively sped up as the spoils of Rupert's offer sunk in. Anything beat mucking about in the mud. He took one step in our direction as Rupert proposed, "Come in here for a bit and look out for Russians while we conduct some *serious* business."

The recruit saluted briefly like an idiot and sped away from the others still digging in the unfinished trenches. Rupert patted Keller on the shoulder. "See?" he pointed out. "There's always time to enjoy the small things, mate." Nobody excelled at enjoying the small things more than Rupert.

Unlike Rupert, however, Keller didn't seem to care about the small things. He grunted and rolled his eyes as the recruit made his way through the concrete entrance.

The young Grenadier turned out to be one of the recruits Rupert was talking to outside the bunker as I arrived. Rupert noticed immediately. "You're one of the shark boys, right?" Without giving time for him to respond, Rupert inquired, “What is your name?”

The recruit saluted again and stated, “Grenadier Fischer, sir!” Even Bruno, a similarly-ranked Grenadier, noticed the unnecessary formality. He raised his chin and squinched his eyes, showing that despite their shared rank, he had earned an extra layer of saltiness by being here longer.

“Hah,” I simpered as I locked eyes with the already grinning Rupert. “How ironic. What are the chances of that?”

Rupert, per usual, found a way to joke about it as well. “How convenient! But you’re not Fischer anymore, Grenadier,” he addressed the recruit. “Get by that MG-42 and keep your eyes peeled for pescatarians, *Guppy*.” I chuckled softly, and Guppy let out a nervous smile. He shuffled towards his new post but briefly hesitated when the unphased blast of Keller’s scowl met the recruit’s eyes.

Noticing that not everybody else got the joke, Rupert explained to everybody else, but mainly to the cross Keller. “I was just talking to him about sharks just a minute ago,” he clarified

Kuhn let out an “ah,” but Keller just groaned. He was still disappointed over having to leave his post, which confused me because really, who wants to be on watch duty, anyway? But he must not have been too upset to play cards instead of watching for attackers, because he sat down in our gaming circle without any further complaints.

Keller took up an open spot on the other side of me, which brought a gust of his scent over to my direction. Fresh shaving powder. He seemed to be pretty cookie-cutter. He must have felt my eyeballs burning into him because he turned towards me. Noticing that we had not yet met, he raised a hand for a shake.

"Hello, I am Obergefreiter Wolfgang Keller." I shook his hand as he added, "I'm your new support gunner. They merged some of the remnants of my squad with yours and placed Grenadier Graf underneath me." Graf didn't have enough experience to be our support gunner, which explained why they gave us Keller, merged from another platoon, and made Graf his assistant.

Silence found its way into our conversation as we reflected over the other week in that dammed city with the marketplace. Our battalion had sustained heavy casualties there, but we didn't lose as many men as some of the other squads in different platoons. The Sturmbannführer was inspecting us while regrouping after our retreat and commented about how we were lucky to have '*only*' lost two men. '*Only*.' What a word for it. How thankful that we had '*only*' lost two men. '*Only*' my long-time mate Moller and '*only*' a boy who knew no better, probably struggling to stay alive right now in a ratty bed in some makeshift medical tent that couldn't even save my foot if it got too fucking wet from the fucking mud they made me dig.

Herrmann looked up from his cards with a glare. "You got big shoes to fill, Keller," he declared, brushing the side of his teeth with his tongue. "Our last guy, Moller, was the best of them. If you're not as good as he was, I'll make-"

"I don't fuck around," Keller retaliated with a fierce scowl.

Everyone, Herrmann especially, was taken aback. "You better not, asshole," Herrmann snapped. Rupert and I made eye contact. Maybe he should intervene?

Thankfully, Keller's rage subsided with a sigh, and his eyes faced the ground. "Look… I knew Moller. He had his bearings. Loved his machine gun and could take it apart blindfolded. It's just that my squad was, uhh, hit pretty bad about a week ago and..." He cleared his voice and made eye contact with all of us individually, beginning and ending with Herrmann. "You're my squad now. I'll do Moller justice here."

Herrmann nodded, accepting Keller's macho form of an apology. Keller nodded back before asking Rupert, "You buried him, so you saw him last, right? He didn't have to struggle, did he?"

Out of the blue, Lindemann suddenly squealed, "Ah, shit!" He squeezed his eyes shut and put an open hand on the side of his head, ferociously snapping to the side like he was trying to air-dry his hair after getting it wet.

I shot a concerned eye to Rupert, realising everybody else had done the same to one another as we all basked in the awkwardness of his convulsion.

Rupert soon broke up the oddness of the moment by reaching reached out to grab Bruno's shoulder. "Is... Everything alright, Lindemann?"

Adjusting himself back to a more normal posture, Lindemann lowered his palm from his head. He glanced around the room before reassuring, "Yeah, sorry, a bug flew in my face."

"Right." Rupert dropped his hand on Bruno's shoulder and returned his attention to Keller. "Moller died how we all want to go. Quick and painless, no struggling at all. I gave him a burial he would have been proud of."

Keller nodded. Noting the seriousness was over, Rupert tried to save the sombre mood by pointing out Keller's glasses. "But hey, welcome to, I'm at least glad another man with spectacles could join us. Udo was getting lonely," he joked.

I always tried to admire Rupert's efforts, so I motioned to adjust my glasses before adding on, "Glasses are an underrated fashion accessory."

Just as deadpan as before, Keller muttered, "Until it rains," before picking up the cards that Herrmann placed to his front. It figured that the same man who was upset about leaving sentry duty would try to drag down the mood as we played cards.

Rupert's eyes narrowed, and his lips tightened. Herrmann, equally as eager to play as to get past whatever had just happened, shuffled in his seat and pled, "Can we start playing already? We've waited long enough."

"Yeah, alright, let's play," Rupert answered. He slapped Lindemann's shoulder, declaring, "Lindemann has been getting better, so let's allow the rookie Grenadier Frank Graf to go first. He'll need it to beat us seasoned card-players."

Ah, so Frank was Graf's first name. Being right was a little win, and it felt nice. Maybe Rupert was right about enjoying all the small things. They were all we had, after all.

Chapter 11

Oberfeldwebel Fritz Martin

As I peered into the mirror to finish eradicating any last trace of stubble, I again remembered how much I detested being inside this luxurious fortress. It was safe, and my men were not geographically far away, but even being half a kilometer displaced from where they were situated at the frontline was too far to effectively command them.

I reveled in the working plumbing as I turned the faucet. Even as a senior enlisted, it was rare to come across running water. As much as I despised being in such a fancy estate while my men labored about in the wet mud, the fresh, chilled liquid that brushed the remainder of the shaving powder off my face was welcome.

After rinsing, I observed my freshly-shaven reflection. Mirrors on the frontlines were not uncommon because shaving was to take place in even the harshest of conditions to maintain discipline. Even so, we rarely had mirrors as large as the one in my quarters. Surrounded by a gold-painted wooden trim, it completely encapsulated the reflected glass. I compared the gilded wood to the adequately-supplied Soviet forces encroaching on us from seemingly all directions. My reflection in the middle, the strained remnants of an energetic soul I once had at the breakout of the war, was a current representation of our exhausted troops. Tired and weary of this dragging war, but still giving forth everything they can to at least put in the effort to shave. I concluded that the shaving part didn't represent my men, but the analogy remained.

My face had changed as the war carried on. The few strands of the hairs on my head were completely gray now, a far cry from the luscious brown hair I used to have years before. My wife says I'm a completely different person. I would be lying if I claimed she was wrong. The constant fighting changes everybody, from the freshest of recruits to the life-long service members like me. I hoped my wife would still love the new me as much as she loved the version of myself I left behind when I departed for the Eastern Front. I suppose I should have taken into account not making it to the war's end, but I was determined to make it as far as I could. Nobody would care for my men as much as I did.

I brushed my hand on the back of my freshly-maintained

head. It went down smoothly, but my hair had been brought so close on the sides that my hand got caught in the stubble sweeping upwards. Complemented with my sheered facial hair, I must admit that I looked proper. If everything else was going to shit, at the very least, we could always try to look our best. Eliminating all of my facial hair was one of the only things I could do with a 100% success rate. Additionally, I needed to lead by example. Soldiers would doubt leadership if we were not clean-cut, despite how lacking some of them are at maintaining these standards.

I removed a few stray hairs protruding from my clothing and gave my trousers one final tug upwards before I was content enough with my uniform to put on my field cap. These new covers were adequate, but I preferred the one I had before. That old cap had seen so much over the years that it made me disappointed to stop using it. I don't argue change, though, because I must act like the example my men should aim to follow. Plus, I have always been categorically against rocking the boat more than necessary.

As I gave myself a final nod and departed towards the door, Sturmbannführer Kolartz appeared with his hands nonchalantly clasping behind his back. As always, his uniform was spotless – his boots were shined, his buttons polished, and his ribbons looked new. Even if he continually persisted in adding difficulty to my day, I could at least admire the effort he had put into maintaining his appearance. Or rather, I could admire the work his assistants had put into it.

"Ah, *Oberfeldwebel* Martin! *Just* the man I was looking for," the Sturmbannführer crowed. We had worked hand-in-hand for months, but he would often specifically choose to address my enlisted rank with extra inflection as some understated means of reminding us that he, an officer, had the final say. It served as a reminder that whatever order followed was law, regardless of my own opinions.

Making no additional gestures as he began strolling down the hallway, Sturmbannführer Kolartz invited, "Come take a walk with me, Oberfeldwebel."

"Yes, Sturmbannführer, sir," I responded, giving forth my best efforts to not sound reluctant in assuming a position by his side to stroll through a lavish corridor instead of returning to my troops.

Sturmbannführer Kolartz was an officer that came from Prussian aristocracy to a well-supplied and industrially-superior

German army. He fought in a decorated unit early in the war on the western front. But Sturmbannführer Kolartz had hardly an idea what it meant to fight as a foot soldier nowadays. France was nothing like here. The might of our capabilities was now far inferior to that of the retaliating Soviets.

The Sturmbannführer leisurely promenaded down the elongated passageway as he observed the architecture surrounding us. "Such a marvelous building. Oradea's nobles have such fine taste," he pointed out to my front with the arm that held his pristine officer cuff-title. "These archways were designed in such a way that emphasizes the meticulous engineering involved to uphold this elegant structure."

An administrative soldier saluted while marching past us as we sauntered down the hallway. The Sturmbannführer hardly more than nodded at the man as he continued his assessment of our building. "Arches are a shape that architects use to maximize the integrity of the structures while simultaneously providing the building with an attractive aesthetic," he shared. "Did you know that, Oberfeldwebel?"

"Yes, sir, my men are constructing similar arches in bunkers on the frontlines as we speak," I replied. What a silly rant during such a frantic time. Such an observation would only be verbalized by somebody whose upbringing had permitted him to be out of touch with the modern reality of this total war.

"You know, Oberfeldwebel," the Sturmbannführer lectured, "I had to work countless long days to get where I am today. It's taken an innumerable amount of hours to earn my current position." I nodded in agreement, but my experience suggested we had a different definition of what a 'long day' constituted.

As the Sturmbannführer scanned the walls, I noticed that the symbols on his cap were utterly free of any scratches. It was as if he had just this day removed it from the decorative box it came in.

The Sturmbannführer then adjusted his gaze to me. "I don't intend to let this strenuous work become compromised from any… Discrepancies in the integrity of our structure," he declared.

I stood up even straighter and stiffened my frown, so Sturmbannführer Kolartz sighed and halted. I mirrored. He indicated the walls and ceiling around us with an open palm.

"This hallway is very uniform. Nothing sticks out as an eyesore, so the ceiling holds," Sturmbannführer Kolartz related as he circled in front of me. He flicked his arms behind his back and faced me head-on before further clarifying, “Consider if one of these archways was not built to the standards of the others. It would put the entire rooftop at risk of collapse. Similarly, any troublesome soldiers that fail to maintain the same required standards of them threaten the overall vitality of our structure.”

The Sturmbannführer was only a few centimeters taller than I was, and yet he attempted to lean over me, carefully lifting himself on the toes of his feet to do so.

“And if these discrepancies are not corrected, I will be sure to allocate the appropriate punishments to all of the offenders,” Sturmbannführer Kolartz proclaimed. His piercing pale blue eyes narrowed before he threatened, “*Including* the men responsible for allowing such discrepancies to go uncorrected on their watch. Do I make myself clear, *Oberfeldwebel*?”

Sturmbannführer Kolartz returned to a more normal position, but his piercingly crisp blue eyes continued their courageous assault to intimidate me. It was ineffective.

When our soldiers would not shave, fail to maintain uniform standards, or lack the effort to address superiors properly, it would get under the Sturmbannführer's skin. He had been turning up the heat on me lately because of the lack of formalities from my men. This ultimatum would have made me waver even a few years ago. But the salty, greyed, and battered version of myself that I saw in the mirror earlier knew by now how to hold his ground. This was war, and I had faced a hell of a lot worse than the Sturmbannführer. I was too old for his fear.

But beyond the Sturmbannführer's petty attempt at intimidation, I agreed that maintaining discipline was vital to some, myself included. The orders, grooming standards, and maintaining clarity of ranks were all parts of being a soldier that I had personally grown accustomed to throughout my years of service. After all my time out here, I had developed a fondness for maintaining this discipline. Despite how well or poorly everything else happens around me, I can always do my best to control how I look. These concepts are essential during training and preparation for war.

Discipline has always been a core principle for any experienced warrior. A soldier without it cannot stick to the constant rules required to survive and fight effectively. But as much as I berated my men otherwise, at the end of the day, discipline for combatting the enemy was entirely different than the discipline in keeping grooming standards. Neither a clean-shaven face nor uniform with shiny, polished buttons will prevent any soldier from getting shot. And hell, if anything, too much discipline can be a bad thing. Saluting an officer out here marks targets for any watching enemy snipers, and always commanding by the book makes it easy for the enemy to predict our plans.

My policies on discipline may have aligned with the Sturmbannführer's during peacetime, but they had evolved through my experiences from being with my soldiers on a day-to-day basis since the outbreak of this conflict. All a crackdown on regulations would do at this point in the war is lower morale. The last thing a common soldier needs on this brutal war against the Soviets is a superior sneaking up on them to reprimand them for not buttoning their tunic correctly.

Most importantly, my men thrived when I didn't enforce standards as hard as the Sturmbannführer wanted. They were a band of misfits that had prioritized doing their job well instead of shining their shoes and shaving every day. I remembered being enraged when I heard them call themselves "mud squad." When I cracked down on Schmidt about it, he resigned as squad leader so he could watch over his comrades, and the gotdamn platoon started calling him 'Overwatch' because of it. Their lack of bearing strengthened their camaraderie because they knew my platoon might be the only one in the entirety of the Heer that allowed them to get away with it. It made them realize that fighting for each other a priority, not fighting for the Reich. Anyone but the most indoctrinated will tell you – we fight for our comrades next to us, not for Nazi Germany.

It does irk me that they do not always adhere to the army policies that appeal to me personally. And it drives me insane when I ask them to do something, and they slack off. Or when they talk back to me. But to compromise their effectiveness in combat, to damage their camaraderie by insisting a sharp uniform will fight off the Soviets, would be nothing short of profound. Every single one of my men, no matter how unkempt he may be, was valuable to me. And they fought damn hard because of it. Harder than any others. So, I could give a fuck if the Sturmbannführer didn't like them.

But this is the price I must pay. I will still give the men grief about their uniforms, but that is my duty as their superior. They reflect on my leadership, and orders are to be followed. However, had my men not appeared as 'threatening' to our Herr Sturmbannführer, then I would not be needlessly kept away from ensuring the construction of our life-saving defenses underwent correctly. I would need to find some sort of compromise to satisfy both the men and the Sturmbannführer.

I could never voice such disagreement to the Sturmbannführer, though. So, I merely agreed with him as convincingly as I could, and we again began walking down the hallways as he continued his in-depth assessment of the elaborate corridor.

After a lengthy detour, I finally was able to slip away from the massive Czechoslovakian château and make it back to my men. I had already visited the defenses under construction by two of my squads. They were working on a bunker and trench line on the north side of the front by the river. Oberleutnant Ross supervised them, which explained why everything seemed to be in working order. I could not deny that he was an efficient soldier.

Feldwebel Uwe Pfeiffer's squad by the southern side of our

defenses was the last group I needed to visit. They were fortunate to have already had a modestly-sized bunker built, although the surrounding area still needed some work. They had only dug a part of the trench connecting their group to the others and reinforced even less of it.

I trekked up an incline towards the main trenches by the southern pillbox, which had already been dug out and sufficiently walled with timber. The rectangle-shaped fighting compartment had a properly-supported mound in the middle to prevent its inhabitants from being completely wiped out by a single explosion. Such a prepared defense was uncommon between the scarce supplies and untrained troops, so catching sight of it reassured me with a justified sense of confidence in my men.

Beyond the bunker was a road that disconnected the continuous trench line. Some of the men were shoveling the edge of our defenses on the other side. A field gun had been set up behind them, on a ridge. Its operators were either digging or somewhere else in the vicinity.

I figured some of the more experienced men were fooling around inside the bunker, but I chose to postpone ending their fun.

Instead, I took a break of sorts of my own by greeting the Feldwebel first to hear how the recruits were faring. I also wanted a second opinion on the Sturmbannführer's rant from earlier.

The Feldwebel had propped himself up against a tree by the field gun on top of the ridge. His position gave him an open view of the edge of the defenses and could ensure the fresh recruits were performing their duties correctly. Always scowling, he looked as if he could use a whip to crack over his new men. He meant well, though, and was a great asset to my command.

"Uwe, comrade, how goes it?" I called from afar.

The Feldwebel's stern gaze almost transformed into one of excitement when he noticed me. "Everything has been running without a hitch, Fritz," he shouted back. He stopped leaning against the tree, steadily edging toward the steep slope to his front before expanding his arms for balance to trot down. After dusting off the debris he had just kicked up from his uniform, he reached forward to shake my hand. "Glad to have you up here with us," he mentioned as I grabbed it.

I sighed. "I'm just appreciative that the Sturmbannführer didn't delay me further."

A sneaky smile crept up on Uwe's face as he reached for a smoke in his pocket. Not even looking up, he declared, "Always more eager to be with your troops than to enjoy running water, aren't you, Fritz?"

I lowered my head as I struggled to hide a rare face of satisfaction. "You know me too well," I reflected as I, too, reached for a smoke. Uwe Pfeiffer was my second in command for the platoon, more seasoned than any of the other squad leaders. He had been with me on this front for longer than anyone else. If anybody understood how I operated by now, it was him.

"What's the old noble have to say this time?" Uwe asked with his cigarette now in his mouth. He reached to light mine before his own.

I puffed within my cheeks, let the tobacco into my lungs, resonated with its burn, and exhaled twice before summarizing the Sturmbannführer's words. "He wants our soldiers to look more like the part," I paraphrased. "Saluting superiors, shaving their faces, you know, boot camp formalities."

"Hah," Uwe retorted before lighting his smoke. He, too, puffed twice before taking a drag. Exhaling away from us, he disclosed, “I am not in the least surprised he’s more worried about fighting a war against facial hair instead of the Russians.”

“Naturally, you’re a proponent for relaxed regulations," I cracked as I slapped the unfastened button at the top of his collar with the back of my hand. Uwe Pfeiffer’s squad, in particular, was notorious for its unkemptness. The easiest way to find the fresh recruits and transfers under his command was by searching for the men who were still entirely within regulations. Between long hair, dirty faces, and a lax atmosphere, it was surprising that they had the discipline to fight as well as they did.

Uwe was amidst one of the widest grins I’d ever seen him make. “They can’t get rid of all of us for a poor uniform, can they?” he challenged rhetorically.

“I wouldn’t be so sure,” I countered. Uwe was right, but I couldn’t let him push the boundaries too far. The Sturmbannführer would be breathing down my neck over it. “You’ve all pushed your luck before. Schmidt especially. I doubt there’s much more that the Sturmbannführer can take before he strikes down again. And when he does, it’ll be harder than before.”

“Fucking Schmidt,” Uwe reflected in a low voice. “That son

of a bitch has been a pain in the Sturmbannführer's ass for a long time." He puffed his smoke again before he raised an eyebrow to ask, "Do you think it's his fault you are getting so much flak over our uniforms and shit?"

"Mmm," I hummed as I gazed off into the sky just above the horizon in the distance. "I think most of your squad is a problem according to the Sturmbannführer, but Schmidt positioned himself to be the ringleader. If he had a less-acceptable service record and was of a lower rank, the Sturmbannführer would have found a better opportunity to make an example out of him."

I took a second to consider what I had just disclosed before I contrasted, "But on the other hand, nobody in your squad puts forth that kind of effort the Sturmbannführer requires. Schmidt may have been the first to stand up against him, but who's to say somebody else wouldn't have taken his place if he wasn't around? Sommer's a lot like Schmidt. Maybe he would have if he ever finds a backbone? And Moller was almost as hardheaded as they came when it came to his uniform. I've never seen a soldier who was that bad at buttoning his tunic. He could have been the one, too."

I paused to tap the chest of Uwe. "Or what about you? You

are of an even higher rank than Schmidt, and your uniform has never been your strong suit. You might have stood up to the Sturmbannführer as well. Especially with the war beating down on us as time goes on, somebody was bound to call out the Sturmbannführer on his mismanaged priorities."

Uwe pondered my opinion for a solid minute while we simply gazed off into the distance to think long and hard about the politics of our military.

The break ended when Uwe speculated about my thoughts aloud. "So, we're all part of the problem, huh?" He rotated towards me and apologized, "In that case, I'm sorry I am failing you, Fritz."

"Ack, Uwe." I placed a hand on his shoulder and rationalized, "As long as your squad stays out here and away from the Sturmbannführer's fancy estate, I couldn't care less what your gotdamn uniforms look like."

Uwe tapped me on the small of my back with a nod. I removed my hand on his shoulder to clarify, "But at the very least, do what you can to hide the unkemptness of our men when the Sturmbannführer is around, alright? Because who knows how much longer I'll be around to cover your asses."

"I can at least see to that," Uwe agreed. A relatively sly look overtook his face as he smirked, "But it's going to take a lot more than some rich Nazi asshole and a couple of Russians to get us, Oberfeldwebel," the seasoned Feldwebel claimed.

"Don't count your blessings yet, Uwe," I cautioned as I took a final puff of my cigarette. "There's still a lot more fighting to be done before the Führer finally says enough is enough."

"That's fair," he compromised.

We shot the shit for a few minutes before a recruit called upon Uwe for advisement on how to properly place some of the boards in his trench. He shot "Duty calls, Fritz," over his shoulder as he sped off to assist him.

"Keep up the good work, Uwe!" I yelled after him. I didn't have many friends anymore. If they weren't injured or at home, they had mostly died out by now. But Uwe Pfeiffer was one of the few that remained. He was not the most intelligent man, but he was one of the few who took everything I said to heart. Plus, he was a great fighter who was borderline obsessed with his line of work, and his experience was invaluable as my best squad leader.

I knew I had put it off long enough – it was time to enter the concrete bunker and break up whatever fooling around was going on inside. I crossed the road and turned the corner of the cement doorway of the pillbox to stumble upon the experienced core of Pfeiffer's squad up in arms over a game of cards.

"That's impossible!" Sommer shouted as he slammed his cards on the floor. Covered head-to-toe in mud, the dark green of his uniform was hardly still visible. Schmidt was pacing around in a circle with one hand holding cards on his hip and the thumb and index finger of his other on his forehead, partially hiding his unacceptably long hair. Lindemann and Graf's unshaven mouths were agape. The new machine gunner, Keller, brandished a scorn as his eyes frantically darted over the cards. As a transfer, his uniform was more acceptable than a slightly muddied Fischer, who was beaming over whatever he had just observed. The generally respectable Kuhn was laughing so hard, his unbooted feet were kicking in the air. But Herrmann was the worst, as he displayed an ear-to-ear grin while leaning back with his hands behind his head, exposing an out-of-regulation tattoo I had previously known nothing about across his chest between an unbuttoned top.

"How can you win *three times* in a row against *six* other

players?" Graf demanded, also throwing his cards down on the crate in the center of them all.

"You had to be cheating," Schmidt declared with a hand swinging from his forehead to point with all of his fingers palm-up at Herrmann.

"Check my sleeves, boys," Herrmann snorted back. "You'll find that I'm free of such an illusion. All that is up there is a natural skill for Skat."

Keller growled as he took up Herrmann's offer, yanking his arms from behind Herrmann's head to search his sleeves before proceeding to inspect the rest of his clothing.

"Go on, Keller, the hate keeps me warm," Herrmann sneered as he was manhandled.

"Argh!" shouted Sommer as he face-palmed. Kuhn's characteristically polite laughter had been swapped for an uproarious howl, and his face turned even more beet-red.

This was precisely the lack of etiquette that the Sturmbannführer spoke of earlier. If they weren't fucking around so much, maybe the trenches would be built. Maybe I wouldn't have to endure hell from the Sturmbannführer. Maybe they would have done so much as acknowledged that I had entered the room. It all wound me the hell up. I balled up my fists and exploded, "That's enough!"

Schmidt couldn't have cared less. "But Feldwebel, Herrmann must be enchanted by some form of dark magic! There's no way he could have won again!" he cracked.

"I just don't see how that's possible…" Lindemann muttered, face still dumbfounded after losing another game of cards.

"I said *enough*!" I demanded with a thunderous stomp. They really knew how to work me up. "Do you realize how close the Sturmbannführer is to sending you all to a disciplinary battalion?"

"At this point, I'd welcome such an act as long as the warlock himself isn't there with his trickery," Schmidt joked. Sommer and Lindemann giggled at the continuation of his description, while Kuhn began wheezing from laughing so hard.

I was up to the brim with all of their goofing off and couldn't hold myself back, so I stormed up to Schmidt and shoved him against the wall. The room immediately silenced and faces locked up. Schmidt lifted his hands with perplexed eyebrows, surprised at my violent outburst.

I instantly regretted lashing out, but I had to double down to justify my actions. “Listen. All of you,” I began, taking the pressure off Schmidt with a step back. “Command has been giving me all sorts of shit lately over how undisciplined you all are.” I expected a sarcastic comment from somebody, but they stayed quiet. Except for Kuhn, who without hesitation began silently putting on his boots. He was cordial enough to not let a moment pass before he took to heart my request.

Still a bit remorseful over putting my hands on Schmidt, I dulled down my tone. Perhaps they would listen better if I approached them as just another soldier instead of as a superior.

“Look. The Sturmbannführer has been putting me under a lot of pressure lately,” I admitted. “You should know especially, Schmidt, that he can be quick to make rash decisions. He pulled me aside again today and told me that he was not going to have any more of it.”

A few of the soldiers shot looks at one another. Schmidt’s hands lowered as he asked for clarification. “What do you mean, Feldwebel?”

I clenched the side of my mouth and nodded side to side, contemplating what to say before specifying, “I don’t just fear for you. Or for anyone else in the squad. I fear for myself now, Schmidt." He nodded, so I added, "I really need you all to pull yourselves together. The Sturmbannführer is on our tail, and you, specifically, Schmidt, need to act more like a role model out here."

Cautious over being asked to be a better soldier, Schmidt's face gave away his concern, so I compromised with the same proposal I had just given Pfeiffer. "I'm not asking you to be a squad leader again. I'm just asking for an effort. If you must, you can still be the goofy slob you are at heart. Just try to pull it together if it means preparing for battle, and especially in front of the Sturmbannführer, alright?"

To my surprise, the humble tone I had experimented with had struck Schmidt's soft spot. After a second of scratching his chin, he nodded and accepted my proposal. "I can make an effort at that for you, Fritz. Sorry to have burdened your position as much as I have," he apologized.

"It comes with the job, Schmidt," I unenthusiastically replied. It wasn't often I could reach through to him, so I appreciated it. Maybe I should try asking him to do things as personal favors instead of as orders more often. I waved my hand over the rest of the men in the bunker as I used the same technique I had just learned to call upon them to do the same. "That goes for all of you. Do it for me, if you must."

They all glanced around at each other before sounding out their agreements. Maybe pulling together this squad wouldn't be so impossible after all.

Even so, I still had to be tough on the recruits. They had not yet earned the same sympathy from me. They must first learn about the hardships of war before they are allowed to place any doubt on the command structure. So, I pointed to Fischer and commanded, "And you, get back out there and help Feldwebel Pfeiffer with dig-"

A familiar noise sounded off in the distance and swept into our ears, postponing my order. The men with experience glanced at each other with widened eyes. Graf and Lindemann caught on after a second, and Fischer knew something was going on, but couldn't figure it out.

Confirming the worst of my fears, Pfeiffer shouted a warning to the digging recruits across the road, alarmingly without any swearing, which echoed through the unsealed crevices of the bunker: "Artillery! Everybody get down!"

Chapter 12

Unterfeldwebel Rupert Schmidt

It's unfortunate how quickly our moods can drop out here. One minute, we're just a bunch of comrades playing cards, and mere seconds later, we're thrown back into being soldiers, just trying to stay alive.

I didn't even really remember grabbing my rifle, but the next thing I knew, I was already hunkered against the side of the bunker with my hand yanking on Lindemann's shoulder, pulling him against the concrete wall beside me.

We were both relatively ready to go, with our rifles in-hand and our helmets now on our heads. However, as I looked around the bunker, I realised that I had some work to do before I could again become the pristine role model that Oberfeldwebel Martin requested. I shouldn't have let Herrmann unbutton his shirt, and probably should have kindly suggested to warm Kuhn to keep his boots fastened. We also should have probably dug the trenches instead of playing cards. Our squad really was a mess.

Any additional efforts to help the unprepared others would have hindered them, so I just stayed put next to Lindemann. I did, however, find a bit of time to watch everyone else get their gear in order. To no surprise, the more senior a soldier was, the more he knew was concerned about the others below them. Oberfeldwebel Martin was helping Herrmann button his tunic, and Obergefreiter Keller seemed to be ineffectively trying to calm down the panicking Guppy. The poor recruit struggled to handle his first taste of combat as Keller retook his position at the machine gun.

The need for a veteran soldier to overwatch his duckings of sorts stems from the complete lack of knowledge the freshest of recruits have at their disposal when a session of shelling begins. Indirect fire is different from a tank's main gun or an anti-tank cannon in that its trajectory has an arc and its landing spot could often provide for enough time to be anticipated. As time goes on, experience can teach a soldier how big of a shell was fired, what it was probably aiming at, how steep of an ark it will have, and if done quickly enough, could provide him with enough time to avoid where lands. Contrary to popular belief, the colossal artillery pieces are surprisingly the easier ones to anticipate. They're much louder. It's hardest to train a recruit's ear to tune in for the quieter, smaller shells that tend to hit without notice. And when you do teach them, they often panic when it actually happens, and they forget. Regardless, though, as I've seen before and am bound to see again, experience can't always save you. We'd either avoid the shells and live or get hit and possibly die. We were doing our best by staying in the bunker, although I doubted its cement would matter too much if we took a direct hit.

Not after long, we had all took up spots along the inside of the bunker walls to wait out the bombardment, save Keller, who was eager to resume his position as the watch by the open slot at the front of our pillbox.

The first of the shells soon splashed around the landscape surrounding us, tailed almost immediately by the terrified Guppy shrieking in fear. After he had finished dealing with Herrmann, Oberfeldwebel Martin switched his attention to Guppy. He had been blabbering to him non-stop, providing borderline too much advisement on what to do. But I suppose it's preferable to give too much instruction than not enough.

Martin eventually ran out of things to say, and we all sat in the ringing silence as the explosions blasted around us.

The roar of the shelling had not subsided after several minutes. Still, the lack of shells hitting terribly close to us paired with the assumed strength of our hideout sparked enough confidence amongst us for conversation.

"This is the most tremendous cannonade I have ever heard," Udo declared to nobody in particular.

"It will probably be over soon," Martin advised. "Technology has changed since the first Great War. Siege weapons don't tend to bombard as long."

I didn't believe Martin was in the first Great War. He was the eldest amongst us in terms of rank and age, but I didn't think he was quite that old. So, I decided to ask. "Martin, were you part of the fighting three decades ago?"

He gazed towards me with his stern, callous eyes. "No, I was not," he specified. "Although I am the youngest of four brothers and a sister, so I have heard many stories."

"My father was in it," Graf chimed in. "He told me stories of the terrible fighting he had taken part of. He had hoped there would never be a war like that ever again."

Lindemann fixed his gaze at the rifle in his lap. "I'll never forget my father's face when he found out another war had begun," he muttered. "He was heartbroken when I told him I had signed up to fight… But I knew it was what I needed to do." Lindemann had been experiencing the ups and downs from getting accustomed to the horridness of war. Though typical with new soldiers, it was still worrisome coming from the one directly under my wing. I hoped he'd someday learn to live with it.

Explosions continued to echo from outside. The Soviet's artillery wasn't precise this time, but there sure were a lot of shells.

"Be ready for their assault," Martin butted in to change the tone. "Is everybody's weapon ready? Fischer, let me see yours."

Fischer handed him his rifle with the tip of the barrel swinging past Herrmann, to which Herrmann scolded, "Watch where you're pointing that thing, Guppy!" Hearing that my nickname for the rookie had caught on admittedly raised my spirit, just a little.

We listened to the shells as they continued to fall. After another minute or so, I nudged Lindemann. "We've got to get out of this pillbox as quickly as possible when this bombardment subsides," I explained.

"Why?" he questioned. His broad eyebrows flexed. "This is the safest place. Why would we leave here? What if they shoot more shells at us?"

Unsurprising of him to argue my orders, though I understand why it would make sense for somebody to want to stay in here where it was safe. "They'll be aiming for the bunker," I rationalised. "We'll be of more use elsewhere."

Lindemann made a reluctant but understanding grunt, so I carried on detailing our battle plans. "We'll cross the road and defend that flank. The recruits could use our help. We've done this before – they haven't." I caught the Oberfeldwebel giving me a reassuring nod.

Mentioning Guppy's recruit comrades made him whimper again, and he started squirming as he murmured, "I've got to get out of here, I've got to get out of here, I've got to get out of here…" The poor Guppy was becoming claustrophobic over being bound inside our cramped cement room during the shelling. He was looking for any reason to get out.

Guppy sprung up, but before he made it to his feet, Keller snatched him by his arm and yanked him back towards the wall.

"Where the *fuck* do you think you're going, Grenadier?" he condemned. "You'll die if you leave!"

The delusional recruit kept trying to shake off the Obergefreiter's clamp before Keller yanked him in and forcefully threw him against the wall, with the ping of Guppy's helmet hitting concrete reverbing inside our bunker.

"Get ahold of yourself!" Keller barked. "There's nothing you can do about it now. You're going to have to wait it out like the rest of us!"

Keller's bash seemed to knock some sense into him. The overwhelmed Guppy traded any attempt to escape with hopeless sobbing, making the only noise for the rest of us to hear in the bunker. Well, besides the explosions.

As the onslaught dragged on, I grew to assume the worst for the recruits caught outside the bunker. Paired with the unfamiliarity of where a shell was going to land, their chance of survival was as bleak as a full book's shot at getting read by Denis. Trust me, there's hardly any chance of that, if at all. Especially if that book is a bible.

Preparing for substantial losses, I leant towards Lindemann

to subtly keep him informed, attempting not to let Guppy listen in on my words this time. "They're probably not having the best of times across the street," I whispered. "We'll more than likely have to rush across when the cannonade ends to assist them."

An explosion wrung out dangerously near to the bunker that jolted everybody inside, which further proved my point. Lindemann's eyes then darted over to the quietly sobbing Guppy. He frowned, but surprisingly enough nodded in agreement. For once, he did not put up any resistance to my plans.

There was not much else to do while we waited, so I found myself with a bit of time to think. Ordinarily, I would have taken notice to Ilsa, but I was sure once we would leave this bunker that our bonding time would come.

Instead, my mind remained fascinated with Lindemann. Lately, his changes of mood have been drastic, and he was always so lost in his thoughts, he'd say irrelevant things aloud. Then, often in an instant, he would swiftly transform to the same witty little shit of recruit he had always been. It was as if he was fighting a devil inside as it tried to possess him. Such an imaginative being he was though. His recent peculiarity is likely from some malicious form of shellshock as it seeped its way into his limitless imagination. I hoped he'd be able to keep it under control. Perhaps I should also talk to him if the opportunity arises. But he's been such a challenging egg to crack that I was not sure if such a chance would ever transpire.

The bussing of a fly near my ear briefly separated itself from the ambient explosions and Guppy's sniffles as he continued to weep. Such a terrible thing, war can be, especially for the young recruits. They were so young when they joined the military and were never given another chance at adulthood before this war swept them away. Their lives were cut short of experiencing what life could have been like before fighting in war became their only trade. This was true for many of the seasoned veterans that had been here since the start of the fighting as well. Instead of war, we could have started a line of work, gone to school, maybe even fallen in love. I've had enough time to accept such a fate, but poor Lindemann has not, and it doesn't make it any easier to watch him struggle with it. It's destroying him from the inside out.

"Ivans!" Keller abruptly barked. "They're in the distance! Get ready!" He licked the top of his lips as his fingers on the grip of the weapon flared to get one final stretch before being put to continual use. Despite the risk of shrapnel, he had boldly been manning his MG for the entirety of the salvo. I was glad he did. The Soviets would sometimes charge our lines before their cannons had even stopped sounding off.

We were lucky this time, though. When the shells discontinued their devastation of our defences, the Soviets were still a fair bit out. I reckoned it would be about half a minute or so before their ground forces were close enough to engage. Even so, I gave it a 10-second count after the last shell fell from the sky just to be safe before I nodded at Lindemann, beckoning him to follow me out.

We were the first two men out of the pillbox. I turned the corner of the cement door frame and made a dead sprint across the exposed street to the trenches across. The anti-tank gun was still in one piece, already being tended to by a couple of men. I was thankful it had survived. It would be surprising if the Russians neglected to extend the invitation to their armour.

I glanced around as I dashed. The slight hill behind the flank's trench had once contained a few trees before a pair of houses, separating our first line of defence from the Sturmbannführer's luxurious ballroom. The trees were missing, and the once-green hilltop had turned brown and black from the explosions. Even so, it piqued my interest as a potentially ideal vantage point.

After I made it to the other side, I immediately snapped my head around. Lindemann had not dashed with me. Though the enemy was far away, I still took a knee and pointed Ilsa over the road to provide cover while he crossed. Without needing me to give him the go-ahead, he sprinted across with his rifle in one hand and his other pumping. He was learning, that he was.

Lindemann halted after he made it to me, so I nodded and entered the trenches. I was surprised at how intact the flank's trenches were. In fact, a majority of their trenches were unscathed, and the few parts that the barrage affected had only sustained limited damage. Thank Pfeiffer for that – he ruled over those recruits with an iron fist, but the hard work Guppy and his friends put in was of good use.

I couldn't see much from my low vantage points in the trench, but I caught a glimpse forward, through the uneven ground and fallen trees. Shell holes were everywhere, and a building not too far in the distance had been knocked over, spreading a mound of brick across the road ahead. The destruction will provide them with extra cover as they advance.

My first priority was to rally these shellshocked recruits. Most of them were still crammed in the corners of the trench, fearing more shells will land. “Get ready, boys!” I screamed as I grabbed one by his arms to hoist him up. Maybe the Oberfeldwebel’s request was sinking in. But they needed to be ready to fight. If they weren’t, they would die. We could all die.

As I did my best to invigorate the terrified boys, I somehow didn’t notice Pfeiffer’s voice as he did the same from the other end of the trench. I almost ran past him before he called our names. “Schmidt? Lindemann?”

Lindemann gave a rifle back to one of the frightened Grenadiers on my side as he beat me to a response. “We’re ready, Feldwebel,” he growled.

I was a bit thrown off at the initiative Lindemann took but quickly assembled a brief status report of the other half of our squad. “Our pillbox is unscathed and ready for this,” I informed.

“We better gotdamn hope so,” Pfeiffer grunted as he brushed past us to continue a final rally before the assault began. “On the front of the trench, men!” he roared.

Pfeiffer seemed as if he could handle it from there, so I tapped Lindemann again as he consulted a recruit. I pointed to the battered ridge behind the trenches to show him that was where we were heading. He nodded back.

I climbed up the wooden walls on the backside of the trench and then up the slope behind it. I watched my footing on the way down the less steep decline on the other side. The area behind the first trenches was indeed scorched. Some fires were still burning on the corpses of fallen trees, and the buildings beyond the crater holes were battered but still standing.

Lindemann had already taken up aiming from behind our ridge, but before I joined him, I took a second to marvel at the ideal position we were about to defend.

Well, in all reality, my unit's defence as a whole was less than ideal. Our platoon's other two squads where Denis was to our left and closer to the river at had taken quite a beating. Their foremost pillbox had taken a direct hit by one of the Soviet's gargantuan shells, likely wiping out its inhabitants. I was a bit worried about their flank.

But on a smaller scale, I found pleasure in my own squad's

defences. Keller's scant bunker overlooked a slight indent in the landscape, providing it with an advantageous angle over any attackers that may spout from the shelled-out building in front. Most of our squad's veterans gathered in the secure battlements surrounding the fortified defensive position as well, which was bound to give the enemy a bloody nose. The recruits by Lindemann and I, while soft and inexperienced, were in favourable positions and were led by likely the best man in the platoon for the job – the combat-infatuated Feldwebel Pfeiffer. So for us, it could have been much worse.

But what I was really pleased to have as a personal asset was this ridge. Its uneven top would be perfect for constant relocation. In addition to providing us with safety from not always firing from the same places, it could allow Lindemann and I to appear like a much larger force than we were. I couldn't let such a perfect barrier go unnoticed, so I brought it up to Lindemann.

"Do you know why I love this ridge so much?" I quizzed Lindemann as I closed the gap between us. Hopefully, he remembered my teachings from a while back.

"It's perfect for cover and we have great angles," he muttered without prying his eyes off from the sights of his rifle. “We’re going to kill a lot of them today.”

His tone had become monotonous and lacked the life it used to display. The behemoth inside him that would take over during combat was on its way out. It was tragic that he had it to begin with, particularly because of his youth. Still, having such a monster inside had its perks. All of us that had fought enough had something of the likes. The Russians included. Without it, we wouldn’t be soldiers.

A handful of tanks appeared on the horizon. Once they reached the outermost Soviet line, the infantry began following in the wake of their armour as they closed in on our position. The blast of the anti-tank gun next to us was the first shot fired. By some grace of God, it managed to hit one of the tanks on the first attempt, and one of their tanks burst into a tremendous ball of flame. Undeterred, the other tanks navigated around the freshly burning metal carcass and continued their advance into our lines.

Their main guns began sounding off. Especially on the go, their accuracy was nothing to boast about. They had the newer models of T-34s with the bigger cannons, much improved over their older counterparts. But no tank firing on the move was bound to be as capable of a shot over its stable, halted counterpart.

The rounds exploding around our trenches did little to shake Lindemann and I. However, a green recruit to our front audibly shuddered in fear as the ground erupted near to his position. They would all soon have to learn how not to panic.

To my front was a single tree on a slight hill. The top of the tree had come down on an oddly-placed boulder beside it, which could conceal any movement a cheeky Russian might make behind it. Further to my left was another tree, though since it was still standing, it provided much less cover and would likely not be as much of a threat. In the distance beyond it and to the left was the mostly destroyed building, with only two of its stone walls still standing. It was across the road, in front of our bunker.

Besides that, there was a considerable amount of open ground, littered with craters from the artillery. The holes would make it frustrating for their armour to cross, but would indeed give their soldiers cover. The stretch of land from Pfeiffer's trench down to the river where Denis and the others were was the only place on this side of Oradea that their armour could get through. They couldn't get through the mountain and forests beyond our flank to the right, so we were relatively safe from that direction.

Though a few had begun firing further down the line, Lindemann eagerly took the first shot out of our side of the trenches. There's no way he could have hit anyone yet. Awoken by the sound of a comrade firing, the recruits instinctively began firing as well.

"Stop firing! Not yet!" Pfeiffer hollered. "They're not close enough!"

I frowned at Lindemann for firing too soon. He knew better but still gave me the same face back.

I raised Ilsa and placed my sights on the corner of the building, waiting for my first victim to appear. The enemy was still too far away. Their tanks still shielded their soldiers, but the anti-tank gun behind us kept firing away.

In due course, Keller's machine gun started barking when they got within effective range. I carefully surveyed the area around the building with Ilsa, favouring the same spot beside the building. As they got close to it, another tank again fell victim to our anti-tank gun. The soldiers behind it transferred to behind the structure. The hair on the back of my neck stood on end, and I squeezed my hand around Ilsa's neck, anticipating for soldiers to charge out from the cover provided by the remnants of the building at any minute.

I was careful to expose just enough of my body to aim for one specific spot, with the rocks and hill surrounding me from taking crossfire from other directions. The tip of Ilsa's barrel, right under her front sight, rested on the dirt about halfway up a peak of the ridge to stabilise her scope. It was indubitably a terrific spot. We had the jump on them.

At last, they burst from behind the tanks and the distraught wall in bulk, mindlessly rushing towards our lines. I tried to follow the bulk of the pack at first, but Ilsa quickly adjusted her sights to the still Ivan providing cover from the corner of the building, similar to what I was doing earlier when Lindemann crossed the road.

I found myself already searching for another target when I realised Ilsa's trigger had already been pulled on our first kill of the day, hitting him square in the chest and penetrating the poor man's heart. At the snap of one's fingers, he was pried from our world and cast into the dark unknown, killed in an instant. He fell to the ground, and the gravity of taking another life added more weight to the ball and chain already connected to the ankles of my spirit.

At that moment, I became one with Ilsa. She was as soothing

as always. My hand hugged her metal bolt handle as I tugged it back. The reassuring noise of the receiver ejecting a spent shell casing graced my ears. My hands picked up every subtle crack in her frame. Her name I carved into the front of her receiver gave me a wee extra bit of tactile feedback, just for these moments. "It's okay," she would console through our touch. "It's my fault, too. We don't have a choice."

She was right. The brief damper in my mood promptly mended itself. Ilsa remained my lifeline out here, and I was positive she would last with me until the bitter end.

My eyes found themselves scouring the area to determine who my next target would be. After just a couple seconds, another Russian popped out on the same wall of the building as he, too, tried to provide cover for the others advancing. I had already demonstrated how zeroed in I was on his location, so I calmly squeezed the trigger for the second time of the day until the familiar recoil from my closest partner during these times of both physical and mental peril punched back into my shoulder.

Chapter 13

Feldwebel Uwe Pfeiffer

These gotdamn Bolsheviks never eased off. First, we kill 10 of them, and they come back with 20. Then we kill those 20, and they come back with 40. Then we strain to kill those 40, and they come back with, uh, 80. Someone said it before, and they were right – one of our men is as good as 10 of theirs, but they always have 11.

That's how our day had been going. But for some gotdamned reason, we've been able to hold them back so far. We didn't get hit too hard by their artillery, so we repelled the first wave without a problem. The next attack, we could manage as well. But now we're about to be on the third attack? Maybe the fourth? And we couldn't hold out forever.

That was no thanks to these green bastards around me. They couldn't hit a cow with a shotgun if it shitting on the grass by their feet. And that's if you could get the fuckers to shoot their weapons in the first place instead of cowering in fear.

Shit, again? "Eiche!" The wide-eyed recruit rocking in the

fetal position at the edge of the trench snapped to me. Tears rolled down his cheeks as if his mother had just taken away his stuffed animal. "Get your ass off the ground, or I'll throw you out of my gotdamn trench!"

He whimpered something and picked up his rifle while slowly getting up. It wasn't fast enough for me, though.

"Move your ass!" I howled as I took a hand off of my submachine gun to yank him up. Before he made it to his feet, I shoved him against the wooden frame supporting the trench. He didn't make another peep but still shook in fear. If the rest of them suck as much as him, we'll all die.

I continued checking on the other recruits in the dugout. These men – or rather, these gotdamn children – were terrible excuses for soldiers. Replacements keep getting younger, weaker, and less useful. By the rate we were going at, we'll damn sure be seeing fucking toddlers charging with swastika-laden armbands into battle.

I could deal with training a few new soldiers. But what was really chapping my ass was how many of the new bastards I got this time. Fritz put extra recruits and some otherwise untrained administration staff under my command to make our part of the line as strong as the other squads. They had two bunkers and held out together. We were on our own.

The Oberfeldwebel also kept sizing me up for leadership, which I haven't decided on. I know I could do it. Hell, I'd kick ass at it. But I'd have to shoot the sunshine up the Sturmbannführer's skirt. And I hated that shit.

The Soviets were preparing to attack again, readying themselves in the distance. Within eyesight, but out of our range. They were taunting us, knowing there was hardly any chance for us to have anything that could reach out and hit them.

It was my worst fear, too – more tanks this time. In the first wave, they had a couple. After that, they only attacked with infantry. More tanks were bound to happen sooner or later, but it worried me because of how little we could do against them. Some Teller anti-vehicle mines we had planted earlier scared them off. Especially paired with the Pak anti-tank gun right behind our trench. By some grace of God, its crew was performing like it was their final hour. I'll mention it to Fritz when it's over.

Besides the Pak, we still had a couple of Panzerfausts, and

some spare Teller mines stocked up. The disposable infantry-held rockets could knock out a tank, but you'd have to get close to use it. Not as close as you'd need to be to take one out with a mine, thank God, but still closer than I'd like to be to one of those fucking things. But even if one of them got close enough, the recruits would find a way to fuck up using the Panzerfaust. It's one gotdamn lever, but they'd still find a way. So, it would be up to us veterans. That's if they'd even be able to penetrate. Otherwise, we'd have to get crafty with the mines.

The tanks began their push in the distance. "They're coming again soon, boys!" I shouted to my men. "Hold your fire until they're close enough for you fuckers to actually hit them this time!"

Just as I had stacked up against the wooden side of the trench facing the approaching communists, I heard my name called. "Uwe, comrade!" I knew that voice. I spun around to see my superior and friend, Oberfeldwebel Fritz Martin.

A smile slipped past my war face. "Knew they couldn't do shit to you, Fritz." His military bearing was sharper than mine, and he managed to hold back the smile he would have otherwise let out as he stacked against the wall next to me.

Fritz leaned his weapon on the wall to observe the approaching enemy through his field goggles. "These tanks are going to be the death of us," he murmured. There was a streak of blood on the forearm of his ordinarily pristine uniform. It didn't seem to hinder his arm's movement, so I didn't address it.

"Those men on the gun behind us have had a heyday on them," I informed, gesturing to the burning tank on the road, right ahead of our position. A timely round fired off from the anti-tank gun behind us, engulfing us with smoke from the muzzle blast. It cleared to reveal a smoking crater in the distance. It missed, but one of their tanks shuddered away from the explosion, heeding the danger.

Fritz grunted. "You'd think a cannon with so many stripes on its barrel would perform better when we needed it to." Field guns and tanks liked to put their hits right before the muzzle brakes on their machines to show their experience. It boosted morale and made them look fiercer in the face of our enemies. The one behind us had several white stripes on it. Great proof of its experience.

But they missed, so I didn't defend the crew's reputation. I beckoned at Fritz's bloody uniform and asked, "Other squads have any trouble?"

Without moving his head or the binoculars, he slightly raised his arm and subtly shook his wrist to point out the stained sleeves of his top. "Yes," he stated.

With a flat tone, I cracked, "Ah, anything but your uniform."

My jest didn't please him. "Schmidt's humor is rubbing off on you," he responded, still searching through his binoculars. "Speaking of Schmidt, I asked him to pull his shit together today."

I took two small steps in place, repositioning myself on the wall of the trench. "How'd that go?"

"I tried approaching him as a friend," he shared. "It worked."

Fritz wasn't usually one for friends. But neither was I. Maybe that's why we got along. But I reacted with a nod because I trusted his judgment.

Fritz again changed the course of our conversation. "How are these recruits doing? Think they'll hold up?"

"They're just kids," I replied while pulling the magazine out of my MP-40 to make sure I still had some rounds in it. "But I've done my best to prepare them. I make sure they have ammo. I tell them when to shoot. But most importantly, I made sure they built a strong fucking trench that will save them when their skills won't."

"That is why I placed them under you." Fritz sighed as he put down his binoculars to look at me. "Uwe, friend," he beckoned with a serious tone. His jaw shifted as he prepared what to say with a deep breath.

Finally, Fritz spoke. "Look, I know you have not been for it, but I need you to consider a promotion," he coaxed. Knew he'd bring it up again. I winced and looked away, but he pressed on. "You've denied it before, but we lost a lot of men over there, and we are going to lose a lot more. Newer and less experienced soldiers are replacing the leadership. Not many platoons are led by Oberfeldwebels anymore."

"But command is crammed in that fucking mansion. They're not going to die enough for you to fill their shoes," I interrupted. I didn't think Fritz thought he was going to die. He'd made it through too much. But Fritz would never abandon his men. He'd also decline an offer for advancement so he could keep a closer eye on us. He was probably bringing it up because command wanted his expertise in the safe confines of wherever the rest of them reside.

"Just do me a favor," Fritz asked. He turned towards the

enemy and brought the field goggles back up to his eyes. “Think it over for me, will you? There’s nobody else in the platoon I’d trust more for the role.”

He made it hard to disagree with. “I’ll think it over, Fritz,” I answered. I’m against being anything more than a squad leader, but you never know. Shit happens. Maybe I wouldn’t get to choose. Either way, I’ll mull it over.

Silence took over. The late afternoon sun had cast a shadow on the ground around us. For all I knew, it could be the last day I ever saw the sunlight. Huh. If Fritz could stay in a good light with the command, maybe it wouldn’t end up being so bad.

My thoughts were cut short when the Oberfeldwebel whispered, “They’re almost within firing range,” under his breath. Right after, he hollered the same thing at our men. It was time.

“Keep shooting!” I screamed to the men beside me. I rose above the battlements to spray a burst of fire from my MP-40 into the seemingly endless onslaught of the Soviets ahead until it clicked. Another empty magazine. I was running low. There were more of them this time.

I crouched back down and propped my back against the battlements. As I swapped out my dry magazine for a new one, a bullet smacked the other side of the trench. A bolt-action rifle sprawled on the ground, following a tremendous red splash. I jolted my head to the side just in time for the thump of another recruit hitting the floor. He had taken a bullet through the neck.

The Oberfeldwebel stopped firing his weapon and ducked down. “Fuck!” he cursed from next to me. There was no saving the recruit. “We’re going to run out of men at this rate.”

Enraged at the responsibility of losing yet another man under my command, I shot back up with a mighty roar, unloading my weapon into the wave of enemies in the distance. I held the trigger down. I wasn’t accurate. But I was fed the fuck up.

“Control yourself, Uwe!” advised Fritz, who had remained calm throughout the battle. “Do what’s best for the men and control yourself!”

Fritz was right. I stopped firing before I wasted the rest of the magazine. I was low on bullets, after all.

The tree in front of us erupted as it took a shell from one of their tanks. Splinters splattered everywhere. I covered my face with my arm to avoid any injuries. Another recruit further down the line cried out. The terror-stricken boy screamed like a lunatic at the hefty chunk of wood sticking out of his forearm. But he wasn't that bad. That was worth a free trip home if he survived this battle.

I peeked back over the wall with my weapon. Our bunker to the left was holding out for now, but the MG inside couldn't watch my side as well. It left us with a lot of work.

Fortunately, we had Schmidt and Lindemann behind us. They were focused more on the enemies further away, so I didn't get to see much of the effects of their shooting until the Bolsheviks had gotten close enough. Charging enemies that had survived fire from the new soldiers would attempt storming our trenches from the front or side. They'd catch a timely round, sometimes two, from sharpshooting duo behind us. I always hated the fucking nickname, but having the Overwatch on our side of the flank was a reassuring safety net.

That Lindemann, though. That kid fucking scares me. The fighting started fucking him up. His mood would change without warning. We all saw his twitches. The weird jolting that happens when he remembers what he saw in the fights prior. But I could give a shit about it right now. The boy could shoot, and that's what I needed. He could twitch around all day long for all I care, as long as he kept firing his fucking rifle at the enemy.

I scoured over the trench just in time for a dashing communist take one right in the stomach from the Oberfeldwebel. Any satisfaction Fritz may have gotten was interrupted by another blast to our front, showering us with mud.

The T-34 that had just barely missed us sped towards us. Our anti-tank gun fired another round, cratering the ground to the side of it. The hulking communist machine took note and halted in its tracks to line up a shot in our direction. Fritz also took note and reached to drag me into cover, but I was already squatting down to get out of its line of sight.

The bullets from the tank's coaxial machine gun peppered around us. They started landing to our front but soon were kicking up dirt on the higher ridge behind us. Not long after, the coaxial had zeroed in enough to clip the man in charge of aiming the anti-tank piece. The impact of catching the bullet dragged him to the side, exposing him. His cannon's metal shield was hardly competent enough to protect its nobs and shit from small arms fire, let alone to offer adequate protection for his crew. The wounded aimer had no chance, and he soaked up a few more rounds.

The other men fumbled to take over the aiming process, stalling them long enough for the tank to fire its cannon into the tip of the ridge right next to them, blasting chunks of rock and dirt everywhere.

I covered my eyes right as it hit. First, I checked my body. Sometimes your blood races so fast that you might not notice when you're wounded. I was fine, so I checked my men. They were too far away to have gotten hurt. Then, Fritz, who was also alright. Thank God. I followed his eyes to where they were fixed. None of the cannon's crew members had emerged from behind after getting hit. Hardly wasting a second, Fritz ordered, "Come on!" as he took off around the ridge back to the cannon.

I followed on his tail, up to the other side of the ridge that Schmidt and Lindemann were on. We got around and found a mutilated corpse with his entrails strewn across several meters of the blackened ground, an unresponsive man lying face-down by the first man's side, and another soldier who silently stared at his severed leg, lying a few meters away from the rest his body. There was previously one more soldier on the anti-tank gun, but he was nowhere in sight.

I was already lifting an unfired shell when Fritz told me to reload. He was fucking with the wheels on the left side of the piece that controlled aiming the cannon. The round was more than half a meter long and around seven kilograms of metal. It didn't look like one of the ones with tungsten in it. Those were growing rare. But hopefully, it would still be able to penetrate enough.

It'd also been a while since I've used one of these. What was it, a Pak-40? They're all the same. After being in so long, I had a damned good idea of how to use almost anything out here. And this was easy shit. Pull the lever backwards, put the new round in, push the lever forward, take cover, fire, repeat.

As I was stepping around the empty shells on the ground with a new round in my hands, the tank fired off another round. This time, it was at the pillbox to our left across the street. Our bunker was tough, but not tough enough for a direct hit. The cement roof collapsed into the bottom, ending the reign of the machine gun inside. At least two of my gotdamned men were in the bunker.

I roared to the sky in resentment. I was already aggravated

about losing the others, but I was livid over the ones in the bunker. Those were my men. My men with experience! We could get new guns. New gear. More bullets. But we couldn't get lost experience.

"Uwe! Load it!" Fritz hollered. I pulled it together and hurried to slam the shell into the breach of the rifled anti-tank barrel, followed by a mighty shove of the lever. The slam resounded from the back of the piece, shutting to keep the shell in place.

"Loaded!" I informed as I ducked down into the limited cover by the side of the weapon. Fritz finalized adjusting the aim through the sights on the left side and calmly pressed the firing button on the other side.

The entire piece slid back on its carriage with a deafening blast. A burst of exhaust from the front of the barrel briefly our line of sight. I wasn't anticipating the assembly to automatically eject an empty shell casing. I jumped to avoid it hitting my feet. The smoke soon cleared, revealing a blindingly bright hole burning through the front side of the tank. A fire raged out of an open cupola on the top of the T-34. It was a direct hit.

"Another! Coming up on the hill to the right!" hollered Fritz, signaling towards another approaching tank on the far right side. It stampeded up the ridge, callously rolling past the deceased on the ground surrounding it. It had already made it about as close to us as the other one we had just hit.

I fetched another hefty shell as Fritz frantically spun the wheels to adjust our aim. The tank fired at us on the move, but it thankfully went above our heads. A crashing boom sounded off far back to our rear. Hopefully, it hit the Sturmbannführer.

My hands trembled with both fear and excitement as I shoved the next round into the breach. I screamed, "Ready!" before I had even fully finished pushing the breech lock back. Fritz again didn't yell anything before pressing the button to fire.

Another cloud of smoke swallowed our sight and was almost immediately paired with the distinct 'ping' of our worst fears. It had glanced off the front armor of the tank.

Without wasting a second, I began the reloading process. But I glanced up after the smoke had time to clear. Sure enough, I noticed a popping silver streak along the front corner of the front plate of the tank. Our round had dented through its dark green paint, but it hadn't gone through. The beast ground to a halt, but with hardly a delay, it again took off towards us. I wished that our hit would at least stun the gunner.

It had almost made it to the boulder on the top of the hill. I needed to be quick. An experienced crew could shoot off ten of these shells a minute, and although not that familiar with the gun, I went as fast as I could to load -

The next thing I remembered was complete silence, and peacefully the sky above. There weren't many clouds, but they were a few. It reminded me of many, many years ago, when I was just a toddler. I used to lie on a blanket in a park with my mom and watch the clouds. We used to say what shapes they resembled. One passed that looked like a giraffe. I didn't know why I hadn't done it much since. Watching the clouds wasn't that bad.

My ears kicked in with a sharp ringing as the world slowly came back around me. A tank just shot at me. Ah shit, could I move? I wiggled my toes and hands. Okay, good, I could still feel them. I patted over my chest and stomach. Nothing was missing. Great so far.

My men? I rolled my head over to the right. Lindemann was firing his rifle, and Schmidt was crouched or something behind a rock on the ridge. He was gritting his teeth and clenching his empty hands. But he must not have been injured because he withdrew his pistol and sprung up, sprinting like a madman towards the trenches.

Shit, what about Fritz? My strength came back to me at once as I jolted up to find him. I didn't see him on my side, so I crawled over to the other side of the anti-tank gun to search.

The metal barrier of the gun had a clean hole toward the left side. It had hit gone right through the shield mangled the controls on Fritz's side, rendering the piece inoperable. A wave of terror hit me as I pieced together what must have happened to Fritz.

I twisted around. The crewman who had lost a leg earlier was dead now, his chest exposing a gaping wound. The unresponsive man on the floor had been tossed back, perforated by extra shrapnel. Anxiously, I peeked over a giant rock behind our position and caught sight of a foot. I hoofed towards it, following the foot up to a leg, then the leg to a hip, and the hip-

It was Fritz. His torso had been cleaved down his right side from his trapezoid down to his hip. He laid in a pothole. It contained the gore from otherwise spreading about the area, although there wasn't much left to spread out. The blood had been expunged from his exposed innards so quickly that hardly any more of it seeped out.

Still enclosed by his helmet, his emotionless face peered blankly into the sky. My closest comrade, Oberfeldwebel Fritz Martin, had been killed.

I fell to my knees and repeatedly hammered the ground with my fists. Of all people, why Fritz? Why would they take him away? At that moment, I hated war. I hated it more than anything. But mostly, I hated those fucking Russians. I wanted to make them pay for their actions. I wanted to grab my gun and charge right into those fuckers. I didn't care if I die. Where was my weapon?

"Do what's best for the men and control yourself!" echoed Fritz's words from earlier from within my head. I would give anything to be able to avenge the death of my friend. But he would want me to avenge him by doing taking care of our men. That gotdamn Fritz. He always did what was best.

Before departing, I closed the eyes of my deceased comrade. I took one last look at Fritz as the sounds of the battlefield rang around me. I banged the helmet on my head with a closed fist as I hurried to find my weapon and assess the battlefield.

My submachine gun was nowhere to be found, but Fritz' Sturmgewehr was lying a few paces away, partially buried in the dirt. The pouches that held its magazines had flown off Fritz during the explosion, conveniently landing right next to the weapon. I decided his Sturmgewehr would be my new one, so I grabbed them both. I was almost out of ammo for my MP-40, anyway, and Fritz was better than I was at conserving it.

The battle had continued without my attention for enough, so I sprinted back to the ridge and peered over. The tank had advanced past the top of the slight hill on our right flank, now cautiously progressing directly towards our trenches. There were more tanks further back behind the one that had just killed Fritz, with enemy infantry panned out across the battlefield on the ridge in the first one's wake. The few recruits that remained fighting on our flank madly firing their weapons into the fray, too overtaken by fear to aim effectively. The tank discharged its cannon into the dugout, sending a legless recruit into the air with a red poof. Fighting back at this point was useless, especially without our field gun. We needed to retreat.

It didn't stop Schmidt, though. Brandishing his pistol in one hand and a Teller anti-tank mine in the other, he arose in from behind a tree on the furthest side of our flank. He howled like a madman and tore towards the tank, blasting his sidearm in the direction of the advancing foot soldiers in its wake. The Soviets on the ridgeline dropped to the ground to avoid getting hit. Lindemann, who had emerged behind a similar tree, chose to push up deeper on the far right flank, hunting down one of them who had gone prone. Once he made it to the top of the ridge, Lindemann snapped his rifle almost by his feet. The Soviet's head jolted back into sight as Lindemann blasted him at point-blank range.

By then, Schmidt had somehow made it to the side of the metal beast. He tossed the mine on the top of its treads and bolted away, soon diving into a small crater nearby. The treads of the tank brought the mine forward, and sure enough, it erupted with a tremendous explosion. I was fucking proud of Schmidt. Fritz had been avenged.

Even so, we couldn't keep fighting where we were. "Fall back!" I screamed at the top of my lungs. "Squad, fall back to our next line! There's too much enemy armor!"

I dashed down into the trench to organize a retreat for the remaining boys. There were hardly any of them left. The ones that could still move scurried about hectically but with purpose.

Orders came out of me immediately. "Praune! Carry that one over there! Küchen! Inform the men by the bunker of our retreat!" The men took notice and followed my orders as I fired my weapon in semi-automatic, keeping the enemy's heads down for as long as I could.

Soon enough, Schmidt leaped back into our trench and crashed against the wall opposite of me. The slide of the bulky, foreign pistol he held was locked back, empty. Schmidt returned my scowl with piercingly gold eyes and a determined frown of his own, panting from being completely out of breath. He darted to the side as Lindemann landed in our dugout on his feet in front of him.

"You fucking idiots," I commented as I hoisted Schmidt up with a pat on his back. "Now, get these gotdamn men out of here!"

For just a second, Schmidts eyes flared back to their regular shade of light brown as he quipped, "I always try to, platoon leader." He sprinted towards an injured soldier down the trench and immediately began picking him up. Lindemann stacked up on the wall and continued firing into the enemy.

I didn't think about it until I continued suppressing the enemy with my Sturmgewehr, but Schmidt was right. Fritz ended up getting his wish. I was the new platoon leader.

Chapter 14

Feldkuchenunteroffizier Johannes Buhr

Gunshots and explosions reverberated from outside, shaking the walls of our headquarters. All the other men scrambled about the otherwise luxurious command structure. There wasn't much else for me to do besides hunkering down by the radio.

"Yes, we hear you – we have already requested support," went the radioman into the microphone. "We are doing everything we can."

Beside him was Sturmbannführer Kolartz, anxious as his men frantically fought on the frontlines nearby. "A Guards Tank Army? Can we not get any assistance from the 23rd Panzer Division?" the Sturmbannführer pleaded to the radioman.

"It would be unlikely," I chimed in. Being the resident chef gave me ears on everybody I prepared meals for, including some men from the 23rd Panzer Division I had served just yesterday. "They're heading south to counter a breakthrough near Arad."

Strands of the Sturmbannführer's hair slipped out from

underneath his cover, draping across his forehead. He frowned at me and snarled, "Well, maybe you should trade in your ladle for a panzerfaust, and *you* can destroy the Soviet tanks instead, *Feldkuchenunteroffizier*?"

I promptly formulated a response but unwillingly held my tongue. I was senior to Sturmbannführer Kolartz in age, but the power he had over me in rank made us far from equal. He would make some nasty threats, he would be foolish to follow through on such a reactive outburst. We both knew I was much better with my ladle than a rifle, and even he wouldn't insult my cooking.

A stray shell suddenly burst down the hallway of our command centre, sending rock and debris flying past the doorframe. A soldier who had just missed being torn apart from the explosion swore loudly before going about his prior business.

The Sturmbannführer then took his cover off and ran his fingers through his hair before aggressively planting a hand on the radioman's table. "Just put me through to Major General von Radowitz!" he commanded.

The radioman did not flinch, waiting in silence in response to the Sturmbannführer as he received a message through his headset.

Suspense filled the room as we eagerly waited for the transmission coming through.

Soon enough, the radioman chirped up. "Yes, I hear you, that would be most appreciated," he responded into the microphone. The radioman then turned his head towards the Sturmbannführer and announced, "Major General von Radowitz is sending elements of his panzer division to repel the enemy armour one last time before they depart towards Arad. I was told to notify you that after their assistance, the 76th would have sole responsibility for Oradea."

A wave of coolness overtook the Sturmbannführer, who stood up tall and calmly placed his cap back on his head. "Excellent. The Soviet menace shall soon be repelled from Oradea," he declared. "Send our gratitude to the Major General and inform him that we will do whatever is necessary here to guarantee final victory."

Something didn't sit right with me, so I opted to excuse myself from the Sturmbannführer's presence in search of some fresh air. I found a window in the next room, so I carefully opened it and peeked out towards the frontlines. As I breathed in a light breeze from outside, I could make out some faint sparks of rifle fire in the distance. There were quite a few Soviet tanks on the horizon. The intensity of the fighting was apparent, even from so far away.

At least we had some Hungarians assisting us here in Oradea. Their Third Army was around and about with us, dying in vain just like we were. Some of the men had voiced their concerns over the Hungarians seeking an armistice with the Soviets. They thought the Hungarian soldiers would turn on us. Personally, I was sure an armistice between Hungary and the Soviet Union would happen sooner or later. Still, politics won't immediately change the minds of every soldier fighting for his homeland.

Sure, some of our soldiers thought the Hungarians were not a formidable fighting force. I respect their perspectives. The Hungarians helped us, but they weren't trained as well as those of us originating from our warring fascist fatherland. All it did was help promote their ideology of German superiority, even against our allies.

But those same men on their high horses who preach of Germany superiority over everywhere else are nothing short of delusional. They didn't know those Hungarians. If you pushed their backs against the wall, and they'd fight tooth and nail – to the death. This city, Oradea, isn't far from the current Drebecen battlefield – a city where every meter is soaked in Axis blood. The men don't forget that. It was do or die. Everybody knew it: the Nazis, the Hungarians, the Heer, all of our other allies. But for now, we stood alone with our backs to the walls against Ivan's elite, flinging whatever we can to defend our respective nations against the Red Menace. The Hungarians were just as pinched here as we were.

Regardless, the Guards armour was still closing in. Guards were like the Waffen S.S. of the Soviets – better trained, competently equipped, and with a similar zeal for their country. It had been bleak for years, but it seemed particularly desolate as of late. The 23rd Panzer Division had saved us before, but we'd soon be alone. They'll be tens of kilometres south, more focused on protecting more pressing cities of interest like Arad or Drebecen over Oradea. We may put up resistance here, but the Guards would eventually crush us. This city will fall, and like every city we've fought in, the lives taken to defend the Fatherland would be wasted.

This wave of attackers may be held at bay, but the intense fighting for Oradea had only begun. There was just something unwholesome in the air here. I just knew my boys were going to have a hell of a time out there this time around.

Chapter 15

Unterfeldwebel Rupert Schmidt

Everybody has a few things that seem to bug them more than others. For me, it was people who choose to cover their mouths with their hands when they sneeze. It absolutely bewildered me that they couldn't be bothered to blast their spit and germs literally anywhere else on their body except for the part that touches everything. How could they hug their mothers with such disgusting hands? Barbaric savages.

Another peeve of mine is constant repetition. It drove me into boredom, and boredom drives me to insanity. Such insanity is how I had been feeling as of late. We had been fighting nonstop for this city, block for block, for the past few days. They'd take a block, we'd take it back, and they'd just steal it from us again. The process was a losing battle, but so many lives were being uselessly cast away in the process. Undoubtedly, everybody else felt the same way. So when an opportunity came about for a squad to keep watch over the perimeter of a train station in a part of the city away from the fighting, I was keen to volunteer mine to give my men a breather. I was shocked they let us, though, because the Sturmbannführer just found out about Herrmann's chest tattoo and we were reprimanded for it.

My men were scattered across some of the smaller buildings surrounding the plaza, in front of the train station. We were to keep a keen eye out for any bold Russians who might pre-emptively attack it. The station acted as our headquarters in Oradea, so more substantial defences were being readied there to defend it. I found it amusing that the simple presence of some silly building by a couple of unbroken lines of metal bolted onto some wood was worth so much fuss over. But, I could use that same logic for everywhere else we fought.

I made sure to stomp my boots as I climbed the stairs of one of the buildings while making my rounds so Udo Sommer would hear me approaching. I've learned better than to sneak up on a man on watch.

Any trivial thoughts running through my mind ground to a halt as I placed a hand on the doorframe and stepped through. The difference in the atmosphere immediately made itself evident. Udo had propped himself up in a chair with his rifle and his socked feet resting on the table. His helmet laid in his lap, and his boots sat on the ground next to him. Udo had a smoke in his hand, an exceedingly brave move for a man on watch. The red embers at the tip of a cigarette paired with the smog it emitted made it harder to stay hidden from an approaching enemy.

"Ah, squad leader," Sommer remarked with a glance before returning his gaze back out the window into the overcast sky. His voice was lower than usual, and his words were pitched with hardly any effort, seemingly falling out of his mouth. He smoothly kicked a chair out from under the table across him. "Come, have a seat."

"Sure, so long you put out that cigarette," I compromised before sitting down, setting Ilsa on my lap. I wanted to put her on the table, but it just wouldn't have felt right. A certain staleness in the room kept me at bay. "You know you're easier to spot with that thing sticking out of your mouth."

"Hah," Udo unconvincingly laughed. "Let them spot me. Then I wouldn't have to fight anymore." Udo took a long drag. "Having this cigarette is worth the risk."

"Oh?" I questioned. I wanted to put my feet up on the table

like him, but I wasn't quite feeling relaxed enough. Udo was in an offputting mood. "Why's that?"

Udo stayed gazing outside, eyes glistening on nothing specific far in the distance. "I love the burn," he muttered. He took another puff and fixed his stare towards the darkened sky. "I just love the burn."

I ignored my better judgement, deciding that sharing a smoke with my comrade was more important than avoiding being shot. It was the middle of the day, so smoking wouldn't be as risky as during the night as well. Plus, I felt like he wanted to talk. So, I procured a cigarette from my pocket and asked, "You got a light?" with it in the corner of my mouth. I had a match, but I thought it would get him out of his head a bit. Udo temporarily paused his blank stare through the window by blinking twice and then searching his pockets for a match. He soon procured one, leant over to light me up, and I took a puff.

After I took a drag, I tried to break the ice. "You've always been a big smoker," I tested. "When was your first cigarette?"

Udo took a moment to think. "I don't think I have one specific memory of when I started," he finally divulged. "But my father smoked before he died. Makes me think of him."

I was unsure of what would be appropriate to say next. Thankfully Udo continued before I could give some half-ass response. "He died when I was young," he admitted. "His heart went out."

Everything I thought about saying was either horribly unfitting or much too sappy. I could only let out, "That's horrible."

After some more seconds of awkward silence, he detailed, "I had to take over my dad's work at the restaurant after he passed away. That's when I really took up smoking."

"Ah, so smoking reminds you of both your father and the family business," I concluded as I took another drag.

"Maybe that's it," he stated as he switched positions of his feet on the table. I could tell he was starting to warm up. "I worry about my family's business, Rupert. I don't know how they are managing to cook nowadays."

"You as a Feldkuchenunteroffizier," I tried jesting. "I've seen what you'll eat. I can't imagine how good your cooking was."

"It is a hell of a lot better than my uniform," he reacted. We both sort of chuckled, and I mirrored him as he took a puff from his smoke.

"You really think your family is having trouble running the business without you there?" I pondered.

Udo gandered at me. He raised his eyebrows and reflected, "Well, probably not. My mum is tough. She is the greatest person I've ever met. I know she can handle it." His eyes returned to the window. "But I'm sure she could use a hand. My sister is away, too, so she's a few people short."

"Well you know," I hypothesised, "Some of us might need work after the war ends. Maybe we could all lend your mother a hand?"

The corners of Udo's mouth ever so slightly turned up. "I'd really appreciate that. She'd welcome it," he approved. Then, his head lowered, and his tone changed back. "She'll need the help," he addressed, flicking his cigarette on the floor to his side. He quickly changed gears as he pulled out another smoke. "How's it like being squad leader again?"

I had already prepared an amusing answer to such a question. "Well, I don't have to massage the Sturmbannführer's shoulders nearly as much as I thought I'd have to," I kidded.

"Of course," he verbalised with the frailest of smiles. "You always kept it lively."

"Hey, I try." I waited a second before proceeding. "Squad leader is a lot more work than I remember it being, but I get to prod Denis a bit more. Plus, Martin would have wanted me here, so I'll keep doing it I guess."

"It's already changed you," Udo announced. "Look at that, no more stubble. And I'm sure underneath that helmet is a fresh haircut," he jabbed. His blue eyes shimmered as a hopeful beam of sunlight briefly struck him through the clouds outside.

"Not in your wildest dreams," I rebutted. I decided to honour our fallen Oberfeldwebel's wishes by shaving my face to make the transition easier for Pfeiffer, but I would be dammed if I cut my precious hair. "They'll do their worst to make me a cookie-cutter soldier, but who would I be if I didn't press their buttons?"

"I was just telling Lindemann and Graf about your shenanigans just the other week," Udo shared. He looked at me for a little bit and then turned back towards outside. "Fucking Graf, too…"

"Yeah. Another good one, hey," I resonated. We'd lost Graf

at the start of the battle for Oradea. Udo had befriended him, and only now could find the time to reflect on it. We hadn't had much time off over the past few days.

Udo turned towards me. "Hey…" he started. He wasn't the type of person to ask for things, even when he needed them, so I listened up.

"What is it, Udo?" I inquired.

Udo tightened his lips. "You know, you did everything you could with Hans. Just like you did the same for me," he declared.

"Yeah…" I muttered. I winced and looked towards the wall, too caught up in my mind to even bother pretending to care what was through the window. "It's just hard, you know? I cared so much about him."

"So why not do the same with Lindemann?" Udo pressed. He kept the same face.

"Lindemann, uh, he was just placed under me," I reasoned, leaning back in my chair. "I didn't choose him. And he's into all that Nazi shit."

"You didn't choose Hans, either," Udo rebutted with an ever so slightly raised chin. "And you know Lindemann is just a kid."

It was an exceedingly tricky subject for me. Assembling anything else coherent enough to say out loud was just too much.

Udo, however, was ready. "You did your best with us. You made the time we had left worth as much as it could," he reckoned. "I've always admired that about you most. You never gave up on us."

I couldn't remember getting a compliment as meaningful in all of 1944, so I looked up at him with as genuine of a smile as I could muster. "Thanks, Udo. I really appreciate that."

"Never change that, Rupert. And don't be so hard on yourself if it doesn't work out, because you've tried your hardest," Udo advised with a simper as he again faced the window. "You're going to do great things."

"I'll try to," I thanked, reaching over to pat his shoulder. What a heartfelt compliment. "We both will."

"Yeah."

Minutes of silence passed. We simply enjoyed our smokes as we scanned through the window, with the reverbing noises of sporadic firefights from across the town hardly audible in the background. I finished my cigarette after Udo finished his, and we both lit up more, just to soak in the temporary peace. We had nothing else do but relish the piece, thank God. I could keep my bum on this chair all day in the silence next to Udo. We've all done things we regret out here, but Udo was like Kuhn – an example that good people still can exist under the immense pressure of this horrific war. I would do anything to make sure he made it back home. How would Udo's family support their business without him? I trusted Udo with everything, and I was grateful to have him by my side.

Eventually, though, I had to go make the rest of my rounds. I mentioned it to Udo and got up to leave. As I was at the edge of the room, Udo called back, "Hey, Rupert…"

I turned around by the doorframe. Udo held his stare for longer than what would be reasonable. The dark clouds outside behind Udo took a bit of the colour out of his eyes.

Finally, he let out, "After you saved my life… Well, you've made the time since as good as it could have been."

A grin crept up on my face. If there was nothing else I could do in this world, at least I made Udo feel a little better. It really warmed me.

"Likewise, Udo," I responded. "We'll make sure your mother

is doing alright after all this is over. And maybe tonight we'll bust out that vodka we've been saving, eh?"

"Please do." Udo's stare sunk to the floor in front of his seat before returning back to me. His cloud-coloured eyes peered at me for a solid second before he grunted, "Farewell, Rupert." He made an attempt to smile was so weak, it was hardly more light-hearted than his resting face.

I didn't want to leave so soon, but I really did need to continue my rounds, so I said, "We'll make it out of here soon enough. See you soon, Udo," and exited the room, went down the stairs, and left the building.

The worst part about this war for me was seeing somebody like Udo get so down about it all and knowing there was not much else I could do to help. He said I was doing the best I could, but it still didn't feel like enough. But I thought that maybe a couple drinks later in the night would cheer him up. Hell knows it's worked for me in the past.

I was only about a building's length away when I heard a gunshot ring out from back inside Udo's building. My heartbeat rocketed, and without any hesitation, I whipped around and sprinted back into his structure.

Without thinking, I stormed in through the back door of Udo's building so hastily, I still had Ilsa, a bolt-action, in-hand instead of my semi-automatic pistol. I hardly cleared the first floor before I flew up the steps to where Udo was above.

I barged past the doorframe on the second level and stopped dead in my tracks when I finally laid eyes on Udo, dropping the butt of my rifle from my shoulder to my hip. He was in the same chair he was in earlier, with the gold ray of sunlight peering through a hole in the clouds, surrounding him in a silhouette. His socked toe was stuck in the trigger guard of his weapon, still propped up in-between his legs. A mess of blood had been painted on the ceiling above him, dripping into a growing pool beneath him. A gargantuan opening on the tip of Udo's head added to it as it flopped over the back of his chair.

For better or for worse, I have always had a sluggish reaction when taking in any drastic news. So, I just stood there, soaking up the scene, for minutes on end. I didn't even remember breathing. I just… Stood.

Chapter 16

Feldkuchenunteroffizier Johannes Buhr

"Do you understand?" The Sturmbannführer's order would likely save my life but was still hard to accept. As great of a speaker as he could be, his rooted self-interest deep within proved to be quite the turnip for me to uproot.

"Yes, Sturmbannführer," I responded with a salute. I had been here long enough to get away without such a formal action. Even though we tended to not salute in the field, somewhere between being in a so-called safer area, remembering how proper the Sturmbannführer prefers us to be, and admittedly not caring as much about his wellbeing, I decided to raise my right palm to the side of my brow anyway.

"Very well," the Nazi commented with a nod before departing, his peons following on his tail. Naturally, Sturmbannführer Kolartz couldn't possibly be bothered to return a salute to a soldier of such an inferior rank such as myself. Perhaps he was still bitter over losing his lavish command centre in the days prior.

So, I got back to packing up my cooking devices. After being a chef for so long, I had managed to accumulate quite an impressive amount of utensils. A surprising amount of work went into cooking meals for as many men as I cooked for, which warranted for as much equipment as I had. Anything left behind was not likely to get replaced.

I was the central area of the train station, with an enormous internal room that rivalled the size of an empty warehouse. Around my cooking station bustled the fast walkers, the medics carrying the wounded, the hobbling, and the officers. Hungarians were among us, too. I kept an open mind with them. We could use as much help as we could get. It was indeed a clusterfuck in the final days of our foothold in Oradea.

While packing up my gear, I glanced up to find one of my favourite boys approaching with an uncannily tense pace. "Ah, squad leader Unterfeldwebel Rupert Schmidt," I teased. "How goes it?"

Rupert waved, stopping when he got close enough and placing his hands on his hip. "Still kicking," he remarked. A set of bloodshot eyes looked around blankly for a few seconds. "Do you, uh…" He pointed to my tins lying around in disarray. "Need any help?"

I nodded to the side and promptly changed subjects. "I heard about Udo…" I tried.

Rupert's eyes crept away as he pinched his lips. He took a half-step backwards and let out, "At least he won't have to try your cooking again, will he?"

I saw right through the walls he had put up. "You know, it's okay to let yourself grieve," I consoled with a pat on his arm.

With a monotonous voice, he disclosed, "The last thing you'll see me do is letting my own personal quarrels infect those around me."

Always too worried much about others, he had neglected taking care of himself in the process. So, I reiterated, "That's what I'm here for. You can always vent with me."

"Thanks, Johannes," he grumbled. Rupert grew weary of the sincerity directed at him, even from me, and took the opportunity to change subjects after a fake cough to split things up. "You cooked us a meal though, right? My men have grown hungry."

I was still hung up on his wellbeing and couldn't shake the concern from my face while shifting my weight from one leg to the other. "Of course. There's some food in the carrier over there." I pointed to the oversized canteen with backpack straps that held his squad's dinner.

Rupert went to pick it up as I consoled again, "Sorry, Rupert."

He shot me with a battered look, drained about all the talking about him. My eyes rolled before making it over to him. "About it being oatmeal," I saved. "It's all I could prepare."

He sighed and closed his eyelids. I added, "Not the most extravagant of dishes, but it will, at the very least, fill your men up."

After a half-second, Rupert nodded in both relief and exhaustion. "You always look out for us, Johannes," he noted as I assisted him in lugging the heavy container up to his shoulders.

"Somebody needs to," I hinted. Rupert was always too hard on himself. Remembering that I needed to relieve the pressure of the conversation about him off him, I again attempted to change the meaning of my words. "You're all skin and bones lately! Eat up today, will you?"

"Yeah, whatever, mum," he jabbed with a faint smile. "Speaking of which, I was thinking that you should go help Udo's mother with their restaurant after the war. She could probably use the help."

"Of course I will, my boy," I responded with a smile. But I knew what he needed right then, so I pulled him in by his shoulder. He looked at me before facing ahead as I whispered, "About that thing you gave me to hold on to a while back that we were saving for a rainy day…"

Rupert brandished a well-needed smile as a familiar mischievousness sparked through his strained eyes. "Yeah?"

"I think you should use it tonight," I remarked while leaning over to fumble through my gear. "To be frank, I'm surprised I carried it this long." Several pans and ladles crashed about out before I chuckled, "Ah, here it is," standing straight with a full bottle of clear liquor with Cyrillic writing on the side. "You're lucky I don't drink as much as I used to. Otherwise, I would have drank it all by now."

Rupert smirked as I placed the bottle in his hands. "So, this is the special occasion you were waiting for." The aura around him transformed like a discontented child who had just been served dessert. He examined it and sighed, "I guess you could say I promised someone we would do something like this tonight."

I immediately understood that he spoke of Udo. Most of the men drank from time to time, but we saved this particular bottle of fine Russian vodka for several months. Rupert was generally not a man who enjoyed the lavish spoils of life, but this time, the bottle especially seemed to suit his fancy. I'd be concerned if drinking became a habit, but one bottle wasn't going to do any harm, especially when he would inevitably share it amongst his men.

Noting my attempts to read into him, he returned his gaze to me to change the focus of the conversation. "So, what's going on with you?" he inquired.

I crossed my arms. "Generalleutnant Abraham declared that the most valuable men were to begin evacuating with the wounded," I shared. "And apparently, the Sturmbannführer is considering me valuable."

"Of course, how could the Sturmbannführer live without your luxury cooking experience?" Rupert quipped. He knew I would have favoured staying here with the rest of the men, even as old and useless at fighting as I was. Still, he couldn't resist a prod at the Nazi officer.

"Quite easily, I'd assume. Weren't you just making fun of my cooking?" I shot back. We brandished as confident of smiles as we could whilst remaining appropriate until they grew stale.

Mine found its way into a frown as I decided to give one final attempt to get through to my old friend a go. "I worry about your men. And I worry for you, Rupert," I confided with a deep voice. "Please, though, don't beat yourself up about Udo. You remember how he used to be. If it weren't for you, he would have done that a long time ago, and in a much worse off place."

Rupert made a sigh, but not in a rude way, and then flicked his eyes up towards the ceiling. He reflected there for a short while as men stormed about around us in the station. I let him think amongst himself for a bit.

But he reacted well with humour, so I opted to sugarcoat my bit of wisdom with a wisecrack. Maybe that would get through to him. "Just do your best to get out of here safe, and maybe – just maybe – I'll be able to find some beef for you after we're out of Oradea."

Rupert's smile renewed. "Now there's some motivation," he reflected. "I'll do what I can, Johannes."

I slapped his shoulder before one of the officers beckoned me from afar. "Duty calls, Rupert. Good luck," I encouraged before departed. Rupert gave his thanks and patted my shoulder back as he left the cooking station with the giant container of oatmeal on his back.

As I approached the officer, my mind remained concerned about Rupert's well-being. It was remarkable that he could keep up the sarcasm after experiencing as much as he did first-hand. I just hoped he could learn to recognise the value of his own life. I was terrified when I thought he was gone not too long ago. We all were. I don't know what we would do without his vivacious spirit around and about. But unfortunately, we didn't have much of a choice.

Chapter 17

Grenadier Bruno Lindemann

"Men!" Schmidt shouted as he marched through the door of our room. The rest of the squad fixed their eyes on him as he promenaded to the center of us. "I have good news and bad news."

Herrmann groaned as he sat up from leaning against the wall. "Ah, shit, can we start with the good news?"

"No," Schmidt responded. "*As* your squad leader," he teased as the cocky prick he was known to be, "I find it more fitting to start with the bad news."

"Abusing the power already," Keller pointed out while adjusting the bandage on his arm. That lucky bastard survived a direct hit from a tank while in a bunker a few days ago with only a minor shrapnel wound on his arm. His injury was not serious enough to be evacuated. It worked fine, but I bet it still hurt. Unluckily, though, we lost Graf, his assistant gunner.

I missed Graf. He was my friend. The only other recruit who had arrived with me. Lying dead out there or cast into some unnamed mass grave dug by the communists. It disgusted me.

"Exactly," absorbed Schmidt. Without wasting a moment, he got right to the bad news. "We're going to be one of the last groups left behind. We need to support the retreat of the staff and the wounded."

There was a unanimous groan, topped off with Keller yelling, "Fuck!" The news dampened my chances for survival. I didn't want to fight anymore. But I knew I was going to survive, no matter where they put me. I would do anything I needed to do.

"This is *your* fault!" Herrmann lashed out. "If you had just got along better with the Sturmbannführer, we'd be allowed to regroup with everybody else!"

"Now, now, we don't know that," Kuhn denied after he finished taking a sip from his canteen. Of course, his soft personality prevented him from taking a stab at Schmidt. He was too nice for confrontation.

"My ass it isn't," Herrmann blurted as he folded his arms. "The Sturmbannführer has always had it out for you."

"We literally just got railed by him because of your chest tattoo," Schmidt countered with a squint directed at Herrmann. "But anyway, only the vital soldiers are evacuating. And the Hungarians will be helping here as well. We'll make our retreat as soon as the others are safe."

I didn't trust those Hungarians. They were just waiting for a chance to turn on us. Like everyone else, they just proved the only one that cared about me was myself.

"Yeah, yeah," Herrmann clipped. He leered back at Schmidt with slightly narrowed eyes. "Then what's the good news?" That scavenger Herrmann, always on the hunt for spoils. What kind of good news could soften the blows of an order that would likely be our squad's demise?

"Well first off, we have dinner. Fill up, Herrmann, you become a bitch when you are hungry," he kidded as he placed the food carrier on the ground in front of him. Kuhn politely attempted to hide a chuckle. But Herrmann just continued scowling, so Schmidt backed up to announce, "I've also got something special for us tonight, boys," as he pulled a bottle of liquor from inside his uniform top.

Everybody's eyes, even Herrmann's, lit up when they saw the bottle. "Fine Russian vodka!" Kuhn exclaimed.

"Udo Sommer always enjoyed the burn of his cigarettes. Tonight, we are going to enjoy the burn of this for him," Schmidt decreed. He placed it on the ground in the middle of us all. His hand remained on its top, and he stared at it without saying a word for a bit too long. We all knew that something was up, so the mood shifted.

"It, uh, was my last promise to him," Schmidt finally muttered.

Out of respect for the recent loss of Udo Sommer, the squad reflected in silence. God, I missed Udo, too. I was losing everyone out here.

Keller broke the standstill with a concluding, "For the fallen, then."

The men nodded in agreement with a few grunts as Schmidt found a seat on the ground, and we all began devouring our food and drink. I gathered in with them. I didn't know what I was feeling right then, so I joined them.

It was dark out. Or maybe it was dark out before? I had only just noticed because it was difficult to observe anything other than the oddly lively banter that that was taking place within our squad's circle.

"I'm telling you, the ladies melt when they see a man wearing a coach hat!" shouted Keller. To everybody's surprise, he was a rather uplifting drunk, starkly contrasting his ordinarily bound and determined demeanor. "That's what you need to boost your game, Kuhn! A gotdamn newsboy hat."

Kuhn daintily sipped from his cup. "Oh, I don't have any trouble with my game, Keller," he casually responded to the amusement of the group.

"Really now, Kuhn?" Herrmann probed with his tongue resting on the top of his lips. He looked like he could be a thirsty fellow. "You like to play, eh? You've got a lady?"

"Well, I wouldn't say *a* lady," Kuhn teased with a smug smile as he took another swig. The loaded squad roared in laughter over the soft-spoken soldier Kuhn apparently having lots of lady friends.

Lady friends. Annette. Oh, Annette. That was my lady friend. I heard her voice, humming in the background as her love warmed me as much as the alcohol in my stomach did. Maybe I should get one of those coach hats? The ones tough guys wore. With the tight side haircut. Yeah, those ones, they looked sharp. Maybe Annette would like the look of one of those on me. But hat or not, I needed her. Relaxed with her memory, I decided the world I lived in must be fantastic for allowing me to have met such a pleasant woman. And to have such hats at our disposal!

"Who would have thought that our very own Kuhn was a lady's man!" Herrmann hollered. He took Schmidt's bottle from the middle of the circle to pour into his glass. The room next to us was stocked full of them, so we made use.

It took Herrmann a couple of seconds to realize that Schmidt's bottle was empty, and he then produced a mostly-empty bottle of liquor of his own from his bag. The squad scavenger had, of course, gotten his hands on such a spoil of war. He poured some for himself before placing it beside Schmidt's empty one in the center to share it with the rest of the squad as an odd change of heart.

"I do alright," Kuhn admitted. Schmidt giggled as he grabbed for Herrmann's bottle to fill up his glass, and Keller grabbed his stomach, laughing so hard that his face turned beet red. "Looks like you don't need some stupid hat after all!"

Herrmann retracted his bottle after Schmidt placed it back, ultimately opting to savor the rest for himself. Guppy, the recruit, had been relatively silent until he noticed that his cup was empty. Searching around the room for the bottle, he asked, “Is there any more?”

Schmidt kicked toward his empty bottle. “Of course Guppy drinks like a fish!” he observed as he gandered at Herrmann. There was hardly any left in his bottle either, which may have justified his shrug as Herrmann slurred, “I need the rest of this. Moller loved to drink, and fuck, do I miss that gotdamn bear of a person.”

The recruit nodded, but his heart visibly sank. He was the only replacement recruit left in our squad after the recent days of vigorous urban fighting, so he needed a drink. Fuck, losing comrades sucked.

The selfless Kuhn took note and interrupted Guppy’s wallow in sorrow as he commented, “I think I can help you out, Guppy.” Kuhn grabbed the empty cup out of the recruit’s hand and filled it up with his canteen.

“Keeping the young Grenadier hydrated! How am I not surprised you’re his guardian angel,” Keller complimented as he took another swig of his own.

The recruit Guppy took a sip from his cup when his eyes widened. He started choking and wheezing. Kuhn promptly began patting his back.

"This isn't water!" Guppy coughed, pulling his head away from his drink. "It's vodka!"

All eyes ogled at Kuhn, who simply smirked as he defended himself by winking, "My little secret." He then added the daintiest of chin raises.

I chuckled as everybody else lost it. Keller started crying. Herrmann and Schmidt made eye contact before tossing their heads back to howl. I didn't see what the others did, but it sure as hell sounded like they reacted the same.

Wiping a tear from his eye, Schmidt concluded, "So, that's how you remain so pleasant all the time!" Kuhn hardly more than nodded with a delicate blink of an eye, both hands on his precious canteen.

"Kuhn, you kill me!" Herrmann cried as the laughter subsided. There was a bit of silence while everybody absorbed Kuhn's secret, so he spoke again. "Fuck, that's good. Hey guys, while we're at it, I have something good to share, too."

"Oh?" Keller provoked, which prompted Herrmann to continue. "Remember that game of Scat we played in the bunker the other day?" Herrmann's beam went from ear-to-ear as he revealed a custom-built compartment on the inside of one of his boots, just big enough to hold a couple of cards.

Keller's eyes gaped as big as his mouth, realizing he had been bamboozled earlier. "You son of a bitch! I *knew* you cheated!" he gasped. The squad again erupted into another fit of laughter. Even Keller ended up getting a hoot out of it, despite being the most upset originally when Herrmann had won.

After everyone regained control, Keller cleared his throat, prompted by the two men to his side admitting to something the others did not know. "Hey, I, uhm, well while we're at it…" he hesitated as he wiped his forehead with the back of his hand. "I, uh, overheard I was being transferred to your squad because they wanted you all to be more serious." His voice was soft and vulnerable. Again, a stark contrast of the callous Keller we had grown to know. He stared down at his drink and muttered, "Apparently, I'm pretty good at bringing down the mood."

Schmidt didn't even wait for a second to respond. "Well, they hadn't seen you drink before, have they?" Schmidt added, patting Keller on the shoulder. "You're one of us, now. Welcome to mud squad, Keller."

Relief overtook Keller like a bubble rising to the top of a pool, and he gave Schmidt something like a smile back. The spokesperson of the squad accepted him, no matter what circumstances. Fucking lucky bastard.

"Welcome to mud squad, Keller," Herrmann chimed in, a bit too forcefully tapping Keller's drink with his own.

"You're too dapper to be in charge of this dirty squad anymore, Schmidt!" Kuhn chimed in, referencing the unfitting cleanliness of the new squad leader's uniform. Kuhn was always keen for a compliment.

"Nah, I'm just as scummy as I've always been," he remarked as he flipped his long hair back and forth. "But on a similar subject, I've got another nifty tidbit to add to our cauldron of secret information." Herrmann and Kuhn leaned in to hear, and with grand gestures, Schmidt continued. "I always, *always*, try to get mud on Oberleutnant Ross' uniform. Sometimes I'll even bribe other soldiers to do my bidding for me. He has yet to figure out I'm behind the mastermind behind his untidiness."

We all found that to be humorous as well. "The Sturmbannführer must be livid over it!" chortled Keller as he placed a hand on a grinning Herrmann. "Oh, what a prank!"

Schmidt flipped his palms to face the ceiling. "Hey, somebody needs to keep that piece of shit in check. I'm just doing my job," he chuckled.

All eyes focused on me, being next in the circle. Schmidt was the first to speak. "You've been awfully quiet lately, Lindemann. Why don't you share something with us?"

Putting me on the spot made my mood drop like a duck that had been just shot by a hunter. Me? Why would I want to share with everybody? Why was I supposed to give information up about myself? I had too much going on in my head to worry about these kinds of silly games.

Their eyes. Yes, it was their eyes that drilled into me. Expanding across their faces like an evil empire bent on conquering the land they occupied. Boring into my skull, mercilessly stomping through the barriers that I had set up to protect myself without hesitation. It was painfully uncomfortable. I was driven to grow a sense of panic with all of their attention now gathering in my personal atmosphere.

"Well?" Schmidt evilly sneered. The ridge between his eyes and brow darkened. His uneasy grin exposed the peculiar sharpness of his teeth. In that instant, I became the unarmed Huber, and Schmidt was the Bolshevik on the machine gun, spraying into my already wounded corpse with a devilish appetite.

It made me shiver. No, I couldn't take it. It was too much for me. I needed to escape, to make it back home, to protect Annette, and this was not such a situation that would help me do so. I had to push back, to stand up against this. I will not falter under this pressure. Annette deserves a hero.

"No!" I exclaimed as I threw my cup of villainous liquid to the ground between us all. "These needless games will not protect me from death!"

Herrmann's eager smile transformed into a fierce scowl as my spilled liquor covered him. He fumbled to conquer his intoxication enough to confront me. Kuhn, opting for cautiousness even in aggressive moments, put up an arm to deter him from getting up as Herrmann

I didn't even have time to see how Schmidt reacted before I catapulted from my seat and stormed off out of the storage room next door to escape their haze. I didn't care how new of a recruit I was – they had no right to press me for personal information.

The moonlight shined on me through the only window of my room as I gazed outside at the luminous night landscape. No matter where on earth we were, we all shared one moon. Annette, back in Germany, had that same moon watching over her. What was she doing on this fine night? Perhaps reading a book? At some social gathering? A political rally? She sure loved getting entangled in politics. I should spend more time with Oberleutnant Denis Ross so I can remain knowledgable on the teachings of the Fatherland.

"Herr Moon," I requested aloud as my chest absorbed its mysterious rays, "If you can hear me, please give me a courageous moment in combat. One that would make me worthy enough for Annette. Is that alright, to ask you for your strength?"

The handle of the door slowly rotated, followed by a creak as it crawled open. I didn't need to turn around to know who it was –

Schmidt had finally entered my domain.

I knew Schmidt would eventually check up on me. As demanding of a person he could be, I needed him. He knew how to make it out here. And if I could master his skills, then I'd be able to return a hero.

"Lindemann," Schmidt whispered as he closed the door behind him. He had not gone too deep into my lair, remaining by the relative safety of an escape route the door provided. "That was sure something back there. What *was* that?"

I ignored his question. "There's something about a moon's beam that makes a night magical," I pointed out before clasping my hands behind my back. "Do you think of the moon?"

"Uhm," Schmidt stuttered, rubbing the back of his neck with his arm. "I, uh, suppose the moon is pretty nifty come to think of it…?"

"I converse with the moon during the nights I can't sleep," I stated. "It has been so kind as to offer protection. It helps me."

"Right." Schmidt leaned on a shelf loaded with empty cups, wrapping an arm around one of its posts. "So that's why you bring it up."

I turned to face him directly. "I've been a moon to you for long enough now," I declared. "Now, I want to be the earth."

Schmidt narrowed an eye. His presumed course of conversation had changed routes. "I don't think you're fat enough to be earth," he quipped.

"Always quick to find a joke," I commented while stepping towards his spot on the wooden floor, hands clasped behind my back. I lowered my eyelids when my eyes met his and declared, "I don't want you to look down on me anymore, Schmidt."

"Look down on you?" he questioned as he crossed his arms. "Lindemann, *what* are you even talking about?" he prodded unconvincingly.

"In the other room, you were oppressing–"

"No, Lindemann, I've already had enough," Schmidt interrupted as threw his arms into the air. He was already turning around to leave when he added, "You are taking everything much too seriously."

"But this *is* serious!" I interjected. My hands untied themselves from behind my back to shake in Schmidt's direction. It didn't force him to pause his retreat, so I continued. "Men are *dying* out there! But you audaciously decide to dig into us when we find a break from fighting?"

Schmidt stopped in his tracks, and with his head fixed on the ground, he silently turned back around and took a couple of steps towards me.

After a strained interlude as he stood in the middle of our modestly-sized room, Schmidt raised his head and looked at me directly with the callous pits of his shadowy eyes. "You're delusional if you think that we meant to be anything close to malicious in the other room," he grumbled as he embarked toward the door. I could have sworn that the room just got a bit colder. He spoke deliberately, and with a deeper tone than usual. "Get your shit together, Lindemann."

An unfamiliar feeling hit my system as I realized Schmidt was giving up on me. What was it, sadness? Anger, perhaps? Perhaps with a bit of… Embarrassment? Was it a mix of them all? I didn't know what exactly it was, but it stunned me nonetheless. I couldn't remember such a feeling since I have been out here. How could I keep him from leaving?

Then, I remembered when his letter had referenced me.

"Even so, I wish he'd tell me more about him," I recalled it stating. I read it so many times that I could probably read it out loud.

It enlightened me. Schmidt cared about all of his comrades. Even me. As much as he tried to write me off, he still gave a shit. So if I fed him something personal enough, he wouldn't be able to act like he didn't care. That wasn't the type of person he was. And I needed him to continue trying with me, even if it meant sharing what I would rather keep private about myself to find common ground between us. I would do whatever it takes to accomplish my wartime goals.

Invigorated by my insight, I could only let out one word. "Annette."

Schmidt's shoulders hunched as he whipped around. "What?" he questioned with a raised eyebrow.

I gulped and pointed above my brow to the scar from my rifle during our first skirmish together. "'He still has a mark on his face from when he snapped out of some daydream amid his first battle, just to smack himself with his rifle,'" I quoted. Schmidt's letter ingrained itself into my mind like Huber's violent death. I couldn't forget it. "'I really wish I knew what he was thinking about. Bending over backwards to teach a new recruit is quite the challenge when he remains somebody I hardly know. I haven't quite excelled in similar roles in the past.'"

Schmidt's jaw jarred to the side as he recognized that my words had come from him. I lowered my hand, balling it into a fist as it took its place on my side. Schmidt tipped his head towards the other side.

"Well, her name is Annette," I declared. My chin rose, and I narrowed my eyes to prepare further trekking into the unfamiliar ground. "She's blonde, and her hair is wavy when she's not pulling off a French braid. She's a daydreamer, like me, dreaming of what the world could be like if she could make it ideal. My very soul gets numb when I stare into her irresistibly blue eyes. My heart skips a beat when her letters arrive. She's sassy, but also one of the most driven people I've ever met. I've known her for a while, but I regretfully only started dating her right before I finished school."

Schmidt's face softened as he pieced together what was happening. But to really get through to him, I knew I needed to throw in a lighthearted joke. He'd resonate with that. So, I supplemented, "And she's more than a match for you."

Seeming pleased as he propped himself back on the shelf he had previously rested against, Schmidt simpered, "I've been curious about that a long time."

I wanted a break from sharing about myself. Thankfully, I could use this chance with our guards dropped to change course away from me and regain control of our conversation. So, I rested a hand on my hip and shot the other towards him. Schmidt flinched.

"Why the fuck didn't you ever ask me about it then?" I attacked as I flipped my hand up. If we had any hope of becoming a fully capable duo, I needed to rearrange his motives to keep me in mind.

Schmidt rocked back in his stance away from the shelf before folding his arms. "I, uh, meant to," he fumbled, "I just never really had the opportunity."

"That's bullshit. You had plenty of time," I summarized with a scowl. "Udo, Johannes, fucking Oberleutnant Ross, even the other recruits Weiss and Guppy – you keep everyone else so close. I've seen you ask them about their home, their families, their hobbies. But not with me. After you disappeared and left me all alone, I had to pelt you with a fucking apple for you to finally explain where the fuck you were!"

Schmidt took a full step back. With his mouth blankly open, he rubbed his chin with a set of fingers. But I was relentless.

"And what the fuck happened to the guy before me?" I interrogated. I stood up as straight as I could. "I haven't heard a single thing about him from you. Wouldn't sharing what happened to him help keep me alive? You're supposed to look out for us, Overwatch! Why the fuck do you give a shit about everybody else but me?"

With his hands and arms panicking to find comfortable positions, Schmidt repeatedly readjusted his weight from one leg to another. I knew right then that I had not only punched a hole in Schmidt's motives – I had used his own supposed selflessness to do so. But I was not yet finished. Since Schmidt was keen on remembering details about others, I again took advantage of his vulnerabilities by bringing up his letter for the second time.

"You started your letter with 'my dearest sisters.' You went on about a time you flopped at ice skating with them, for heaven's sake! If you care about them so much, then how the hell is that the only time I've ever heard anything about them?"

Schmidt hid his eyes behind a palm, rubbing his eyebrows with a thumb and pointer finger. I placed my other hand on my hip just like the other and held my glare, using the looming silence to force him to explain himself. It was one of the many useful techniques I picked up from Johannes.

Soon enough, a calmness overtook Schmidt as he dug both hands in his pockets. He began stepping towards me without even looking at me. But he strolled right past me, towards the window. I took a position to the side of him as he peeked out of it, indiscriminately scanning the dimly-lit cityscape outside the station. As he clasped his hands behind his back, a coy smile began to grow on his face.

"My sisters have always meant the world to me," Schmidt reminisced aloud as the moon reflecting off his light chocolate eyes. "I used to worry that I tried too hard to place myself back into their lives. That I was away so long, they no longer had a place for me in their lives. I worried that I would annoy them. That I *did* annoy them. So, I stopped writing them letters nearly as much as I wished to. Not because I didn't want to, but because I didn't want them to stop loving me because I was bothering them too frequently."

The moonlight fluttered as a cloud crossed its beam, draining the vitality from Schmidt's cinnamon-tinted eyes as they fixed themselves outside on the nearby ground. He removed a hand from his pocket to rest it against the side of the windowsill.

"Now, I'm not able to bother them at all," Schmidt let out with a deep sigh. "They died in an allied bombing raid about a year ago."

Taken aback, I was at a complete loss for words. All I could react was with a soft, "Woah."

A sternness overtook Schmidt as he looked further into the darkness outside. "I still write them letters, though. I'll stick them in the leather pouch on Ilsa's stock. I like to think they'll help me protect the only family I have left now."

Schmidt switched his focus from the window to me. His soft, chestnut eyes glimmered as the moonbeam regained its strength through the window from the passing cloud. "Which are you guys. So, I don't care if I die out there. I mean, I don't necessarily want to die, but I'm impartial if I do. Risk neutral, if you will. Because the more of myself I give for my new family, the closer it might bring me to my old one."

We stood in the silence for a good minute before I had anything to say. Schmidt again faced the outside. I kept at him, trying to figure out how it all related to him not caring about me.

Fortunately, Schmidt had more to say. "But this attitude I've adopted isn't safe for others. That's what happened to Hans…"

"Hans?"

"Yeah. Obergrenadier Hans Simon," Schmidt murmured. "We called him Helfen Hans because he'd always try to help us. Like Kuhn, Hans cared about all of us. But, he also had a driving knack for repairing things and would tinker with our gear."

I nodded slowly. "So Hans was the guy before me?"

"Yes." Schmidt gulped, staring high into the starry sky. "Hans was like my brother."

A gust of wind outside softly wiggled the window. "What happened to him?" I inquired when it died down.

"It was a little less than a year ago. About a month after the battle of Kursk." Schmidt took a deep sigh but remained in the same place. "I was in charge of our squad at the time. We were advancing in the wake of our armor through a grassy field. Without warning, Russian AT guns, hidden in some brush ahead of us, began slicing into our tanks. Word came in to fall back."

"But you didn't, did you?"

"No." Schmidt briefly glanced at me and then went back to the window. "Our tanks all started to fall back in reverse, keeping their thicker front armor faced towards the AT guns. Our tank was one of the furthest ones back, so we made it a relatively safe ridge on our side of the meadow first. But another tank more forward than ours received a direct hit from one of their guns. The impact must have killed its driver because it switched directions and charged forward, exposing the foot soldiers who were taking cover behind it. They sprinted towards our line as the tank eventually ground to a halt in the open, closer to the enemy. Amidst small arms fire, a crewman lept out of it hatch on the back. He began hoisting another out behind him when a fire erupted from within the tank. But as he pulled his burning comrade to the top of the tank, he was struck by a bullet in the upper torso, whipping him off in our direction. His comrade, whos legs were ablaze, had rolled to put them out until he, too, fell off the same side of the tank. The duo was helpless behind the narrow carcass of their machine, both unable to run."

I remembered Udo sharing part of this story earlier, but I

never heard it directly from Schmidt. I didn't make any indication that I knew, though, so he'd tell me all of it himself.

"They were hurt, but still very much alive," Schmidt whispered. He closed his eyes. "I can still hear the one with burning legs screaming 'Don't leave us! Please!'" He shook his head side-to-side before opening his eyes. "I knew we had to help those crewmen, but our rally point was further back than the ridge, so the tanks kept falling back. I shouted to our tank's commander, who was crouched inside the open hatch of the turret, requesting him to stay and help, but he said it was too dangerous for him. So, I ordered our men to let our tank retreat without us and provide covering fire for me while I went and got the injured crewmen. As my men spread out from behind the tank, our tank briefly stopped as the commander relayed a message from the Sturmbannführer. He was strict on denying our change of plans. He instead ordered us to get back behind his tank and retreat to the rally point, leaving the men to die."

I was too eager to hear the story and couldn't keep my silence. "But you got stayed anyway, right?"

Schmidt nodded up-and-down as he shifted towards the wall beside the window, letting the moonlight hit the ground between us.

"I told the tank to go on without us, and then I asked Hans to help me get the crewmen. Helfen Hans was selfless, so without any hesitation, he agreed to follow me into the fray. The squad opened fire, and I blitzed into the field. Bullets blazed around me, but I beelined right towards the burning tank in the open. I smacked into its treads next to the injured crewmen with my shoulder, but when I turned around, Hans wasn't there."

Eyes on the ground, Schmidt crossed his arms. "I didn't see it happen. But I was told later that Hans had been struck down almost immediately after we left the ridge."

"Fuck," I commented as I took a half step back.

"Yeah. Under my order, and against the request of the Sturmbannführer, I got Hans killed."

"But did you get the crewmen?"

"One of them. The one with the burned legs. The other had bled out by the time I got there. But Sturmbannführer Kolartz almost sent me to a penal unit for it. Putting my squad at risk for those crewmen made him furious. So, I resigned as our squad leader. I told the Sturmbannführer that from then on, I would only put myself at risk."

I crossed my arms and shifted my weight to one leg. "But they placed me under you. And you're squad leader again."

Schmidt propped his hands between the wall and the small of his back. "Over time, I realized Hans wouldn't have done anything differently, but I was still pissed off that I got him killed. Still, when Fritz assigned you to me, I put up a fight. I didn't want to put anyone else at risk."

A moment of silence passed us before Schmidt stared right at me. The sincerity bled through every subtle expression on his face. "I guess I've been keeping you at bay because I don't want to order somebody to their death again. So I'm sorry I haven't treated you right, Lindemann."

Just like that, it all clicked. Schmidt didn't hate me – he was just scared of losing me. Finally, after all the time we spent out here, it felt tremendous to receive confirmation that he gave a shit about me.

"You know, Schmidt, I would do anything for Annette. Just like you for the men," I tried. "Maybe we're none too different."

"Maybe that's why we don't get along," Schmidt wrangled to quip, running fingers through his hair. A casualness had returned to him.

"Then maybe we should try to," I proposed with a keen squint.

Schmidt rubbed the back of his head with closed eyes as he tried to hold back a grin. He began to take a seat. "Sure, but first I need to address something," he proposed as he lowered to the ground.

I cautiously followed suit across. Schmidt put a smoke in his mouth before offering me one. I hesitated, but when he tightened his eyelids and shook the pack of cigarettes, I nervously accepted his gift. He sparked his lighter and offered it towards me. Anxiously, I declined by demanding, "Well? What is it?"

Schmidt broadened his eyes as he ignited the tip of his smoke. After a few puffs, he finally looked back at me and explained, "There has been something that has been going on with you lately."

I gave him a face, and he continued, "Avoiding people, acting odd, staying quiet, or just not really being there… I fear you're struggling to adapt."

Schmidt wasn't wrong. I was changing. So, I uneasily lit my

cigarette to avoid his stare.

"I deserve a hero," Annette's voice echoed in my brain. She was right. I needed to make her proud.

But I unintentionally mouthed her words as they bounced around my skull, which baffled Schmidt. "What was that?" he questioned.

I needed to say something – anything – to not dwell what Schmidt just observed. "Oh, just saying you're right, Schmidt," I declared before taking another timely drag. Good save, Bruno. "I was scared to arrive out here at first, but I realized that fighting means I'm properly aiding the German war effort. Plus, I'm pretty good at it. It isn't too unlike the hunting I did at home with my father."

Schmidt sluggishly blinked. "Okay, well, that's sure something." There was a brief pause until it was cut short by his empathetic reflection, "But I can see where you got that idea from."

So he wasn't on the same page as me. But I still wanted to find out where he came from, so I inquired, "Why…?"

"Well, uh…" Schmidt began to shift positions against the wall. "I just… I just don't want it to get to you."

I unfolded my arms to cross them the other way. Schmidt understood that thought process perplexed me, so he brushed a hand through his hair and tried again.

"Look, Udo died out there because I didn't talk to him enough…" The bronze of Schmidt's eyes glimmered like the sun off the ocean. "I would have done something if I had just known, but I didn't... He killed himself right after I talked to him. I thought he was doing fine. But he wasn't."

We stood by the windowsill for what seemed like a full minute as Schmidt did puff after puff. "His death taught me that I need to communicate better with those close to me," he finally stated as he hastily looked around the room. "I just… Can't let him die in vain either. So, I just need to make sure you're doing alright, okay?"

I thought I understood his rationale. "I'm can handle it. I just need to prove myself out here to be deserving enough for Annette. She wants somebody who would make Germany proud. I want to take down an entire battalion of those stupid Soviets on my own."

Schmidt tightened his lips. A considerable amount of tense seconds passed as he eyed me over. Finally, Schmidt conceited by shutting his eyes.

“Everybody has an Annette of sorts,” Schmidt concluded. “Even the Russians do. But nobody exists on purpose. Everybody's going to die someday. Stop thinking that doing horrible things out here will make you happy.”

I couldn’t piece together any words, so Schmidt reached out and slapped my arm. “Look, your views on us Germans is absolute rubbish, and you need to fix that.”

Schmidt’s cigarette had gone out. He fired up its end again with his lighter and took a long drag. “But I also need you to focus on controlling yourself,” he urged after a thick cloud of smoke left his mouth.

“Controlling myself?” The direction of his narrative furthered my disorientation. “What do you mean? I control myself in combat better than any of the other Grenadiers.”

Schmidt finished another puff before he clarified. “Part of the troubles you have discovered outside of fighting is due to who you have become when you are in it. All good soldiers have that bloodthirsty demon inside of them. And sure, it has its uses. I use mine to do everything I can to protect our comrades. But you enjoy fighting too much. You need to figure out how to dial it down so you can make the best decisions for the team. That'll also help you turn it off when we're not fighting so that you won't bring the war to all the other facets of your life."

Schmidt took a deep breath and fixed his gaze towards his feet. "Look, I do everything within my abilities to make sure our comrades don't die out there. I would have done anything to prevent Udo from doing what he did, but I did all that I could to keep him alive up to that point..."

A timely cough interrupted Schmidt's train of thought before he carried on. "So, that's why I need to make sure you're doing alright. You've got a life to live after this war. So does the rest of the squad, and it'll be your job to protect them if anything happens to me."

Schmidt raised his hand to shake mine. "Which is why I need you to work on controlling yourself. Okay?"

I thought it was a trick. I could usually tell when a salesman is trying to pull the wool over my eyes. But something about the character of this comrade in front of me prevented me from being able to decline. So, I reached out my hand, and Schmidt cracked a sideways grin as he gave it a firm shake.

It was relieving to at last get along with Schmidt. And I was tired. Tired of scheming, tired of arguing. So, I reeled in my motives, and out of curiosity, babbled, "Alright, so it's settled. Now then, tell me about your family."

Schmidt extended his lighter to rekindle the smoke I had been carrying for too long as he reminisced about his family. He loved his two little sisters with all of his heart. Then he asked about Annette, and I told him all about her. I reflected on his proposed worry that I would not be worthy of Annette if I made it back to her. He believed in me, though. It was odd, being two battle-hardened soldiers, conversing over something as trivial as the affection we have for the ones we loved. But it was welcome. For the first time since I arrived out here, I felt like a real human again.

Minutes turned to hours as our bonding session continued. We eventually took up spots on the ground. At one point, we realised we had used up almost all of our smokes. Schmidt then glanced at his watch and wooed over how late it was.

"We should get some sleep. We've got a big day tomorrow," Schmidt suggested. I agreed as he had stood up. He reached a hand out to help me to my feet. "I'm going to join the rest of the men. You should join us."

As against leaving the cosy room as I was, I didn't want to be alone, so I decided, "Fair enough, Schmidt," as I accepted his hand.

Schmidt yanked me up and held the clasp of our hands as he grew a cockeyed smile. He nudged his chin upwards and requested, "One last thing before we do."

I cautiously studied his face and carefully responded, "Uh oh. What?"

Schmidt let go of my hand to pat my shoulder, and while spinning his torso around to the door, ordered, "Call me Rupert from now on," before turning the knob.

The moment I've been waiting for since I witnessed the breakthrough with Udo had finally arrived. Now that we were on a first-name basis, I felt satisfied that I had gotten through to him. Schmidt – rather, Rupert – was more than just a mentor to me. More than just a tool I needed to survive. He had become part of me.

"Well?" Schmidt hesitated to open the door before I could give my answer.

Comfortable with my new crony, I mocked, "Whatever you say, *Rupert*," with a sly beam.

Rupert grinned as he cracked the door and tiptoed into the room with our other sleeping comrades. I followed and closed it behind us, and we took up two empty spots amongst the rest of our slumbering squadmates to catch a bit of shut-eye.

As my impending sleep made my eyelids grow closer and closer, I could make out Annette from right in the middle of our room. She glared at me with her arms crossed.

Chapter 18

Oberfeldwebel Uwe Pfeiffer

A thud followed the 'ding' noise of metal-on-metal. A familiar sound. I darted my eyes to the side. The pierced helmet on the limp carcass lying in a splatter of gore confirmed my worries. We lost another NCO. This time, next to me. Gotdamnit, at that rate, we were going to run out of troops by the end of the day. But there was nothing I could do then but grab the rest of his ammunition from his submachine gun. Didn't fit in Fitz's Sturmgewehr, but somebody would need it. Always needed more of it.

I was the most senior squad leader after they got Fritz. They needed me to be in charge of this platoon. So much so, they already promoted me to Oberfeldwebel. As if that meant shit. But I already missed being a squad leader. Sure, I was still in charge of a squad. Well, kind of. But there were fewer men in my platoon-level staff group than in my old squad. Also, with the platoon commander, Oberleutnant Ross, it didn't allow for me to make as many of my own decisions as when I was a squad leader.

I fired the Sturmgewehr on semi-automatic through a

window when I heard somebody climbing up the stairs of my building. I yanked the weapon around and gritted my teeth to prepare for a close-quarters brawl. I could have crushed its pistol grip from how hard I was clutching it.

Then, a German boy not even old enough to grow facial hair yet turned around the corner of the doorway. I yelled, and terror immediately took over his youthful face. He jumped.

But I gasped in relief and dropped the barrel of my weapon. The boy removed his hand from his upper chest but remained in the doorframe. "Uh, Oberfeldwebel, sir!" He stressfully shouted with a salute. He shrieked when he noticed the fresh body strewn across the floor, next to another who had been killed not long before.

"Get the fuck down!" I ordered as I sprung from my cover to drag him against the wall below with me. "Don't you *ever* salute out on the field again, you hear me? You just marked me as a fucking target!"

The overstimulated child kept blankly staring at the mutilated corpses. His lip quivered as he realized the reality of his situation. I didn't have time for his coming of age, so I dug into him.

"Well? Why the fuck are you here?" I stammered. The boy

trembled as some of their automatic weaponry strafed the outside our building. He ducked down, but I shook him. He reached a shaky hand into his pocket to produce a note. I immediately stole it from his hands.

It was from the Sturmbannführer. From behind the frontlines. Typical officer bullshit. Always so willing to look out for themselves. He had ordered my platoon to fall back to the rally point. Fall back again. There was nothing we could do to prevent retreating, but I hated doing it.

The platoon needed to know. I popped my head outside to scream, "Men! Fall back to the rally point! Everybody! Fall back!"

I waited until my orders were echoed back before I began readying myself. Besides the child runner, the only other man that remained accompanying me inside the building was already stowing what could still be salvageable of our busted radio. It caught the bullet that went through one of my men earlier. My new radioman used to be a stretcher bearer, but I needed him back here with me. So, I repurposed him to fuck with the radio.

The child runner shook as he rose to his feet, trying to leave. I decided to take advantage of my new rank by again jerking him by his arm, back down to the ground. “Oh no, you don’t,” I scowled. In his confusion, the boy couldn’t muster up a word. I grabbed the MP-40 off of the dead corpse next to us and threw it in his hands. “You’re with me now,” I explained.

“But… I’m a runner,” the deer-eyed recruit begged. He carefully examined the weapon, blatantly unfamiliar with it. “I’m not supposed to fight.”

“I don’t need a fucking runner right now, son! Runners aren’t going to prevent these gotdamn Bolsheviks from killing my men. I need more gotdamn soldiers!” I snarled. Command always wanted to take away my resources. But I was fed up. Pointing to his new weapon, I asked, “Do you know how to use one of those?”

“I think so…” he muttered as he played with the magazine release. Not convincing, but I didn’t have time to play teacher. I was already down two men.

“Well you better fucking figure out,” I instructed, throwing him some a magazine. He’d have to survive long enough to earn the others in my pouches. “Welcome to my platoon, son.”

The child frantically searched around the room. He wanted to find a reason to weasel out of this, so I pushed him over to the window between the two bodies, grumbling, “You gotdamn boot.”

I didn’t have time to soak up his reaction. He’ll have to learn. I just spun around and fired Fitz’s weapon out of the window to cover my squad’s retreat. Maybe I could get used to being an Oberfeldwebel.

Chapter 19

Unterfeldwebel Rupert Schmidt

Blood was everywhere. On the walls, on my hands, on the ground, and all over my clothes. As part of Martin's last request, I had been trying to clean myself up lately to ease Pfeiffer's transition into our new platoon leader. I had a great reason to come back with such a stained uniform, but command would still probably give me flak for it. The Sturmbannführer thinks I was the one who poured the rusty nails into his granola. Though, if given the opportunity, I would definitely be that person.

"I need another gauze pad! Quick! Mine's soaked through!" I shouted to my squad as they desperately tried to hold our position. We were on the second floor of a large building that overlooked a street crossing. For better or for worse, our corner was a crucial position. It intercepted multiple roads, being a stubborn thorn in the side of our encroaching Soviet friends.

"I got an extra," Herrmann responded from against the front wall. He dug around his belt until he procured a first-aid pouch to chuck my way. I gave my thanks before failing to catch it, and it smacked against my face.

But I recovered quickly and kept doing my best to stop the bleeding with the equipment inside the first aid. The bullet somehow did not go all the way through him, which was less than desirable because it left a rogue chunk of metal floating around his insides. Also, it entered him by his right lung, which gave even more of a possibility for something to go wrong if I caught any wise ideas to try to remove it.

"Fall back! Fall back!" Keller echoed out his window while reloading his MG-42. He batted an eye at me and repeated himself. "Schmidt, our platoon is falling back!"

"Hold this position until we can stabilise Guppy!" I ordered before re-fixing my attention back to the wounded boy before me. Keller grunted and repeated my order to everybody else in the vicinity. I caught Bruno whispering something from his corner of the room as he fired his rifle. I had my own worries about Bruno, but right now, I was just glad that berserk was on our side.

The poor teenager Guppy coughed up more blood as fluid filled in his lungs. To my displeasure, he splattered some on my face, but I couldn't waste a moment wiping it off. I thought it would be a good idea to give calming him a go. "Easy now, Guppy, you're going to be alright."

Neither my words nor the bullets whizzing inside our building made an impact on the poor recruit. Out of the blue, Guppy questioned, "Do you know what did before the war?"

While frantically trying to halt the flow of blood with the last of my latest gauze pad, a drip of Guppy's blood fell off the bridge of my nose and onto the ground between us. I wiped my face with my shoulder, and somewhat calmly responded, "Not at all, boy. What did you do?"

"I worked at a tile store," he murmured. He feebly wheezed up more blood before he specified, "My family's tile store."

The second dressing was soaking up Guppy's wound almost too well. I figured that I only had enough unsoiled gauze to push down for a little longer, or I will have no choice but to resort to using bits clothing. I'd prefer to avoid using bits of uniform to touch his open wound. It would just get him infected, only torturously dragging out his death.

"Do you know what it was called, *Doctor* Schmidt?" The

words were cast out by his tongue with so little velocity that they practically fell out of his mouth. “I bet you’ll *die*.”

“You reckon? Try me,” I replied. I had to keep him conscious. Getting him to talk could keep him awake and could also mitigate the effects of losing so much of his bodily fluids. I just needed to keep the pressure on the wound for just a wee bit more. It just had to stop bleeding.

I thought we may have found hope – the blood stopped enough to where all I would hopefully need to do was secure the pads to his chest. But the recruit casually kept staring in my direction with eyes that seemed to focus beyond me. Then, with a frail smile, Guppy declared, “Fischer Fliesen.”

Fisher Tiles. What a title. The punch line of Guppy’s joke set in and I couldn’t help but let out a strained chuckle while securing the bandage around my dying comrade. “How brilliant that your family’s store name is an alliteration!”

“A what?” Guppy asked. His eyelids had grown weak, though I was encouraged he could still maintain a conversation.

“It means you’re a doofus, Fischer,” I clarified as I finished securing the bandage. Guppy’s eyes focused on me as a soft beam emerged from his exhausted face. It gave me a superb feeling of satisfaction over trying so hard to keep him alive. I delicately patted him on the opposite shoulder before I grabbed my rifle and shuffled to one of the windows on the ledge to relieve Kuhn and Herrmann. "Go get Guppy ready to retreat," I asked. "Be careful, and keep him talking! We'll head back when you're ready."

I lifted Ilsa above the window and viewed the area through my scope. There were a lot of them, most of whom Keller had kept at bay with his machine gun. There were still a few promising targets, though, namely one in a building a few down from the one across the street. The barrel of his weapon slyly crept through a window on the second floor. He carefully turned the tip of his front sight towards us, thinking he was savvy enough to stay hidden amidst the chaos of the firefight.

Ilsa trained her sights right on the Russian as he exposed more and more of himself. I might have been able to hit him if I shot, but it probably wouldn't be a clean kill. He could still try something cheeky maneuvers if he only got wounded, so I waited a few seconds until just enough of his head showed.

I had partially squeezed Ilsa's trigger when a rifle next to me cracked. My target's rifle sprung up, and his head jostled forwards before slumping from view. A maroon splatter peppered the wall behind him.

"He thought he was invisible," a voice sneered, tone ripe with inflection. I ducked behind the wall and flashed to Bruno Lindemann on my side, whose lips were ajar enough to expose his canines. He mischievously donned a crooked smile while staring into the scope of his rifle. "But I can see the invisible!"

Bruno's current face thwarted my best effort to continue fighting. He donned a peculiar smirk. Not one from a joke though – it was too devious. He fired his rifle again when his agape beam increased in strength as he licked the corner of his lips before changing aim. His bold eyebrows accented his look, easily capable of singlehandedly capturing the essence of his cruel intentions. But what dominated his demeanour were his eyes. They had darkened from their standard shade of a medium brown into an inky black. It was as if they were the windows into a bottomless abyss riddled with lightless flames.

I was aware that Bruno was changing, but it took until that very moment for me to fully comprehend who he had transformed into. Gone was the innocence of the eager boy that had first stepped off the train. The pure, care-free child that couldn't comprehend the horrors of war with a face that could make no other reaction to violence but sheer terror, such as Huber in his final moments. In a mere couple of months, the brutalities of this conflict had taken over this boy – rather, this man – into a callous machine of death. Especially after what he mentioned the previous night, it sent chills down my spine to realise that this new Bruno Lindemann seemingly *enjoyed* this.

A scream broke out behind me, and Kuhn cried out, "Schmidt! We have an issue!" I snapped around to find Guppy writhing in pain as Kuhn continued. "The gauze isn't holding up and he bleeds too much when we move him," he babbled with a deeply concerned expression, devastated over Guppy's condition. "He can't go anywhere!"

I stood up from my cover to get closer to them. "Have you tried-"

Without warning, a burning pain shot up from the lower part of my torso, above the hip bone on my left side. "Schmidt!" Kuhn shrieked as I dropped Ilsa and fell face-first to the floor. How foolish of me to leave my cover in such a careless fashion! I couldn't catch the first aid pouch earlier, but you could bet your sweet ass I still managed to catch a bullet.

I laid there for a few seconds, eventually coming to from a terrifying roar originating from Bruno's position. I found myself on my back with Kuhn already applying a bandage to the front of my wound with Herrmann assisting him as best as he could.

After a tense minute contrasted with the two very different screams from Guppy and Bruno, Kuhn declared, "There! It's not perfect, but if somebody supports him, we should be able to get him back to the rally position."

"I'll carry him," Herrmann volunteered as he packed up his medical pouch.

My senses came to me as I remembered Guppy. "But wait – argh!" I winced as I placed a hand over my unpleasant wound. "What about Guppy? Two men need to carry him."

Kuhn couldn't withhold his heartbroken expression while exchanging a glance with Herrmann, who took over by tapping Kuhn's shoulder. "We can't take him, Schmidt," he announced.

Keller's machine gun kept sputtering in the background, with

Lindemann occasionally chiming in with his rifle. The rest of us looked at Guppy, who had pulled it together enough energy to grasp what was going on.

"What?" Guppy gasped, pupils as wide as dinner plates. "No! Don't leave me! *Please!*"

I winced, struggling to sit up. Kuhn noticed and assisted me. "We have enough people to carry him," I commanded. "Leave me! I'll be fine, get Guppy out of here!"

"Dammit, Schmidt!" Herrmann pounded the ground with a fist as he crouched. "Carrying your ass back is already plenty of work, and you wouldn't need as much assistance!"

Contemplation overtook the room as Keller's MG stopped firing to reload. "I only have one belt left, we have to make our move!" he hollered.

"No… I don't want to die alone!" Guppy begged, looking at each of us individually. Tears filled his eyes as he sobbed, "I never wanted this!"

I was tired of losing men. But they were right, so I ordered, "Then leave us both." The gears in Kuhn's mind promptly began to turn, desperately trying to find a counter-argument, so I halted him.

"Carrying me would slow the squad down. Plus, what if one of you gets hit on the way back?" I pointed out. "I can still shoot – I'll cover your retreat."

Kuhn leaned towards me. His heart was too big to willingly leave a comrade behind, so he tried, "We can't leave you, Schmidt!"

I looked back at Guppy. His eyes were as wide as the moon. "And I can't leave Guppy like this."

Herrmann wiped the brow of his forehead with the back of a palm. "Who will be in charge?"

"Keller!" I shouted as I grabbed Ilsa and begun scooting towards the window. Moving didn't quite make my wound feel any better.

Keller continued firing his weapon, not even turning his head to respond, "What?"

"You've received a field promotion! You are the squad leader now. Get these men out of here!" I instructed as I hunkered against the brick front of the building.

Keller was perplexed enough to stop firing the MG for just a split second as he reacted, "Wait, *what*?" before picking up firing again.

“That’s an order, Keller!” I demanded, propping Ilsa’s butt on the floor next to me. Herrmann was visibly devastated, and Kuhn was even worse, so I gestured for both of them to get going. “Now move! All of you!”

Herrmann slid some of Guppy’s unused ammunition on the floor towards me while grabbing his weapon as he murmured, “Thanks, Schmidt. I’ll be seeing you.”

A teensy smile found its way to my face, and I found it fitting to jest, “Oh, you’ll be around to loot my corpse.”

Herrmann struggled to mirror my affection as he shuffled off through a door on a wall beside the windows to the other room with stairs. “Good luck, Guppy,” he shouted behind his back after he crossed the doorframe.

Kuhn approached me, putting a hand on my shoulder and closed his eyes as he pressed the forehead of his helmet against mine for just a second. “Thanks for everything, Schmidt,” he whispered as he lightly tapped my helmet. Kuhn pulled away from me and scooted over to Guppy to do something similar. I gave him a second before hollering, “Sing stories about me to your lady friends, Kuhn,” which interrupted his heartfelt moment with the recruit. He gave me a sullen look and a slight nod before he set off to the stairs. I immediately began missing his warm and genuine spirit.

I whipped Ilsa through the window and fired off a shot into the general direction of the enemies, giving Keller the okay to leave. He stopped firing and sprung from his position, sprinting to the door with his MG at his hip. He bid farewell with a grunt as he rushed past me before making it through the door.

"Hey," Keller remembered, popping his head back through the doorway. Bruno was still firing to my side, which allowed me to turn my head around for the hardened soldier Keller state with a tenacious expression of affection, "You're a bulldog, Schmidt," before he nodded and disappeared through the doorframe with the others. Keller couldn't be bothered with a sentimental act. His final statement to me meant a lot, coming from the soldier who thought he was placed into our squad to bring down the mood.

"Get drunk more often, Keller!" I hollered after him as I flung Ilsa back above the windowsill.

I fired my rifle a couple more times out the window when I noticed that my loyal counterpart had not yet made his escape. "Bruno!" I shouted as one of Ilsa's rounds smacked against the wall next to my intended target further down the street. "Get out of here, quick!"

"No!" the boy insisted with a voice as cold as stone before his rifle sounded off again. A Soviet soldier in the corner of my sights plunged to the ground in the distance. The man's weapon, one of their DP light machine guns with a pan-shaped magazine, flew from his arms as he tumbled, sliding along the brick footpath ahead of him into the sunlight. The cunning Russian attempted a clandestine advance through the shadows on the sidewalk closest to the buildings. But Bruno saw right through it, thwarting his efforts from an impressive couple 100+ metres away with only a 1.5x magnification scope aiding his aim.

"Go! Before it's too late!" I exclaimed as I slammed Ilsa's bolt forward. Guppy gently cooed in the background. A boy as young as him should not have to come to terms with dying. It revigorated my intention to stay with him.

"I need to save you!" Bruno retaliated. He slammed his back against the wall next to his window, then ripped back the bolt of his rifle back to cram it with more rounds. "This is it! This is finally it!"

I struggled on the ground toward his position, careful this

time to keep below the windows. Bruno had just finished loading a bullet into his rifle as I grabbed his arm and heaved him down to me. The dark pits of his eyes clashed with mine, and he let out an angsty groan as he fiercely squirmed. I gambled on him not attacking me, but it was hard to be certain. It didn't matter if he was on my side – getting that close to somebody in such an animalistic state could be risky.

"Forget me! I'm stuck here!" I reasoned. Bruno's shriek intensified as he convulsed. After a strenuous few seconds, he struck my head with enough strength to make my helmet ring. It succeeded in loosening my grip, and he scurried to a window slightly further away to keep fighting.

"Lindemann! Where are you?" shouted Keller from downstairs. Bruno was jeopardizing the entire squad. Reaching through to a soldier in his form was always a daunting task, but he showed no signs of the sensible Bruno that I had bonded with into the wee hours of last night. A selfish obsession with his agenda had again compromised him. I was dumbfounded.

Last night. That was it! I knew what I needed to do. Hassling to prop myself up against the wall, I flopped my head in his direction and collectedly mentioned, "You won't make it back to her if you don't snap out of it."

As if I hid behind my hands while playing peek-a-boo, Bruno froze in confusion like a baffled baby. After a second, he regained his aggression with a frenzied rattle of his head and continued firing.

But I pressed on the subject, slamming my hand against the wall to get his attention. "What does Annette prefer, Bruno? You dying here needlessly or you returning to her alive?"

At first, Bruno didn't pause the operation of his weapon. But soon after, he abruptly crashed the butt of his rifle against the ground with a shout. A hand slid down its receiver like a fireman's pole as his back sunk against the wall. "Fuck!" he conceded, wiping his forehead with his eyes fixated on the ground. "I can't make it back to her if I lose you!"

"Nobody wants to lose anyone. But you're putting everyone else at risk by staying here," I reasoned. Bruno avoided eye contact as my words sunk in. But when I made another scoot toward him, I discovered he was actually focused on the pouch on Ilsa's stock. Just a corner of my latest letter to my sisters stuck out through its leather flap. Bruno returned his gaze to greet mine. His feeble eyes returned to the shade they once were when he first arrived.

A machinegun sounded off across the street, strafing the walls outside our structure. Guppy shrieked as we ducked even further below our cover as more bullets whizzed past.

"Dammit, Bruno!" I snapped as the rest of our squad returned fire from the connected room. The hard love somewhat worked in our first battle together. Perhaps it would suffice this time around. "Do you *not even remember* what we spoke about last night? I trained you specifically in case this happened to me! You need to make sure our men make it back to their own Annettes! That'll make you enough of a gotdamn hero!"

Keller again called for Bruno to hurry from the other room. I stretched out to smack Bruno on the calf. "*You* are the Overwatch now!"

Bruno's face tightened as the power of his new title invigorated him. He then understood that he needed to leave.

Confident with my efforts, I used Ilsa to prop myself back up against up to the wall. Bruno nodded in approval and stacked up against the bricks as well. Without saying a word, we both popped into view and fired our weapons in sync to suppress the enemy.

After a couple of shots, I ordered, "Go!" and he dashed across the room to the door as I continued providing cover for him.

I kept Ilsa pointed towards the onslaught of Soviet troops. The weapons from the rest of the squad downstairs died off one-by-one as their footsteps signified their retreat. The last rifle to sound off from downstairs was a bolt-action. It could have been Kuhn's, but I was pretty sure it Bruno's.

As the last footsteps began their departure, I recalled I had one final order of utmost importance to issue. "Oh, and remind Oberleutnant Ross that he is still a piece of shit for me!" I hollered.

I was a tad surprised at, by hook or by crook, how long I had held out. It had been what, ten minutes? As a lone man with merely a bolt-action rifle that could only output maybe a few more than ten rounds a minute max, it was no small feat. But my life's clock was ticking, and I knew I wouldn't last forever.

"How are you doing, Guppy?" I shouted over a shoulder as I continued operating my weapon. A round struck the outside wall beneath me, but I couldn't figure out from where.

From behind me, the fading recruit uttered, "Easy like

Sunday morning, Schmidt," before he started humming. Dying soldiers do all sorts of peculiar things when they are too injured to fight but too alive to stop talking. The poor boy had grown delirious over losing so much blood, so he'd taken up humming. Nonetheless, I was determined to be with him during our final moments, as he may be the last person I ever talk to.

"I'm Rupert to you now, Guppy!" I insisted with another shot of my rifle. Guppy hiccuped before continuing to hum, which I interpreted as a sign of affirmation.

Another round whizzed past my head. I didn't even flinch as I pulled the trigger, striking the man who had just unsuccessfully tried to kill me from the side of a building down one of the streets. Ordinarily, I would console myself by getting swept up with hugging Ilsa's bolt, but there was no time for such monkeyshines. There were just too many enemies, so I kept my eyes searching for more of them instead.

Guppy stopped humming, which drew my attention. "Hey, *Rupert*," he whimpered in an almost sassy fashion.

I slammed my back behind the cover of the wall to begin individually press more bullets down Ilsa's disengaged top before I could reply, "What is it, Guppy?"

The wounded boy took a few seconds to piece together his statement. Enemy fire echoed from all around, but I was too curious about what he had to say to give it too much attention.

"I never said thanks," Guppy soon whispered. He rolled his head over to look at me. His eyes were bloodshot, and his normally rosy, youthful skin had a ghostly yellow tint. "So, thank you."

It astonished me that a recruit who I met only a week or two before had still scrounged up enough energy while on his deathbed to show me his appreciation. I knew right then that staying behind with Guppy was indeed the right choice. Sure, it was better for the rest of the squad, too. But I was nothing short of honoured to be by the side of this comrade during his – pardon me, our – final moments.

"Hey, I just needed to demonstrate how to fight off the sharks," I cracked with a grin. Guppy simpered. Another joke well-placed, I thought. Good job, Rupert.

As I scampered to a different niche along the second floor of the storefront, a splitting pain below my chest reminded me of my wound from earlier. Kuhn's bandage was working alright at best on my front, but he didn't seem to put as much attention on the exit wound. I took note of it when he was patching me up, but I wasn't going to let myself tie them down here any longer. So after they left, I managed to place a makeshift gauze pad out of some torn cloth from my undershirt around the exit wound and then jury-rigged my belt to keep the pressure on both punctures through me. It worked for now, but it wasn't perfect by any means.

I rose above the window and peered through Ilsa's scope. Just as I noticed the DP machine gun was no longer in the sunny part of the sidewalk further down the street, a wave of gunfire erupted from across the street. There was hardly enough time to duck back down before bullets zoomed overhead. The wall shook as it took a couple of hits, but thankfully, did not penetrate. If our building wasn't mostly brick, I would have been in much more trouble.

"But the tiles! We just got Persian Ivory back in stock!" Guppy grew unhinged from the energy he had found as the walls around were torn up by enemy fire and had begun sputtering gibberish. He would soon bleed out, and I would be alone with Ilsa. I had decided long ago that if I had to go, it would be with Ilsa and me giving it our all. I guess I had my pistol, too, but Ilsa was my lifeline.

I struggled over to another window and darted above to take a potshot at the MG as I noticed troops storming towards my building. I didn't have time to deal with that machine gun – they were moving to invade our outpost.

"This is it, comrade!" I roared to Guppy as ducked down I topped off my rifle with a few more rounds. "This is it!"

For just a moment, all of my senses dulled as my body adjusted to the extra blood that began pumping through my veins. My right hand gripped Ilsa with tremendous force, and my left hand palmed the side of my helmet, trying to crush it with the tips of my fingers. Like a werewolf in a full moon, I felt my skin stretching to keep a monster inside that desperately wanted to escape. I had feared of such a demon possessing Bruno multiple times, but he was untamed. It came out when the full moon was not overhead. Mine was the culmination of too many years fighting, a beast that I had almost fully managed to keep under wraps except for these very circumstances.

I had denounced the need for war multiple times, but I'd be lying if I stated that something was addicting about the adrenaline that pumped through my body during those times of challenging.

Perhaps it was the excitement that would overtake me. Nonetheless, I relished the captivation of my transformation as my head snapped up, and I painted with an agape draw. The veiny skin throughout the entirety of my body became tense as if it had grown armour strong enough to ward off gunfire. I wanted to roar like a rabid wolf towards the sky, but I had more pressing matters that demanded my attention. It was time.

With a frenzy of energy overtaking me, I rose to a crouch and bolted past a humming Guppy, no longer feeling my wound. I barged through the doorframe where my squad retreated from, dropping to the floor to get a better angle down the set of stairs. Ilsa and I were just in time for approaching feet to jeopardize themselves through an open doorway and window by the base of the stairs at the ground level. I quickly fired at the first torso that appeared from the feet. Ilsa discharged a second round so rapidly that it hit my victim again before he hit the ground.

Another Russian behind the first stuttered to conceal enough of himself behind the outside wall, out of my sights. I landed one on his exposed leg, which unfortunately for him, yanked his whole body down into my line of sight, revealing his helmet. He was ended there.

Only then did I realise I wasn't even aiming down my scope. Ilsa just seemed to know where to point herself. The magnification was too strong for such close quarters, anyways.

A PPSh arose from around a window downstairs and fired blindly inside, showering copious bits of metal around my position. It forced me to hide, so I rolled on my back behind another set of stairs going up.

As their fire peppered the was while my head faced up, memories of the past flashed across my mind. I remembered Johannes, one of my most valued friends. God, I'd miss him. He had helped me through so much. I hoped that salty cook had made it out of Oradea alright. But I just knew he would. He always came out on top.

The volley soon subsided, so I rolled back to the top of the stairs. Ilsa orientated herself towards the window that the PPSh had appeared from. In the blink of an eye, another arm appeared and tossed a grenade inside my room before I could react.

By some undeserved mercy from God, it hit about two-thirds of the way up the stairs and bounced right back through the door outside. I rolled out of view again as a distraught shriek reverberated from outside. The explosion silenced it.

Seizing the opportunity, I mustered all my strength and hustled down the stairs to get the jump on them while they were dismayed. I only made it a couple of steps down when I realised that I had made a terrible mistake. My gut was in an excrusiating pain, and I could feel the blood oozing out from underneath my uniform. On top of it all, I was still covered in Guppy's blood from earlier, too. I must have been a horrendous sight.

When I got down the stairs, I lurched in tremendous agony against the inside part of the exterior wall. I hurriedly pushed my weight against the ground and climbed up Ilsa until I could peek above the window. The remnants of the men from the grenade's blast made a grisly scene. Legs, arms, torsos – all covered in blood.

Before I had the chance to pull Ilsa up, I caught sight of a giant Soviet tank through the intersection, far down the street. It was too distant to have previously heard, but near enough for me to catch it rotating its turret in my direction. It took everything I had to get out of there as quickly as I did. The machine gun from across the street opened up on me from behind as I disappeared back up the stairs. The outside wall by the base of the steps detonated, its shockwave tailing me as I made it back inside the room on the second floor.

I put pressure on my wound as I brushed past the serenely humming Guppy. Ramming into the second-story wall beneath the windows, I pulled off a shot into a horde of men closing into my position. Another single round whizzed passed my head, right before I noticed the tank's turret fixed its sights on me in the second story. There was nothing I could do against armour this time, so I did my best to displace myself from the window as much as possible before another eruption rocked from behind me, flinging my body against the wall like food thrown from an unruly toddler.

The raw power of the tank's main cannon had revitalized any forgotten pains from my previous injuries. The wound through my abdomen from earlier had seeped too much blood during my heart's finest hour for me to continue. Splinters peppered my body from the explosion. Blood from Guppy and myself alike covered my uniform. The adrenaline that my veins contained had pardoned enough of itself from my body, draining the excess energy from my body.

"You still with me, Guppy?" I sputtered as I rolled my head

to the side. The boy had ended up underneath some dust and rubble by my rifle down the back of the wall. Guppy had not enough life left in him to survive such a forceful blast. As I always thought it would be, Ilsa was the only one still with me during my final moments.

Still, I called forth the last bits of my strength to shuffle down the wall towards a spot between the duo. Ilsa was out of ammunition, which was fine because I couldn't be bothered to load her back up again. I just wanted her with me. But when I struggled close enough to her, I also lacked the energy to yank her from the rubble. So, I just rested my hand on her stock, where some blood-stained letters jutting out of their leather container.

Weary from just losing another comrade, I strafed the fingers on my other hand through the hair of the fallen recruit. "We did it, Guppy. We let the others escape," I sputtered before turning away to wheeze. Blood had come up from my lungs, splattering it over the rubble. My body wanted to cough more, but I just didn't have the vigour. I just accepted the lump in my throat.

My eyelids grew heavy as my fingers struggled to course through the fallen recruit's hair. A meagre burst of energy awoke me when enemy footsteps echoed from the stairwell of the connected room. The hand on Guppy instinctively twitched towards the pistol on my belt. My other hand around Ilsa's stock even reached for her neck, where I could pull her trigger. But there was no more need to fight, so I relaxed my hands. We had stalled the Soviets enough to allow the squad to evacuate. With our mission accomplished, nobody else needed to die.

Well, maybe just one more person needed to. At last, I finally accepted my body's request to close my eyes to get the rest I had only dreamt of. I no longer fought the weariness as it consumed me, and began drifting into slumber.

As footsteps stormed around me, I thought about how fruitful a life I had lived. Quite a bit of living had been packed into my few years on this earth. I've been in more countries over the past few years than most have their whole life, so I couldn't complain.

Even so, I felt sorrow. I was sorrowful for leaving all my mates. Johannes, Kuhn, Keller, Herrmann, Pfeiffer, hell, even Denis. And I was especially sorry that I had to leave Bruno. I hoped he could pull it together for the men. But most of all, I was sorrowful for all the killing I did. I killed so many. I truly regretted it.

Oddly enough, a sensation of peace found itself as my final thought before I danced off. I could be reunited with my family. Or, perhaps, families – both those of my sisters and my fallen comrades. That seemed nice.

So, this is what it's like. I'd be lying if I said I haven't always been curious...

Chapter 20

Grenadier Bruno Lindemann

"Where's Schmidt?" Pfeiffer adjusted his grip on his submachine gun to the middle of its frame while reaching underneath one of Herrmann's arms to help Kuhn lug him down the street. The men with him remained in the cover a nearby house provided, firing their weapons at the encroaching enemy. I joined them and took up a position to guard our retreat. Maybe I could ward them away from Rupert.

Herrmann groaned as his weight was shifted around. A recent wound above his thigh made it inconvenient for him to retreat. He spun his head the side and taunted, "Get me below the ass while I'm not looking, why don't you? You bastards wouldn't dare hit me straight on!"

"Easy now, Herrmann," Kuhn thoughtfully consoled to his wounded comrade before he addressed the Feldwebel. "He's…" Kuhn winced as a burst of enemy fire struck the building beside him.

Keller rose from behind some rubble he had propped himself

up beside to chime in. "I'm squad leader now," he explained, matching his pace with the group. His sizable weapon remained trained on the rear as he held it by the grip and bipod, the last belt of ammunition swaying to the sides with every step backward. Kuhn shot him a look of relief. Keller caught Kuhn's eyes but didn't make any further gestures.

I wanted to stay as close to Rupert as possible, but I had to overwatch the others. It was his last order. So, I reluctantly retreated past Herrmann and the posse to another safe spot I could provide cover from slightly ahead. I temporarily muffled the voices of concern in my head when I passed them to overhear Pfeiffer uttering, "Thought he was a lucky one."

After a while of pulling back, the other men providing cover figured out that shooting at enemies so far away was ineffective and wasteful, so their firing tapered off. Still desperate to do anything to save my counterpart, I took a couple of useless shots after they had ceased. But I ultimately gave in, unenthusiastically accepting that I would no longer be able to defend Rupert.

After another block or so of fleeing through the destroyed town, we met up with the other squads in our platoon. They took fewer casualties, freeing me of the responsibility of providing cover, so I joined the bulk of the others.

Oberleutnant Ross promptly noticed Schmidt was missing. When Pfeiffer told him, he didn't say a word. He just tightened his lips with a nod and kept running.

I took the opportunity to grab his attention. "Oberleutnant Ross, sir," I beckoned as we made our way back.

The officer seemed surprised to notice it was I who was speaking to him. "What do you want, Grenadier?"

I didn't know how to handle losing Rupert. Part of me didn't believe it yet. He had done this before, after all. But I decided that digging into Oberleutnant Ross might relieve my disorientation. Besides, Rupert would have been proud of me. So I puffed out my chest and declared, "Unterfeldwebel Schmidt's last request was to remind you that you are a piece of shit."

The Oberleutnant was taken back by such a snide comment made by a soldier so far underneath him in rank. He scowled, so I swiftly raised my hand almost up to my shoulders to demonstrate I would have mocked him with salute if not on the field with an added, "Sir." Yeah, Rupert would have liked that.

Oberleutnant Ross first seemed like he was going to lash out at me, but ultimately ended up sighing, "Very well, Grenadier." His eyes drifted to the ground. "Those *would* be his final words," he moaned.

We fell all the way back to the plaza in front of our train station headquarters, passing our men preparing more fortifications in the surrounding buildings. We really were going to defend this town, tooth and nail.

Past the plaza and by the front of the train station stood Sturmbannführer Kolartz. He studied a piece of paper in front of the train station amongst some others until he noticed us.

"Ah, Oberleutnant Ross, glad to see you've made it," the Sturmbannführer mentioned as we got closer. He shifted his eyes up from his document, taking his monocle off and stuffing it into his pocket as he examined our men. His ears perked up. "Where is Unterfeldwebel Schmidt?"

There was a moment of silence before somebody responded. "We were losing men, so he sacrificed himself to cover our retreat, sir," Oberleutnant Ross answered after he had attracted some nearby medical personnel to take Herrmann to a medical station.

"How fortunate," the Sturmbannführer reacted, folding his document. After an unsettling pause, he continued, "…That he had so much to give for the Fatherland."

My fist clenched over his poor choice of timing. That sick fuck was actually pleased Rupert was gone. I wanted to strike that callous prick down from his high horse. Yeah, how 'fortunate' would that be, sir? I stepped forward, towards the side of the unsuspecting Sturmbannführer when Rupert's voice interrupted me. "Relax, Bruno," he advised. "I don't want you to get in trouble over me."

Then, I couldn't control my hand. It flared open on its own, stretching the tendons on the back of my palm. It was as if Rupert had taken command of me for just a split second. It startled me just long enough for Keller to speak up about the Sturmbannführer's reaction before I could act out.

"Bullshit," Keller declared, lowering his machine gun from over his shoulder to the front his waist. He approached the Sturmbannführer, teetering on the border of the socially allowed distance between a man and an officer. Some of the Sturmbannführer's S.S. bodyguards stopped talking amongst themselves and took notice. Pfeiffer winced.

Keller stared deep into the officer's eyes and proclaimed, "If that's how you react to the death of one of your men, then I am given the illusion that you are unfit for command."

Returning Keller's glare with a pompous smirk, he nonchalantly plucked a smoke from his tunic. He took his time lighting it up before he unconvincingly clarified, "I can assure you that I am free of such illusions, *Obergefreiter*." Officers were positioned as superiors to all enlisted personnel, and they were habitually quick to indicate it.

Keller growled, and Kuhn grabbed at his sleeve from behind. Keller shot dangerous eyes back to him at first, but his aggression subsided as the more senior Pfeiffer stepped in front of Keller to take over communicating with the Sturmbannführer. Pfeiffer knew he might have more sway as a platoon leader.

"He is just shell-shocked," Pfeiffer apologized. The Sturmbannführer recognized his excuse with a hum. Keller grunted again, and Pfeiffer recognized the necessity of piecing together an appropriate enough statement to the officer on Keller's behalf, or else he would say something less than appropriate himself.

"It's just, uh," Pfeiffer began, "Schmidt could have made it. He held them off."

The Sturmbannführer took a long drag of his smoke. "That does not concern me, Feldwebel," he flaunted.

Keller rumbled, wound up by the unexpected hostility of the Sturmbannführer's response. He shook off Kuhn's grip and took another strong-willed step towards the senior officer.

One of the Nazi bodyguards began to step into Pfeiffer's path. He was held back with the head officer's hand, allowing Keller to enter the Sturmbannführer's breathing room.

Sturmbannführer Kolartz casually examined Keller's face, but ultimately looked back at Pfeiffer. "But since your men display such a vitality over ensuring other comrades have retreated," the noble-turned-officer teased, "I will assign your men to such a position that will surely maximize your skillsets. I'm sure the Jewish resettlement here in Oradea could use your expertise."

All of the men in our platoon shifted around in discomfort, shooting looks and whispering to one another while scratching areas on their bodies that didn't really itch. We knew something wrong went down in those so-called 'resettlements.' Soviets didn't capture the Germans working them. They killed them on the spot, even more often than they did on the battlefield. Such an order was a death sentence.

Oberleutnant Ross must have known because he was the first to speak up over the orders. “Sir, I can assure you that we can assist the defenses best from around this train station,” he hastily proposed as he pulled Keller back. He knew he would be involved in such a proposal, and having the highest rank out of any of us, felt he could most adequately speak up to him. “We have too few men to provide an effective buffer for the enemy from anywhere further.”

Sturmbannführer Kolartz nodded to act as if Ross’ proposal was a better idea to his phony motion. “Very well, Oberleutnant,” he conceited. “Have your men resupplied.” He clasped his hands behind his back and turned towards the station behind him. Then he rewound to recall, “Oh, and Oberleutnant, I need to see you regarding an order by Generalleutnant Abraham. We need to destroy a munitions dump before we evacuate this city.”

“Better get our bullets quick,” Pfeiffer mentioned to us all in general as he pulled the magazine out of his weapon to check how many rounds it had left.

"We're evacuating the city, sir?" Ross responded with a finger in the air.

"The Generalleutnant declared that the defense of this town is no longer possible. We are to regroup about ten kilometers to the northwest," the Sturmbannführer specified as he stepped backward before proceeding to creep back into the station. "Come with me, and afterward, we can find where your men are best suited," he echoed from inside.

Sturmbannführer Kolarz strolled away, with Oberleutnant Ross on his heels. About a full minute passed before anybody dared to comment on what had just happened. We needed the Sturmbannführer to be far away before we said a word.

"Fuck him!" We all turned in disbelief to see Kuhn of all men showing an emotion we had no idea he was capable of: anger.

Kuhn took the news of protecting the resettlement camp the hardest. Such a hateful environment would have been too much for a selfless man like Kuhn. The severity of Keller's frown dampened when he noticed, so he announced, "I heard Lieutenant-Colonel Péterffy evacuated that camp months ago. Plus, he'd never send Heer forces to defend that kind of place. That's an S.S. job. The

Sturmbannführer was just trying to jerk us around."

Still shaken up, Kuhn's dreary eyes stayed fixed on Keller, who piggybacked, "And I'm not endangering *my* squad for some political shit like that."

Kuhn partially mirrored Keller's stern face. His hands trembled as he struggled to unwind the cap of his canteen. When he finally had it undone, he took gulp after gulp.

Keller again calmed him down. "Woah there, Kuhn. Relax on that stuff!" He reached in to pull the canteen down from Kuhn's mouth. Kuhn painted heavily.

Pfeiffer, who wasn't part of our bender the previous night, raised an eyelid. "That stuff?"

Though it was the only remotely humorous thing that had happened that day, I was still trying to figure out how to process everything. Without Rupert's guidance, I just didn't know how to act.

The fog that sunk in was welcome. Though it dampened the effectiveness of my scope, it kept me out of sight enough from the third floor of my building. I could easily detect the shapes of enemies through the mist of the open street before they could notice my shadowy figure through the window up here. But the fog would be especially useful for enemy armor. Tanks were loud. Loud enough for our ears to frequently be more valuable than our eyes. So, we'd have the jump on them.

The engine of a tank sputtered in the distance. We didn't have any armor in this city anymore, so another enemy assault was in the works. The second tank we've seen today.

The Soviet armor soon materialized from the fog but didn't even have time to fire off a round before it was destroyed by a mine we placed on the street earlier. The fog conveniently also made mines even harder to detect.

Keller began firing off his machine gun from his building at the end of the street just as the first of them appeared. Soon after, the rest of the squad sounded off from a building on my side of the street. The Soviets dispersed, flinging themselves towards cover or diving on their stomachs.

I held my fire because I planned to take today differently. I needed to keep myself calm and under control. Plus, I wouldn't be worthy of Annette if I couldn't curb another fit.

Well, that wasn't fully it, and I guess it wasn't fully my idea, either. Schmidt told me to go into this building. He told me it was the best position to be the Overwatch, and that the Overwatch would keep calm unless it was otherwise necessary to make the brightest decisions. And I was the Overwatch now.

As the fighting continued along the streets below, some of the Russians grew sly. Some thought they could make their way through the buildings on the other side to get a better angle on our men. Through the cracks between windows, I caught them pushing to more threatening positions.

After about half a minute of searching for them with the tip of my rifle, one busted through a window and began spraying his weapon towards the squad. I was at just the right viewpoint to get a clear shot at him. I accepted that I'd have to take one of them down eventually. No bloodlust today, though – I would do it just to protect the squad. And to survive. For Rupert. For my comrades. And of course, for Annette. Just hit him and carry on. That'd be enough bravery for Annette. So, I cautiously pulled the trigger, and the butt of my rifle kicked back on my shoulder.

The man's head tossed back as a familiar slosh of guts

squished against the wall behind him. His body remained in the exact position by the time his chin jolted back to where it was before my shot, revealing my work on him. Bright red drained from the new crater I gave to his skull. He remained stiff as he sluggishly fell backward and landed with an audible 'thud,' weapon still clenched in his lifeless hands.

I panicked like when I was scolded after my first kill. Was I still calm? Was I supposed to not feel satisfied over protecting the men with another neutralization? Satisfaction was always what Rupert advised against, so I felt embarrassed.

"But I don't want you to end up like Rupert," a soft voice murmured within my mind. My stomach knotted from hearing Annette's voice. "You still value what you have at home. Rupert lost the significance of this. Not all of his teachings were true," she proposed, voice crisply ringing in my ears. "Not all of his teachings will earn your spot back to me."

Annette had a point. Rupert had the tools to fight, but not the will as I had. Maybe he intended for me to improve his ideology all along. That explained why Rupert has been providing his insight directly into my head lately. Like Annette's from back at home,

Rupert *chose* to combine with me. He had also become a part of me. Together, we would make it out. Yes, I needed to be the better form of him, and Annette would guide us. I would honor him by correcting the discrepancies with his lessons.

Why did I feel wrong over shooting this Bolshevik, anyway? It needed to happen. One less dangerous Soviet adversary on the battlefield. It saved the squad, all while improving my chances of getting home. So, Rupert's advice required modernization. If I'm glad to rid these enemies as a threat, perhaps I'll perform better, and be more likely to survive. Rupert stressed shaking my enjoyment of terminating the enemy *after* the fighting, so I could do whatever I wanted during it.

"I'm proud of you, Bruno," Annette declared as I observed my work. "Another job done well." With my target's innards spewed across the wall behind him, the communist had not so much as twitched since he hit the floor. I had chosen to act on the power my rifle gave me to remove the Soviet player from this game of war. A sneer crept on my face as I realized I felt more than okay – I felt *prime*.

Across the street, a balcony bustled with a group of about

three other Bolsheviks who had promptly taken turns firing outside the unfastened doors. My rifle seamlessly floated to their position as I pulled the bolt handle back and returned it forward. “Stay proud, Annette,” I whispered as I shot the first one through his side. He tossed his weapon out of reach and instinctively began squirming on the floor with hardly more than an occasional whimper.

Before I took another shot, one of the Reds began shouting to his comrade before disappearing within their room. I fired a volley of rounds at him before he escaped, narrowly missing him before he jumped out of sight. The metallic ring of an empty shell leaving the receiver echoed on the ground to my side as the sounds of fighting in the streets carried on.

Another window burst open, and the sparks of gunfire flashed in my direction. I swiftly drifted beneath the window as its rounds peppered the wooden side of my building. A couple of them made it near me as they pierced through the wall, but I didn’t so much as flinch.

“Relocate,” Rupert advised. Good idea. From below their eyesight of the windows, I retreated to the stairs to get to the second floor. I didn’t rush into the room, though. I slowly peeped out of the stairwell with my rifle pointed in the enemy's direction until I uncovered his window. He wasn't there, so I patiently waited like an eagle waiting for the right time to strike.

At last, he appeared. I operated my instrument like a master musician, orchestrating a round into the submachine gun in his hands. He howled in agony as he disappeared from sight. I was the conductor, and my weapon sounding off paired with his shriek was a symphony to my ears.

I returned to the third floor, where the better vantage point was, and eagerly lingered for somebody else to appear. In my view were rosy splatters of fresh blood surrounding my first two victims. My second casualty from the balcony was still wiggling in his own blood. He would need attention quickly if they wanted to save him. Maybe I could use him as bait.

But not long after, I grew impatient, and my leg started twitching. I was thirsty for more action. The Soviet who was writhing in pain. He was such an alluring target, in plain view through the balcony. I wanted to shoot him again, but I held back.

"Do it," Huber begged as my rifle slowly locked itself in on the wounded victim. I still held animosity for the Communist monsters because of his callous execution. I could honor Huber by seeking vengeance against the disabled peasant, I argued. Plus, Rupert would be alright with it because I could provide a humane solution for his pain. And perhaps it would scare off the remaining enemies. It could very well be a good option while I waited for more action.

Eh, maybe not. The first man I ever shot was wounded, and Rupert was very upset about that. So, I wasn't entirely sold on the idea of shooting the wounded man.

But then my twitching foot began stomping, and I just couldn't wait anymore. I needed to do it. The Soviet's fussing just kept distracting me. I couldn't focus anywhere else. I didn't have another choice. So, I just kind of let out a bark and yanked the trigger to strike dirty savage again. His body reacted with a twitch, and his movement subsided. It satisfied me.

A shooting pain stabbed at the front of my brain. "No!" Rupert's voice reprimanded. "Overwatch! You need to be the *Overwatch*!" I remembered that I needed to keep an eye on my comrades. My head trembled as I sprinted to the side of the room to get a better view of the rest of my squad's positions.

The dull-green armored bib of a Soviet shock troop discreetly leading other men across the street to the side of my Keller's position made my hair stand on end. I hastily fired a salvo of rounds in their direction, uplifting the dirt around their feet. How could I have been so enveloped that I forgot to keep overwatching my squad? I pulled the trigger again, and it clicked. Gotdamnit, it was empty! I might have been able to stop them, but by the time I topped off my rifle, they had already hidden behind the far wall of Keller's building.

"Keller! They're outside! On the right!" I screamed at the top of my lungs with my rifle trained on their last visible position. The sound of his MG-42 stopped as, by the grace of God, he heard my warning. He spun around while yanking his sidearm from its holster, his replacement assistant machine gunner on his heels as he sprinted out of my sight deeper into the room. Flashes of light promptly dazzled from within his building, escorted by the mixed sounds of different weapons sounding off.

How foolish of me! I was so enraged by my incompetence that my legs gave out, casting me to the floor. I pummeled the sides of my helmet. The inside rang like a bell. How could I forget

Rupert's main request? I had one job, and I had already failed it!

I frantically shook my head from side to side. My fists tightened as they fixed themselves to my helmet, moving with my head as it twisted. My muscles tensed up, and my skin grew strained. "Argh!" I screeched. I couldn't control myself. My elbows twitched fiercely, and my eyelids scrunched shut. I saw stars in the darkness. The physical pain my body had brought on made me uncomfortable. My head autonomously rocketed back. Red clouding my peripherals as I stared at the ceiling, I let out a mighty howl like a wolf at the full moon.

"Well? Get down there!" Rupert ordered. He was right. Maybe I could redeem myself. My rifle found its way back in my hands as I shuddered while rising to my feet. I was out of breath. But I knew I had more energy. A lot more. And I needed to use it to make them proud. To make them all proud.

Chapter 21

Obergefreiter Wolfgang Keller

I was the new guy in this squad. Hadn't been here as long as some of the others. But gotdamn, I already saw the benefits of having this so-called "Overwatch."

I would have just kept the pressure on them at the end of the street, where I thought they all were. But then I heard Lindemann's warning and kicked it into full gear. I had just made it to the exit's hallway when the Soviets stormed through a doorway on the opposite side of the room. My tenderfoot assistant machine gunner behind me bumped into a chair and decided to engage them from there. He got the first guy that stormed in but was gunned down from the next Soviet's submachine gun, gasping as he sprawled on the floor in the middle of the room.

I hoisted my sidearm up as the first communist fell, his piece sliding across the ground in front of him as he nailed the floor. I fired onto the direction of the second, hurriedly stepping out from the hallway to drag my wounded comrade to safety. Most of my rounds made it through the doorway, which kept them at bay.

My pistol clicked, and I yanked my fallen assistant gunner through the doorframe and fell on my rear to reload, his torso landing on my legs. I needed to get a loaded magazine back in quick before they would appear again.

The empty magazine fell out of the grip of my P-38 as I automatically reloaded. My eyes followed the magazine down to where it and hit the floor between my legs, close to my assistant. He had taken at least four bullets through the torso. There was no saving him. I didn't really know him. He was just some replacement admin solder unfortunately assigned to me back by the train station. But it still wasn't good. We couldn't afford those one-for-one trades anymore. Way too many of them compared to us.

The same Soviet who had killed my assistant machine gunner leaned around the wooden defense of the doorframe and again fired his weapon, first strafing blindly throughout the room and then in my direction after he figured out where I had gone. I had scarcely enough time to cock my pistol's slide before I leaned on my back to trade rounds, my comrade propped on my feet in front of me like a lean-to.

As I returned fire, I glanced down at my ally's carcass after it twitched. I didn't plan on using my fallen comrade's body as a meat shield, but I was damned thankful I did as his body jerked when a round hit him. My wife would kill me if I got shot, especially where I would have if this unlucky guy hadn't been suspended on my toes.

A metallic kink dinged from where the enemy was. Excitedly recalling such a distinct noise, I snapped my attention back across the room. The soldier I was trading rounds with had retracted behind cover as another Bolshevik donned in a dull swamp green vest dashed from behind the doorframe to get on the other side. It was a gotdamn Russian with steel armor, and I had hit him instead. My pistol couldn't do anything to one of those, even at this range.

I reloaded my pistol at a blinding speed. Last magazine. Fuck, I missed my MG-42. It would tear through the side of their building and that fucking armor like paper. I kicked the carcass of my dead comrade off my feet and shuffled to a crouch behind the cover the hallway's doorframe and wall provided.

I took a fraction of a second too long in deciding to floor it to the exit. The Soviet in the steel bib appeared from behind his cover, unloading a PPS at his hip in my direction while marching forward with dominating, deliberate steps. One of the Russians followed him in, but his other comrades aimed at me from the doorframe. Everybody held their fire but the armored infantry, content on letting him do his reckoning alone. I retaliated with my meager pistol behind the unconvincing safety of the wood-reinforced doorframe.

The shock trooper thoughtlessly unloaded in my general vicinity with hardly a care where he aimed. Bullets zipped into the tables, chairs, and the thin wooden walls between us, smashing through the safety of my cover. I fell to the ground behind the doorframe, partially to make myself a smaller target.

Worst of all, the juggernaut's armor fully absorbed a hit my measly little pistol placed on him. He hardly so much as balked as he steamrolled toward me, trucking through chairs in his way instead of going around them. With metal ricocheting everywhere, the last magazine in my pistol grew closer and closer to empty, and I gripped the sharpened screwdriver in my boot with my other hand tighter and tighter. Soon, it would be my only weapon. I further leaned behind the wooden frame, desperately dodging the rounds as they pierced the walls around me. "Oh God, Erma," I thought. "I am so sorry…"

Without warning, the shock trooper's head unexpectedly

exploded inside his helmet like a watermelon. He plopped on the ground slightly askew from where he would have marched, weapon tumbling on the floor towards me.

A terrorizing shriek originating from the building's front window my machine gun remained resting on. It gave me goosebumps as the lone Russian in the room slammed backward into a freshly painted canvas of his own blood. The Russians in the doorframe snapped their weapons towards the front of the room and yanked their triggers.

I gasped for air like an engine with a choke at my new chance at life before instinctively scurrying up to crouch behind the perforated doorframe. Knowing what I had to do, I clenched my teeth and took the opportunity to dive on my belly into the room. I needed to steal one of the weapons on the ground while the Russians men were distracted by whatever the hell was going on outside.

One of the two Reds left took notice, whipping his rifle around just as I picked up the shock trooper's PPS. Luck was on my side again, and I got him first, his buddy catching on and taking cover. My target twitched with every shot, pinching his face as his chest ingested my bullets. My submachine gun jacked my target backward until he tripped on the ground outside. I still held the trigger down until the weapon in my hands clicked empty because I had just stared death in the face and was not fucking around.

The last threat outside the room panicked, fleeing away from his spot along the doorframe. I hastily grabbed another weapon from the floor when a shadow dashed past the front window, charging in the direction that the last man had escaped.

First, there was a shriek from outside. Then a thud. Wailing and growling soon mixed in. I cautiously approached the doorframe to find out what was going on, weapon at the ready.

I cautiously peeked through the doorframe. A Bolshevik soldier was on the ground with a bloodthirsty Grenadier Lindemann on top of him. Both were unarmed. Their weapons were scattered on the ground a few meters from where they tussled. Lindemann's scoped rifle had caught a bullet on the barrel, rendering it useless. He'd need to find a new one.

I wanted to help my squadmate, but the area needed to be secured first. I popped my weapon through the doorway to make sure nobody else was planning to interrupt. Gunfire still cracked off from the rest of the squad's building and at the end of the street. It sounded like the rest of the attacking Soviets were still mostly by the carcass of the destroyed tank at the beginning of the road, so there was nobody else in the immediate vicinity.

I again took notice of the brawl going on beside me as their concerning noises reached my ears. I didn't need to join in. Lindemann was holding his own. But the Russian man sounded like he was begging for mercy, shouting something in his foreign dialect with his hands only on the defensive, trying to block the Grenadier's blows. Lindemann was like a wolf, tearing apart his prey. His victim shrieked in pain. It was brutal, but I couldn't stop them.

Finally, Lindemann ripped off his helmet and started bashing his prey with it. Even I was disgusted by the crunching of the Russian boy's skull from the torque of Lindemann's battery.

After a few more strikes paired with homicidal roars, I knew I needed to step in. There was no need for Lindemann to continue his desecration of the limp human beneath him. So, I dashed from the cover of my doorway to get the Grenadier off the body.

"Lindemann!" I loudly whispered while smacking the back of his shirt with one arm, weapon still pointing off in the distance. The Grenadier's arms flailed, shaking me off.

The growing concern for Lindemann's assault tingled my sixth sense for the battlefield. Russians would be quick to seek revenge if they oversaw what was going on to one of their fallen comrades. Lindemann was becoming a liability. So, with the heel of my boot, I launched him off the dead man. He rolled on the ground and sprung to his feet, teeth brandished. He stepped at me, red-stained helmet ready to bash another skull in. I feared he had become rabid and pointed my weapon at him. He stepped at me, lodging his stomach into the tip of the barrel. The barbarian's distant gaze came into focus as we locked eyes as he raised his helmet about halfway up his body. He was challenging me.

Lindemann's pupils were pitch-black as if they had lost feeling. His breath smelled like he had just run several kilometers. I thought he would try something, even with my weapon imprinted in his gut. I understood his mood. But I had just stared death in the eyes and had no fear of backing down at the recruit, no matter what he was capable of doing. Shit was tough for him, but he had no idea what it was like to do this for years. Not yet, he didn't. So, I dug the barrel deeper into his gut. My lip under the left side of my nose rose as my scowl intensified.

After half a dozen tense seconds in our stance as the gunshots rang out from where the others fought, the engine for Lindemann's rampage ran dry on fuel. The color of his humanity had gently regained its way back into his headlights as he lowered his bloodied helmet to his side. I felt it was safe enough to low the tip of my rifle, but my eyes stayed undaunted as we remained fixed on each other.

The boy's legs started to tremble. The shock of his actions was reaching his mind. As the ranking soldier, I was obligated to look after him. So, I peeked to our sides before dragging him through the doorway by the middle of his tunic.

"Grab a weapon," I advised while stepping over the corpses towards my much-missed MG-42. Fuck, I needed her earlier. I almost kissed her as I picked her up, vowing never to leave her again.

We needed to focus on the battle taking place down the street. "Lindemann," I called while redeploying the bipod on the window sill. Hopefully, keeping him busy would preoccupy his conflicted mind. "You're in here with me now. Get over here and help me with this."

After my MG was all ready to fire again, I aimed, searching

for any more Soviets through the fog. I didn't find any. The building nearby that was occupied by the rest of the squad intermittently echoed with the noise of German gunfire, but the returning fire from the edge of the street had soon subsided, was a good sign. It sounded like they were just taking a couple of crack shots at a fleeing enemy force. We could still hold our position.

Lindemann propped up a newly-acquired PPSh -41 against the wall beside me before digging into a nearby ammunition box for my MG, preparing another belt to be loaded when needed. He then retrieved his newfound weapon and took up a position near the door they flanked us from in case they came again.

Seconds of waiting turned into minutes. Lindemann hadn't said a word. Probably still lost over what he had just been through. And from losing Schmidt earlier. I remembered losing my first friends years ago. Still think about it, too. But now, this squad was my responsibility. I may not be the best person for it, but I knew I should try to prevent his mind from further dismantling itself.

"Good choice," I mentioned. Lindemann's eyeballs burned into the side of my cheeks. I stayed focused on the foreground. "They always preached about how superior our German engineering was to that of the Bolshevik's," I proceeded. "And most of the time, they're right." I affectionately patted the top of my MG-42.

I shifted my stance from foot to foot. "But the PPSh is an excellent weapon, superior to our submachine guns," I explained. "Cycles faster, a more rugged chassis. You'll like it."

I thought something moved behind a building. But right after, a newspaper flew out. False alarm. To be safe, I kept my weapon trained on it for a good minute before I assumed it was nothing.

Lindemann was too busy examining his new tool by the doorway to notice. "I've only been used to my Karabiner 98k…" he admitted. "I was getting used to that scope on it."

"Uh-huh," I remarked. "Kid, by the way you fought a couple of minutes ago, I doubt you'll be missing your old rifle."

I felt the muffled excitement radiating from the boy on the other side of the room as he tinkered with it. "Just be sure to grab lots of extra ammunition," I advised. He nodded and went back to search the bodies of the fallen. "PPS magazines don't fit into a PPSh," I remembered aloud.

I gave him a few minutes to search before bothering him again. "Oh, and here's something else for you," I remembered.

Without looking, I grabbed the sharpened screwdriver from my boot and held it out to him until I felt him take it.

The boy looked it over before I described it. "My family owned a garage," I started. "Grew up with automobiles from a very young age."

I would generally rather keep as much of myself private as possible, but this was my squad now, and Lindemann needed it. So, I sighed and carried on. "Look, I kept that screwdriver from home in my boot in case I ever needed it. But I'm only going to rely on my machine gun from now on." I slapped the stock of my MG-42. "But by the look of it, you could use it more. Hell of a lot easier than using your helmet."

Lindemann didn't seem sure how to react as he took up the position back by the door. "Wow… Thanks, Keller."

I grunted but didn't say anything else. That was enough of an effort. As squad leader, it was time I got an issued knife, anyway. I'd take less shit from command. So, we waited in more of the silence.

Then, the hum of a tank engine echoed through the fog. I tightened my grip on my weapon.

"Hey, over here. Make sure the Panzerfaust is ready," I

alerted Lindemann. He dashed over beside me and fumbled with the torch-shaped device by the ammunition box. I just grunted. “You know how to use one of those, right?”

Before he had time to respond, figures in the distance bustled around, hardly visible through the fog. Lindemann caught on and crouched above the wooden barrier with the panzerfaust. I hot-stepped behind my weapon, ready to engage.

The first man appeared along the side of the road ahead, cautiously passing the burning tank and the bodies of the fallen. I waited.

Once I could make out two or three more of them through the grey haze, I opened up. My first burst caught two men before they could react, and I nipped another in his wheels as he sprinted to a storefront, collapsing him to the ground. The others returned fire soon after, but I kept them pinned down.

We had scarcely begun another round of fighting when the tank charged through the street, smashing the burning carcass of the other out of its way. I could tell through the mist that it was a Joseph Stalin tank, with bigger cannons and much heavier armor than their T-34 counterparts. They were rugged beasts. Still formidable machinery, though.

"Lindemann! Shoot!" I shouted while attempting to keep the enemy soldiers occupied. He aimed for about half a second and fired off the rocket. It just glanced off the thick armor at the front.

The massive product of Soviet industry took notice, and its hull machine gun opened up on our position. We had angered their mechanical monster.

"Hallway! Now!" I screamed as I picked up my weapon with a belt of ammunition. I shoved Lindemann in front of me to make sure he left first. I didn't want to lose another assistant gunner. I was tired of losing them. I was tired of losing any men.

The tank fired its primary weapon. We narrowly escaped an explosion from behind that destroyed the main room littered with the Soviet corpses. I directed Lindemann toward the others' building and slung the extra belt of cartridges around the back of my neck. We needed to fall back to the station where the AT guns resided. Those were all we had that could take their tanks head-on.

Chapter 22

Grenadier Bruno Lindemann

"He's dead – leave him!" Keller howled. Kuhn's impervious humanity prevented him from giving up on another one of our comrades just yet, so Keller cracked down by pulling him off the perforated corpse.

"We have to get out of here!" Keller barked again. Kuhn unsteadily ascended to his feet and followed the last of the other men, hurrying down the stairs to exit the building. Keller again ushered me to leave in front of him and followed me out.

Once we were outside, I noticed that the growl of the tank's engine was louder than when we had first entered the structure. The men panicked and largely stood still until Keller came out. With an aggressive hand gesture, he singled towards the opposite direction of the noise. "Go!"

We all sprinted away, towards the outer layer of the battlements prepared in front of the train station. Thankfully, the tank wasn't as quick as us.

There were about six of us total, but I was only familiar with Kuhn and Keller. The rest of the men with us were replacements, from either armored units that lost their vehicles, mortarmen who no longer had their mortars, and I think an anti-tank gun crewman. They were re-assigned to us, so we had a fuller squad. I hadn't gotten to talk to any of them, though.

Gunfire cracked around the city as we waded through the fog back towards the train station. Once we made it, I could make out fighting that had already erupted on the other side of the cement grounds of the plaza towards the front of the station's marketplace. Makeshift defenses littered the area amongst a couple of concrete bunkers. Most of the surrounding buildings were in rubble. It was a bleak defense.

We sped past the unoccupied left flank of the first line, catching sight of a handful of Soviets across the open ground on our way the next line trading fire with our defenders. Their assault on the plaza's right flank had compromised at least one entire line of defenses, already forcing our men to pull back to the second line. Why the hell didn't anybody tell us about this? We were holding a building further practically behind the enemy's lines for no reason.

The communists could have crept up on our rear.

When we reached the edge of the first line, an unexpected volley of machinegun fire opened up on us from the second line. Rounds pelted the dirt and rock structures around. We all hit the ground or otherwise took cover. One of the others with us screamed, catching a round in his leg. I peeked from my cover and saw it was one of the new men. Thankfully, not Keller or Kuhn.

Keller was the first to prop up his weapon to retaliate but paused when he realized the bunker that opened fire on us on the second line of defense was still manned by men wearing our same distinct helmets. "What the hell!" he gasped.

The wounded man amongst us rocked on his back, cradling his bloodied shin as the ground tore up around him. Kuhn couldn't take it anymore and shot up an arm up like a rocket amidst an onslaught of gunfire.

"Stop! We're Germans!" Kuhn shouted at the top of his lungs, slowly rising from behind a stone barrier. He flailed both arms wildly above his head, making it to a stand. "Don't shoot! Don't shoot!"

The fire continued, clipping the ground in front of Kuhn. He hopped but kept waving his arms. But thankfully, after that, they hesitated. Keller and I exchanged looks before we raised an arm and got back on our feet to follow Kuhn forward. He could have died, but if he didn't do what we just did, we could have all perished by our own comrades. It was only another testimony to his unrelenting selflessness.

We all approached the bunker and were greeted by one of the men from another squad in our platoon. "Mud squad? They told us you were gone," the soldier explained to us as two Hungarians helped the wounded man hobble inside the bunker. "Completely wiped out."

"Like hell, we were!" Keller lashed out, stepping square to the front of the soldier. His stark visage contrasted the weakening embarrassment of the man who had just strafed his own allies. Keller was probably a few years younger than the man, but his hardened mug distinctly asserted that he had more grit. "Who told you that?"

Another man in our platoon behind the first chimed in. "They were our orders, sir! We were told anybody who approached would be an enemy!"

Keller growled and remarked, "Don't call me, 'sir,'" before

storming off to the exit at the back of the bunker leading to the next line of defenses. Our squad's replacements cast their eyes among themselves. I shrugged at one of them and followed Keller out, a couple of the others with Kuhn on my heels.

We stepped out the back of the side of the bunker and marched towards the next line of defenses. On the street between the two lines, we passed crew moving their anti-tank gun to the corner of the bunker. I looked it over before taking notice of the battered remains of a cement structure that seemed to be bustling with troops on the third line.

From outside, I caught a glimpse of Pfeiffer pointing at a map on a makeshift table beside one of the other squad leaders, Fritz's Sturmgewehr leaning on the wall next to him. Keller stormed into the premise. I went after him, but the rest of them stayed outside as a sparse number of soldiers brushed past us on their way towards the second line. It was too packed for the others to follow, anyway.

Nobody noticed Keller and I had entered. The troops just kept hustling about, paying no attention to the blood-splattered soldier menacingly standing by the door frame. Keller held his MG-42 on his hip as he deliberately racked its bolt. Though a belt of ammunition hung from its side, it still made a distinct noise.

It caught the eyes of a few of the men as they hotfooted about, but not Pfeiffer's. Keller grew agitated, so he grabbed his machinegun by the pistol grip and bipod and aimed it up. He yanked its trigger, firing about seven or eight rounds into the sky. The remaining commotion from the other men around stopped as they witnessed the scene. Among a few others who stopped, Pfeiffer finally looked up, armed with a scowl.

Pfeiffer's puckered frown dropped when he laid eyes on a stone-cold Keller standing before him. "Keller…" he gawked, stepping around the table to cautiously approach Keller. "I thought your squad-"

The tip of Keller's MG-42 flung toward Pfeiffer, with the smoking, cone-shaped flash hider just centimeters from his stomach. Pfeiffer peeked down and returned Keller's stare with sheer bewilderment. Nobody made a noise, with only the distant echoes of gunfire making any sound at all. I could only hear Keller's breathing.

Keller's unwavering monotone pierced through the silence like nails on a chalkboard. "Why wasn't my squad told we were all falling back to the marketplace?" he accused. The strain of his hands was audibly warping the grips of his machine gun. "Why the fuck did you tell your men we weren't still out there?"

Pfeiffer's resting scowl returned. His fingers opened from the palms at his side, and then again closed. "You really I thought you all were still alive?" He placed his hands on his hips, lurching his head forward in defiance.

Seconds seemed like hours as time sluggishly crept on. Their vehement stares remained in a belligerent lock, neither willing to let up. None of the other men did so much as flinch. All eyes stayed trained on what the salty veterans were going to do.

"What the hell is going on here?" Oberleutnant Ross broke in as he entered the structure from the other side. Keller kept his eyes trained on Pfeiffer as he adjusted the tip of his MG-42 towards the officer.

The Oberleutnant raised his hands in surprise, eyes almost popping out of his head. "Woah!" he exclaimed.

"Who told you my squad was gone?" Keller demanded, voice still void of any emotion. His eyes stayed clashing with Pfeiffer's.

Oberleutnant Ross took a slow step backward.

"Sturmbannführer Kolartz said the artillery would have wiped your squad out if you didn't make it back with the rest of our unit."

I winced and scratched my cheeks. "He's lying," Rupert's voice whispered. The itch grew from my cheeks, to my neck, and to my back. "Nobody knows this little man like I do." I tightened the grip on my new weapon. "He's a piece of shit, remember?"

Like when you stand up too quickly, my vision clouded, and all the noise faded. I don't recall what happened for a handful of seconds, but when my senses faded back in, I was towering over the mortified officer on his back. He had propped himself up on an elbow with his other hand blocking his face, the cold, gray tip of my submachine gun but centimeters away. I held the weapon away from my body as if I had just skewed him with an invisible bayonet. I was now involved in this negotiation.

"There was no fucking artillery!" I cleared up as a drop of blood fell from the brim of my helmet onto the ground. I greeted the butt of my weapon with my shoulder as one of my feet stepped in between the officer's legs.

"I know! I questioned the Sturmbannführer about it!" Oberleutnant Ross cried. "I swear I did, but he insisted you were gone!"

The anti-tank gun by the bunker opened up at around the same time a nearby machine gun kicked off its chatter. The Soviet assault on the plaza had spread to our side of the flank. "Quickly, finish him," Annette proposed. "He compromised you. He doesn't deserve to live."

"No, you must learn to be better," I muttered Rupert's advice aloud as he stated it in my head.

Oberleutnant Ross scooted back. "I…" he began, carefully rising to a sitting position against a wall behind him. A hand remained held up in front of his face. "I will learn how to from now on."

A group of soldiers rushed through from outside, having no idea what had just happened here. Some of the other men that had watched the whole ordeal took the opportunity to flee from the scene.

A cold hand gently resided itself on my shoulder. "Comrade," Pfeiffer began. I remained immobile, trigger finger still itching to paint the ground with blood. "We will take care of this later."

Rupert again chimed in. "Use this energy to defend the others."

"That's the idea," Pfeiffer intoned. "But first, we must make it out of this city. Too many green fucks on the left flank. We need you there."

"Lindemann," Keller called. His glasses flickered, reflecting off the light from a nearby lamp as he turned his head. "Come. We have retreating Germans to execute," he quipped before throwing his MG over his shoulder and heading back towards the second line of defenses.

A second or two passed before I agreed and lowered my weapon and turned around. Kuhn's head was leaning around the door. Judging by his eyes, which were as wide as a rabbit's in headlights, he had witnessed the whole thing.

When Keller caught a glance of the mortified Kuhn, he became compelled to shove one final stake into the heart of it all. As he paused to brace an arm on the remnants of a doorframe, his deep, monotonous voice reverberated in the stale atmosphere of the structure. "If the Sturmbannführer thinks my squad is dead, he's wrong. And if he thinks he's safe…" Keller cranked to the side to catch the agast Oberleutnant out of the peripherals of his resolute, emerald eyes. "…I'm coming for him."

Keller held the silence to let his warning sink before storming back to the front. I gave Ross one last leer before I exited in Keller's wake. Pfeiffer gave me a nod on the way out.

Damn, Keller was dangerous. Thank God he was on my side.

To nobody's surprise, things again went from bad to worse almost immediately. Everyone else besides our squad proved to be useless, and the enemy was relentless.

Keller manned his MG-42 inside the bunker as Kuhn fiddled around with its spare barrels. We were all trying to not stumble over our dead littered inside on the second line. Hungarians and Germans alike laid strewn across our cement coffin, but it nonetheless remained the safest spot.

I sprayed my new weapon to one side of a burning tank outside the window as Keller clipped down some of the men on the other side of it. The inflamed Soviet beast was poorly positioned, directly in our line of sight. But thankfully, it was inactive. The AT gun we had seen advance towards the side of the bunker earlier had done its job.

"Kuhn! Barrel!" Keller barked. I reloaded a fresh magazine into my PPSh, ready to give cover once they were swapping out barrels.

"Ready!" I announced. I began firing when Keller smacked a lever on the side of his MG-42. A red-hot barrel slid out and clinked on the floor, and Kuhn promptly undertook the installation of a colder new one.

I had a wide angle to cover, but it was no problem with the absurd rate of fire of my new weapon. I favored it more than my old rifle. The meager scope on my Karabiner was useless in this haze, and this new PPSh could put down enough rounds to where it didn't need to be as accurate. The Overwatch didn't need to be far away to best suit the men, I decided. Rupert, again, was incorrect.

In my fusillade, I mowed down a lone Bolshevik peasant, hitting him with a handful of bullets. "Yes, my love," Annette mentioned. "Do it for me." Oh, I will, Annette. I absolutely will.

Keller picked up firing near after, dispersing a herd of the swine from the front. We were performing competently, but we couldn't hold out forever.

"Bullets! Bullets" Keller screeched after about half a minute. The top of his MG-42 flung open immediately after. "Hurry! More bullets!" he stammered on as Kuhn fumbled around the box of bullets with a pair of trembling hands.

I was at the end of my drum magazine, so I reached for a fresh one as quickly as I could. I only had stick magazines left, but they would do. But as I did, a horde of men appeared in the fray, dashing towards the side of our bunker. I crammed in the new magazine but could only fire a salvo at some of them before at least one had made it out of our line of sight. He threatened the safety of our bunker by heading towards the side entrance on our bunker's flank. Sensing danger, I roared, spun around, and charged to meet him.

Keller caught the wind of me storming outside and knew the position was no longer safe. "Fall back!" he shouted to Kuhn, becoming aware of the futility of holding out with just one other man against an entire army. "To the next line!"

I leaped around the bunker's archway into the cement corridor outside, happening to smash right into the communist before he could fire. The metal receiver of his similar weapon clashed together with protruding magazine on mine with a thunderous crack. I took the initiative and slammed him into the concrete wall across from the bunker. Before he could react, I bashed into his head with the top of my helmet.

But the Soviet flung the butt of his submachine gun up towards my lips, knocking me back half a step. "Don't let him damage your face," Annette warned. The taste of my own blood paired with her words sparked my fuse, driving me red with rage. I charged head-first right back into the Soviet before he could finagle the tip of his weapon at me from in between us.

"Lindemann!" Kuhn shrilled as emerged from the bunker. He focused his weapon at us both, but I couldn't halt tussling with that fucking Soviet who damaged my lip. *My* lip, the lip Annette likes! He needed to be punished, and I was the reckoner!

Keller stormed through the bunker's archway with his MG in the assault stance. He instantly opened fire towards the front of the hallway, holding off some of the other rude Soviets keen on interrupting my judgment.

After a few more seconds of struggling, I delivered a blow with my elbow to the jaw of the Communist, knocking him to the side. Using the opportunity to my advantage, I kicked him down the wall, forcing him to trip over some crates in the way as I released a tremendous volley into him with my submachine gun.

Blood splattered everywhere. It flicked on the front of my uniform, and bit even sprinkled on my lips. But I held down the trigger until my PPSh clicked. “Do you remember what it tastes like?” Annette asked. It tasted salty, like the crackers we would have on our picnic dates. I missed her.

Kuhn also received a spray from the insides of the Soviet peasant as well, but he didn’t seem to savor it as much as I did. He was too soft to understand my rationale for its enjoyment, but I supposed that the glistening crimson layer of gore was a horrid color scheme for camouflage. Plus, nobody likes being wet.

The MG-42 clicked as the remnants of Keller’s belt of ammunition dried up, and he ordered, “Let’s get out of here!” He grabbed Kuhn by the shoulder just as another Soviet rocketed from around the corner at the end of the outdoor hallway, lit Molotov cocktail in hand.

Without missing a beat, I instinctively flung my empty PPSh at the Soviet. Thank goodness I did because Kuhn, the only man with a loaded weapon, merely gasped and slammed his eyes shut.

The submachine gun smacked against the Bolshevik's neck, disrupting his throw. The Molotov fell short, hitting some crates in the concrete hallway. But before the Soviet could react, I was already on top of him. His helmet flung off as we hit the earth together, and I threw my fists at his head and body.

I struck blow after blow to his face and neck as he ineffectively tried warding me off. As the flames devoured the containers, Keller soon hailed, "Lindemann!"

The growing inferno from the crates spread like wildfire, catching the camouflage netting on the top of the bunker, setting the entire area ablaze. I hardly so much as flinched – I was too immersed into dismantling the dirty communist's face.

Muffled coughing squawked from the other side of the rubble, followed by incoming footsteps from the other direction. I gave the Soviet pig a tremendous final blow to the skull with my elbow, rendering him unresponsive, before swiping his weapon and getting to my feet. He had a PPD.

Suddenly, my frame rattled uncontrollably, and my vision blurred out. I tumbled back to the ground with a resounding thud.

"Bruno!" Annette watched on in horror from in front of the flames as I instinctively crawled closer towards the relative safety the concealment from the billowing pillars of smoke provided. Shit, I had been hit!

A cough from the smoke echoed from my side. I impulsively whipped my weapon towards where it originated from and tugged the trigger for an abbreviated burst. I remained static in the dense fog and smoke, preparing my body for another salvo of gunfire.

Finally, a faint clank followed the vibration of something metal hitting the gravel. I sighed. I got him.

"Your body!" Oh no, she warned me not to return battered! I reached down and patted my wounds. I got hit more than once, right above my hip! What is she going to do with me if I returned with all these holes through my body?

My concern mutated into infuriation. How dare someone – especially a filthy, *disgusting* Soviet savage – make me less perfect for Annette? As the flames from the bunker enveloped all around, I knew I had to seek her vengeance.

The pain from my fresh wounds that awoke as I tried struggling to my feet only accelerated my determination for payback.

Even so, I could only crawl. I began poking through the clouds during my search for the Red bastard that tarnished my pristine body.

Weapon ready in one hand for anything else, I used my free arm to struggle towards where the noise originated from. Soon, I could make out a figure through the dense black and gray, lying on the ground with his weapon just an arm's length from reach.

I had soon made it about a meter away from the wounded Soviet. He had taken a couple of bullets, some by his lungs, which strained his breathing. He couldn't make a peep, but his eyes stretched as wide as they could go when I emerged amidst the fires next to his side.

Still, the pitiful Ivan kept struggling to verbalize something in a language I didn't care to learn. "Don't listen to his begging," Annette reacted. "This communist peasant is only desperately clinging to the brink of a life he doesn't deserve, anyway."

The tip of my PPD sifted towards his perforated chest. His hands trembled as he feebly lifted them between us. I brushed past them to shove the tip of my weapon into his heart. Too weak to push it away, he just grabbed the barrel. His voice tried to make noises but could only exhale, and somehow his eyes managed to expand even further than I thought possible.

"Make him pay," Annette ordered. I grinned, reflecting on how eager I was to carry out her requests. I would do anything for her. So, I savored every millisecond while further pressing the tip of my weapon further into the dying barbarian's chest against his wishes.

"Rupert was never capable of such power," Annette declared. She was right, too. Us Germans were better than anyone else. Rupert and I were the best German warriors out here, but I was the most superior form Rupert could have been. I had become even more powerful than him. The only person who was worthy of me was Annette. Together, we would rule the world.

I was so concentrated on seeking vengeance, my vision tunneled, and the ambient noises grew louder and louder. This one would be for you, my love. "Yes, yes, yes…" her voice egged on, pitch dropping in a manic frenzy with her every word from the pain I could make him experience. The only thing I could hear was his painting, and the only thing I could feel was his suffering.

But instead of joy, a monumental force kicked me out of

nowhere, knocking me to the side away from my weapon. Disoriented, I tried to stagger to my back, just for my assailant to continue stomping me. One of his kicks came towards my weapon, casting into the smoke. I kept trying to turn around, but his foot kept coming down. How *dare* this bastard ruin my moment!

I managed to grab his leg amidst one of his stomps and pulled him to the ground with me. He landed on his face. Using all of the power left in me, I threw myself on top of him, and we rolled on the ground towards the flames.

I was completely blind in the thickness of the smoke, but I wanted this soulless pig to look his killer in the eyes before I end him. Then they'd know they've met their maker.

He was tenacious, but I held my own against the man while the smoke blew in between our faces. Finally, the wind picked up, and the smoke began to thin out.

My adversary let out a soul separating roar, as he elbowed me and flipped around. In the most intense sense of unadulterated terror I had ever experienced, the fumes cleared between us enough for me to lock eyes through a mutilated face with none other than a blood-lusting Rupert Schmidt.

I throbbed in horror as Rupert struck my face with an open palm. “I saw it happen earlier!” He wretched as blood dripped from his lips onto my cheeks. Oh God, he spoke the wounded Soviet on the balcony I had executed earlier!

Rupert grabbed me by my helmet and repeatedly slammed it against the ground. I screeched, seeing my worst nightmare back from the dead. “I told you I’d kill you myself if you did that again!” he recalled. His teeth were pointed, hungering for blood like a gluttonous shark.

“I’m sorry! I didn’t mean to!” I babbled. I swatted at his head with a panicking forearm. It somehow pushed him back enough for me to kick him and crawl out of his grasp. His vibrantly gold eyes pierced through the smog as the flames surrounded him like a boxing ring.

I flipped over to my back, but he rolled into a crouch before I could even try to get to my feet. I attempted to crawl towards my weapon, but the lurking fiend converged towards me. “You’re a liar! You were just about to do it again!”

Rupert lunged at me through the smoke, a devilish tongue flopping from his mouth. He booted me in my chin before he dropped on top of me. “You made me do this, *Grenadier*,” he remarked while clutching my neck with one hand and hitting me with a salvo of blows with the other.

“No!” I coughed as I futilely tried to prevent him from dismembering my face. It was the worst kind of pain I could ever imagine – with every pummel, the memories of my horrid acts came to mind. Every malevolent kill I made flashed before my eyes. The surrendering one during my first battle, the man bleeding out on the bridge in the marketplace, all of the men I had killed in Oradea. Oh, God, it was horrid!

Rupert then jabbed a fist at my gut, right on top of one of the fresh wounds I had neglected to think about. I howled like I had been lit ablaze, recalling my comrades that had perished. Huber, Graf, Guppy, Oberfeldwebel Martin, Udo Sommer, even Rupert. I had insulted what they died for by reconstructing myself into the vilest person possible. Tears rolled into the open cuts on my face. The pain was indescribably unbearable. I had to make it stop. I needed to make it stop!

The screwdriver. I had Keller’s screwdriver! I made a desperate jab at Rupert's throat with my fist, dazing him enough to again kick him off me. Rupert faded into the darkness as I scurried backward to sitting position and desperately searched around my person for that blasted screwdriver. Where did I put it?

"I'll teach you the wrongs of your actions if I have to come back from the afterlife and drag you to hell myself, Bruno!" he squealed from behind the smog.

That's right, my boot! Keller told me to keep the screwdriver there so that I could access it easily. How stupid of me, I could have used it earlier! I frantically reached for my boot, trying to produce the only weapon still on me.

I withdrew the shining blade screwdriver and held it at my side, ready for his counterattack. I was prepared to shove it right into the side of his ugly face. Taking down my old mentor with a melee weapon like this would be brutal, but I had no other choice. I needed him to stop.

Soon enough, Rupert materialized through the smoke. My eyes cried as I caught the submachine gun in his hands. There was nothing Keller's screwdriver could do to save me. I was fucked.

Rupert's weapon began to spark as it slammed me into the wall of the burning bunker. My head repeatedly bounced against the concrete, but I didn't feel a thing as the rounds impacted my chest. He no longer moved – he just exhaled at me through a snarl with his musky, putrid breath. I stared deep into his gilded eyes as I absorbed the bullets. They wanted to do this.

Rupert fired until his weapon clicked. He pulled out the empty magazine, giving me one last lookover before he pelted me with it. He spun around and commented, "Scum," over his shoulder before disappearing into the fog.

It was over. I no longer found the energy to move. The gravity of my wounds set in. I had been shot countless times, and I had been losing blood. I was tired, as if I'd been awake for days on end.

Sobbing sifted through the crackles of the emerging fire from the man I had shot just before Rupert attacked. Another Russian began to talk to him, consoling him in his final moments. He was hardly able to speak, verbalizing something I couldn't understand.

Then it all hit me – he was crying for his comrades. His family. His sisters. His *Annette*. I had focused so intensely on the rush of becoming a hero that I had lost touch with the humanity I had prided Annette with bestowing upon me. I had warped that same motivation to live into a desire to fight. I shuddered in shame as I realized that these Soviets – these *people* – I had killed were none too different than myself. Rupert returned for the betterment of all the Annettes in the world that longed for their respective Brunos.

Gunshots continually resounded from near and far. The footsteps of Russian troops passed around me. They might not have seen me through the smoke, but if they did, they paid no further attention to me as they stormed by. But I didn't stay upset. I found myself relieved – no longer would I have to deal with the stressors of war. It was going to be peaceful soon. I may not deserve rest, but after this prolonged fighting such a brutal war, I needed it.

I closed my eyelids, and like a newsreel, watched the serene memories of Annette and me together. The melancholy from being forced to leave the world, the joy of merely existing enough to experience those incredible times – it was overwhelming. I haven't cried in years, but in my final moments, I couldn't hold it back.

How brilliant that I dreamt such a fulfilling inner monologue in my final moments. I should thank Rupert when I next see him.

Epilogue

A flickering television sporadically illuminated the otherwise dimly moonlight room. Some curtains on the wall ruffled as a light breeze sifted through an open window. The greyish-brown hair on the head of an older man sitting on an armchair flowed from the gust as he snored. His fingers remained clenched around empty beer in his hand.

As the television broadcast some late-night program, the snoring of the older man stopped. He began jostling in his sleep, with his head jolting to the side. The noise of his slumber returned, but gone were the peaceful snores of before. Strained breathing took its place as his eyelids and fingers tightened. His head snapped from one side to the other. His free hand briefly raised above his head, gripping the back of his headrest. “Bullets, bullets,” he begged, voice hardly more than a whisper.

After a few struggled breathes, the older man’s plea grew more intense, “Hurry! More bullets!” The arm above him came crashing down on the armrest table next to him, throwing its empty beer glasses across the floor.

The empty bottles on the table smashed as they hit the ground. The older man's eyes could not have gone to a more opposite position as they sprung open. He reactively threw the bottle in his hand upwards in panic.

No time to waste, the tired man jumped out of his chair with youthful agility his body would otherwise be incapable of. He hit the ground in front of his seat, ignoring all the protesting his seasoned joints gave him before the bottle he previously tossed upwards shattered as it hit the ground around him.

The man dragged his back to the base of the chair with his frail fingers giving their best attempt at gripping the floor. A muffled voice approached as beads of sweat slipped down the side of his face. He frantically slapped his torso with the arm that previously held his empty beer as if he was searching for something that his life depended on. The voice grew louder and louder. The flailing of his hand on his chest grew more and more intense. The enemy kept getting closer and closer. Where was his pistol? Where was his pistol?

"Honey!" the voice cried out as a distraught woman saw the

emptiness in her husband's eyes.

With a gasp, the real world came back to the old man. The situation he had found himself in was just as distressing as the horrible things he had seen in the war prior. Shame overtook him, and silence swept the room, only interrupted by the panting of the troubled veteran.

After the longest ten seconds or so of their relationship, the conflicted warhorse turned around and grabbed a half-empty case of beers beside the chair he had slept on.

"Uh, I'd like it if you joined me at the balcony," he tried.

The woman had seen similar things happen before, but she was still shook over what had just happened and wasn't sure how to proceed. "Uh… Sure," she delicately responded.

The man disappeared through the doors of the balcony. The wife stood around for another few seconds before cautiously following him.

She soon made her way through the doorframe. Her spouse sat stoically in a rocking chair, slowly rolling back and forth with his eyes fixated on the dimly lit yard before him. The case of beer laid between him and another empty rocking chair.

“Take a seat, grab a beer,” the old man simpered, eyes fixated on the same spot as before.

Beckoned by the request of her husband, the woman shifted around to the front of the seat and fell back into it. She declined the beer.

The man, uneasy with the tone on the porch, relied on his drinking experience and took a hearty sip. He fumbled with a pack of cigarettes in his lap before ultimately deciding not to offer one to his wife, putting them on the armrest opposite to him.

“Do you know why I go back every year?” the man asked after a couple of seconds. “To Rottenberg?”

The woman shifted around in her seat, preparing for the serious conversation that was about to take place. “Yes, it’s because you want to meet up with your comrades from the war.”

Another gust of air filled the silence as the vulnerable veteran pieced together his words. “Well, that’s part of it,” he shared before taking a long drag on his cigarette.

The wife sensed there was much more to it than just that, so she tried again. “Isn’t it also because you were friends with Udo Sommer’s son, and wanted to help out her and Johannes with their restaurant?"

"Sure." The man reached for a cigarette inside his packet and put a new one in his lips. He hesitated with the pack in his hand, nodded side to side to himself, and offered it to his wife. "Here, have one."

With her sombre mood interrupted, the woman's eyes lit up as she gingerly selected a cigarette from the middle. The husband withdrew the packet, lit a match, and reached over towards his wife. "I know you try to smoke these in secret," the old man teased. The woman nodded as she leaned over the arm of the chair and lit up his cigarette, taking a few puffs before she laid back into her seat.

"Mrs Sommer's son was a man in my squad," the reminiscing veteran started. He lit his cigarette and took a couple of hearty puffs before he continued. "We were comrades."

The woman, though often lively, had not often seen her husband get into a mood like the one he was in. "What happened to him?" she finally asked, hesitant if that was the right question for the situation.

"He couldn't take the pressure," the man uttered. The woman stared intently at her husband. She caught a glint from behind his circular glasses. His eye sparkled as it reflected the light of the half-moon.

After another puff, the man toyed with his cigarette, rolling it around in his hands. “Well, Erma, you have a right to know by now.” His gaze drifted down to a scar on his arm. “It was about mid-October of ’44 in Oradea, now Romania. I was a machine gunner. I should have died. But instead, I had to watch as we lost almost everybody else in my squad. Wiped out one-by-one.”

It was then that Keller finally described the last days of the German occupation of Oradea. Erma was all ears, having never having heard the full story about her spouse's time in the war. She had only known from the little bits he occasionally shared. So, Keller went into as much detail as he could on how his comrades had perished one by one. It was challenging for a tough man like Keller to talk about something so personally damaging, but he knew it had to be done. His wife had put up with his quirks from the war for more than a decade, and she deserved to know why he struggled.

“Woah,” The woman responded after Keller finished. Her cigarette slowly burned a small bit of itself up with a slight gust of wind as she held it in motionless hands. “I’m sorry…”

Keller grunted as he examined his beer. "Erma, we've been married for many years. But do you know why I drink so much?"

Erma nodded side to side. "No, Wolfgang, I don't know any specific reason."

Keller grunted. "Those were the worst days of my life. But an old friend told me that I was more fun when I drank. Our squad leader. Schmidt. The quirky guy. It was a small compliment, but I hadn't been called 'fun' since before it all started. It was the first time since before the war began that I thought about life outside fighting."

Erma, attentive as always, nodded. Keller took a long sip from the beer before continuing. "Not too long after Kuhn and I had made it out of Oradea, the war ended. And like everybody else who survived, we tried to find ways to deal with what we had gone through." Keller delicately ran his fingers through his hair. "Most went back to whatever they did before the war. Like Herrmann, if you remember him, going back into some sketchy shit. Others used their kindness to look out for future generations. Like Kuhn, the school teacher."

Another breeze scattered the brittle leaves across the ground, and Keller waited for the crackling to stop before carrying on.

“For me, I travelled for years to figure out what I could do to make the most out of my life. But long after all the fighting had stopped, the war still had its grasp on me. I didn’t care if I lived or died. Just like when I was a soldier. I didn’t necessarily want to, but it would have been fine if I did. I’d just join the fallen. The only time I felt anything else at all was when I’d drink, bringing me closer to that night in Oradea.”

A troubled Keller stared at the moon, soaking in its beam as he formulated what to say next. “But it was always only a temporary fix. I always remained empty.”

Those that had been through the war hated these kinds of conversations, and Keller was no exception. He hated them with every bone in his body. But he knew he had to get through it for his wife, so he pressed on.

“I started getting in contact with some of the men I fought with. Found out they met up at Mrs Sommer’s restaurant. Primarily because the Chef, er, Johannes, worked there after the war. Asked him if I could come visit. We began talking about our experiences. And I learned something important.”

The woman's eyes lit up. “What was that, Wolfgang?”

Keller looked up towards the half-moon, his eyes sparking a feint gold through the circular glasses resting on his nose. “It’s that I’m fucked, Erma. I’m just… Fucked.”

The dismayed vet’s eyes grew watery, but the seasoned veteran was far beyond being able to cry. The many years of pain had hardened him to the point that he no longer knew how to. He turned towards his wife. “I’m so sorry about what happened in the other room. I’m so, so sorry you had to put up with shit like that since I came back.”

Erma’s eyes watered as he turned away. Keller couldn’t take the shame of looking at his caring wife in the eyes. He needed a few seconds to recompose himself before carrying on. He breathed heavily, fighting it all down.

Finally, Keller was ready again. “I was a good soldier, Erma. I fought. I killed. I did what I had to.” Keller gulped. “But it fucked me up inside. I tried to run. I tried to find ways to fix it. But it never fully fixed itself. I got better. But I’ll never be fully fixed. And I was still one of the better ones off. You’ve seen Kuhn. Real good guy at heart. But he was never the same after the Soviets returned him.”

Keller shook his head side to side. “So, I’d talk to the Chef about it. He told me the real reason why Schmidt gave us all that booze on the only night of the war I enjoyed. To try to enjoy all the small things after Mrs Sommer’s son had passed.”

“Oh, wow…” Erma marveled at the sincerity in her husband’s gilded eyes as she soaked everything in. It was quite an experience for her, but she knew it was a conversation she’d remember for the rest of their lives.

“I learned that I was too focused on the big picture, on what was next, than just to enjoy the moment,” Keller continued. “Most of my comrades are dead. So, it’s more than just helping out at the restaurant. I focus on living every little moment in life. That’s the best way I could honour them. It’s easy to always mourn them. It’s easy to die for those you love. But they wouldn’t want that. It’s much harder to live for them.”

Erma wiped a tear from her cheek as she hummed in understanding. Keller sighed, blinking briefly and his eyes returning to their standard green shade. He didn’t like serious conversations in general, but he knew it was important to share what he learned, so his wife would understand why he was like this.

Keller nodded his head to the side as he flicked some ash off the tip of his cigarette. "It's the best way I could honour any of them, really. Dead or living. Because the wounded, the shell-shocked, the ones who were never the same after the war – they lost part of themselves, too. To not at least try to make my life meaningful for them would be a waste of their sacrifice."

The ash on the tip of Erma's cigarette was at least twice that of her husband. The woman was much too fixated on Keller's story than to worry about smoking. Keller, however, took another inhale of his cigarette. He then blew it out and took another generous sip from his beer. Erma finally ashed out her cigarette and mirrored with as puff of her own as she waited for Keller to continue.

Finally, Keller spoke up. "Erma, the war fucked me up. But I'm doing my best to make sure they don't fuck things up for you. But I need you to remember that even when things are at their worst, you'll still have small things to find excitement in. You've got to try to live a good life. If not for you, for those connected to you. For those connected to me."

Keller threw his cigarette beyond the porch. He reached an arm across and grabbed the hand of his wife. He stared deeply into

Erma's dazzling green and brown eyes, slightly tightening his grip. It empowered him to crack a fatigued smile. "And if things don't get better, then it's not really over, is it?"

The End

Author's Note:

Thank you so much for reading through my story. I created this book as a way for me to use my enthusiasm for history to vent about an immoral job I had in the past. Because it was an almost therapeutic activity for me, I honestly didn't expect anybody ever to read this, so it really means a lot to me that you finished it. Yes, each and every one of you that reads this – I appreciate you.

A lot of support from family and friends went into making this piece, so a big shout-out to them for helping me make it this far. You all rock.

If you didn't finish this book and are just reading this page, then congrats on finding this Easter egg early.

Index

Ranks:

Grenadier – The lowest enlisted rank of the German Heer during this period. Equivalent rank of a Private.

Gefreiter – A slightly more experienced enlisted soldier. Equivalent rank of a Lance Corporal.

Obergefreiter – Enlisted soldier ranked above Gefreiter. Equivalent rank of a Corporal.

Unterfeldwebel – Relatively uncommon rank for a non-commissioned officer. Equivalent rank of a Sergeant.

Feldwebel – Lowest senior non-commissioned officer rank. Equivalent rank of Staff Sergeant.

Oberfeldwebel – Senior non-commissioned officer ranked above Feldwebel. Equivalent rank of Sergeant Major.

Oberleutnant – Second lowest officer rank. Equivalent rank of 1st Lieutenant.

Sturmbannführer – More senior officer rank within the SS. Equivalent rank of Major. Note: This rank is for members of the SS, not the Heer like above. Rank procedures are still respected, regardless of branch.

Feldkuchenunteroffizier – Not a formal rank, but a role given to the soldier in charge of food. Literally translates to, "Field Kitchen Non-Commissioned Officer."

Weapons:

Karabiner 98k – Standard-issue rifle for the German forces during WWII. It operated by bolt-action, meaning every bullet must be manually loaded into the chamber by pulling down and cocking back a lever on the right side back by hand. Rate of fire is slow, but the rifle is regarded as accurate. Can be fitted with a scope.

MG-42 (Maschinengewehr 42) – Standard German light machinegun during the late-war period. Uses the same round as the Karabiner 98k. Rate of fire is up to 1200 rounds a minute, which is unparalleled for a support weapon in this period. Very heavy and cannot easily be operated standing up.

MP-40 (Maschinenpistole 40) – Most common German submachine gun during the war. Fires a pistol-calibre round, but is capable of automatic fire. Slower rate-of-fire than Russian counterparts (500-550 rounds a minute) to keep aiming controllable during bursts. Not capable of using the similar-sized but slightly more powerful Russian pistol-calibre round.

STG-44 (Sturmgewehr 44) - Widely regarded as the world's first assault rifle, firing a bullet that is sized between that of a rifle and submachine gun. Capable of both semi-automatic and fully automatic fire. Automatic rate of fire is 500-600 rounds a minute.

PPSh-41 (Pistolet-Pulemyot Shpagina 41) – Standard issue submachine gun for the Russians during the war. Blazing fast rate of fire, capable of 900-1000 rounds a minute. Can use either 35-round stick magazines or 71 round drum magazines. Considered a very rugged weapon, capable of using the similar-sized German submachine gun / pistol ammunition.

PPS – A similar submachine gun instated later on during the war to replace the PPSh due to less-costly machining. Rate of fire is 600-700 rounds a minute. Generally overshadowed by the PPSh, but still considered a very lightweight and effective weapon. Also capable of using the similar-sized German submachine gun / pistol rounds.

Various:

Wehrmacht – Combined German defence forces during WWII, containing the Heer (Army), Luftwaffe (Air Force), and Kriegsmarine (Navy). In theory, the Wehrmacht is separate from the Nazi military powers, however, it often found itself under control of Nazi leadership.

Heer – German standard Army, or the land forces component of the Wehrmacht during WWII.

SS – Schutzstaffel, or the Nazi party's paramilitary organization. Strongly valued Adolf Hitler's ideology. In this book, SS refers to the Waffen-SS, or the military branch of the greater SS. Waffen-SS forces participated in unison with the Heer in conducting combat operations.

For more on Overwatch: 1944, come visit this book's Facebook page, where you can find exclusive videos on the plot, characters, and behind-the-scenes looks at the creation of this book.

You can view the Facebook page by going to this URL: www.facebook.com/overwatch1944book

Made in the USA
Columbia, SC
13 July 2021

41814812R00245